The BEST THING That I Didn't EVER Do

RON RUTLER

www.blacknovapress.com

DEDICATION

*I would like to thank my kids and my family for
their assistance and support.*

CHAPTER 1

As he did every year on his birthday, Crazy Larry would show up for work bright and early at his mob boss, Tommy's, downtown office. Usually, Uncle Tommy, as everyone called him, would have a group of Larry's cronies on hand to surprise the birthday boy. Uncle Tommy would bring in this huge cake that always had something hidden in the middle of it. Every year, he would make the same point to Larry, and anyone else within earshot, by saying, "So Larry, if ever I get tossed into the slammer, don't forget that you can hide just about anything inside of a cake this big." Then it would be business as usual until the end of the day, when he and Larry would stop by Carl & Mary's for a quiet one-on-one malt, an order of Curly-Q fries, and a cheeseburger.

As Larry waited in the hallway outside of Uncle Tommy's office, his mind focused on the upcoming events that lay just the other side of those solid oak double doors.

He looked forward to this day. What a boss Tommy is, he thought. Looking in a mirror, he began practicing the fake "I'm surprised" look that would have to radiate across his mug as he walked through the doors in reaction to everyone yelling "surprise."

With a solid metallic click, the brass handles released the locks, and the doors opened, and there stood Tommy with both hands extended. "Come here, my old friend." Larry walked up to him, and they embraced. As they did, Tommy said, "Happy birthday, my friend." Larry replied with a "Thank you." Still in a manly bear hug, Larry looked around and saw no one else in the room.

Tommy walked over to the coat closet and pulled out a long, slender birthday present wrapped in colorful paper. He handed it to Larry and said, "Happy Birthday, but don't open it just yet. I'll tell you when. Oh, and sorry about the whole no-surprise thing this year, but I'll make it up to you. Just be patient. You see, we've got some important business to take care of today."

Larry's ears perked up at this. He liked the sound of this already. "You know, Larry, how I hate to make house calls. However, it's like what I keep telling Tommy, Jr. Sometimes you just have to do things that you really don't want to do. You see, Larry, it seems that our old pal Victor is way overdue for a monetary visit. Three shipments of cigarettes were hijacked by him and sold, and not one ounce of juice has come our way. I think everyone thinks that I'm growing soft. So, guess what, my old friend? I waited until today, your birthday; to make what I hope will be our last house call."

Larry's eyes got as wide as silver dollars as he said, "You mean today? Really, Tommy?"

"I mean today. Look in the mirror," Tommy told Larry.

"What?"

"Look in the mirror. Next year, this is the face you should practice to look like when you try to act surprised." Larry looked in the mirror.

"It's that bad, huh?"

"Well, let's just say that I don't think that your previous performances are going to be bringing you any Oscar nominations."

"Boss, I've got a feeling this is going to be my best birthday ever." Tommy pulled a few tissues from the box in his desk drawer and handed them to Larry, who wiped away the tears that were sliding down his ski slope of a nose. Uncle Tommy pulled his grandfather's gold pocket watch out. "Hey, we've got to get rolling. Spats tells me Vic gets coffee and a roll down at the neighborhood cafe every morning about 8:45. Then he walks alone the short block and a half to his office. I guess he wants to show how brave he is, walking unguarded. How stupid is that, walking alone every morning at the same time, in the same place? It's a recipe for disaster. Any rookie hit man could figure that one out in his sleep. Well, I guess if you factor in the whole cigarette fiasco, it's plain to see we are not dealing with one of the brightest of people. Now, let's get going."

Larry walked over to the cabinet and opened the doors. Like a proud papa, he smiled approvingly as he saw the solid cherry gun box sitting there on the glass shelf patiently waiting for him. "Hello, old friend. Sorry that I have been away so long." He ran his hands over the rounded brass corners, and then wiped his sleeve across the gold plaque on the top of the box, polishing the inscription that read "The Pearl."

Tommy had given this gun case and the pearl-handled, blue-barreled pistol that was in it to Larry years ago, and it had gone with them on every house call since then. Opening the box, Larry picked up the revolver. Viewing the chamber, Larry's eyes once again welled up. Out of the corner of his eye, he saw a handful of tissues being handed to him by Tommy, who was standing behind him. Larry grabbing the tissues, said, "Thanks, boss," as he wiped his eyes. He was a crier, just like his dad, and he appreciated the fact that Tommy had never embarrassed him about it. He just kept the tissues coming. After verifying the gun was loaded, he pulled his standard revolver out of his shoulder harness and laid it on the shelf next to the box. Then he closed the lid to the gun case and shut the doors to the cabinet.

Standing there in deep thought, he suddenly felt Uncle Tommy's hand on his shoulder as Tommy said, "Larry, you can bring Pearl for old times' sake and protection, but today I have something else in mind. Just keep it in its holster unless you have no other choice. Let's get out of here."

As they headed out the door, Tommy stopped and motioned to the birthday present. "You might want to bring that along," he said.

"Really," Larry replied? "Okay." Larry turned around and picked up his three-foot long, heavy, yet slender birthday present. He turned to Tommy. "Come on, Tommy. Can I open it now?"

"Nope," replied Tommy matter-of-factly.

"Then can you give me a hint? It's driving me crazy not knowing."

"Everything drives you crazy. Why do you think we call you Crazy Larry? Okay, okay, I'll give you a hint. You're going to like it a lot. As a present, it will be a big hit." Larry held it up to his ear and shook it. Arriving at the car, Larry opened the back door for Tommy. Once Tommy slid in and got situated, Larry closed the door and tapped on the window twice with his knuckles. He always did this for good luck.

Opening the passenger door, Larry put his present in the seat. He grabbed the seat belt and fastened it around the treasured gift as it sat upright against the backrest. Larry looked up at Uncle Tommy, who rolled his eyes. Tommy had to smile as he thought of this gentle giant as his protector.

Larry shut the passenger door and walked over to the driver's side, climbed behind the wheel, and drove off. From the back seat, Uncle Tommy asked, "How many of these house calls have we made together?"

"I don't know, boss, but I wish this wasn't our last. I really like working with you on these."

"Yeah," Tommy said, "but the mess. Nope, I'm getting too old for this stuff. And with Tommy, Jr. and all, I want to be around a while." After a quiet 20-minute ride, Tommy broke the silence. "Pull over right up there across from the café and let me out. I'll walk across the street. Then I want you to circle around and position yourself and the car just out of view of the picture window. Keep the engine running and be ready to follow us."

"Keep the engine running," Larry repeated. "I love the way that sounds." Tommy handed Larry another handful of tissues to wipe his eyes. "Like I said, keep the engine running. Be ready to follow us, because I think old Victor and I just might want to take a nice little walk together back to his office."

"Right, boss. I'll be ready." Larry jumped out of the car and briskly walked around to Tommy's side, and opened the door. Once Tommy stepped out, Larry shut the door and walked back around in front of the car, stepping right out in front of an oncoming car. He stretched his arm out, instructing the driver to stop. The car screeched to a halt. Larry pointed at the driver and said, "You wait right there until this man gets across the street."

When Larry and Tommy reached the dividing line, he found a steady stream of uncooperative drivers speeding by. Always ready to accommodate Tommy, Larry, galled at the nerve of these drivers, reached behind his back and tucked his sports jacket behind his holster in a way that exposed Pearl. Then he stretched both hands out in his best crossing guard form, stepped out into traffic, and signaled for the traffic to stop. They did.

Uncle Tommy pulled his fedora a little further down on his forehead to hide his identity. As he walked past his crossing guard, he said, "Larry, next time, could you draw a little more attention to us?"

Larry perked up again. "Next time? Did you say next time? Are you saying that this isn't our last house call?" Tommy just kept on walking and shook his head.

As Larry saw Tommy step up on the curb to the sidewalk, he put down his arms and motioned for the cars to continue on. "Thank you!" he yelled as they drove by. Having walked out to the middle of the street after stepping down from his crossing guard pose, he realized he had stranded himself in the middle of what now were four fast moving lanes of traffic. He turned and looked over the blurs of blue, red, and green tops of the fast-moving cars and saw Tommy just about to step into the door of the neighborhood café. "Holy mother-of-pearl," he said to himself. "I have to hurry and get across the street so that I can be there to cover Tommy's back."

"When in doubt, pull Pearl out," he said to himself. Larry reached under his coat to his shoulder holster and pulled his gun out and pointed it directly at the driver of an approaching vehicle. The driver, seeing Larry standing in the middle of the lane with that cannon pointed at him, slammed on his brakes. The skid of his sudden application of the brakes made his car slide to the right, which brought his car to a stopped position that blocked both the outside and the inside lanes.

Larry walked over to the window of the car that he had fixed his aim at, and with his gun, he lightly tapped on the glass and motioned for the driver to roll down his window. The guy inside the vehicle, realizing that a window wouldn't stop a .22 caliber, let alone a bullet from a gun the size of that cannon, did exactly as he was instructed. As he rolled down the window, the nervous driver said, "Yes? How can I help you, sir?" Larry said, "Do you see that car right there?" With his free hand, he pointed at his car, visible through the guy's front window.

"You mean that big black one?"

"Correct. I'm going to go climb into it, and I am going to make a U-turn. So I don't want you to unblock this traffic until I have had a chance to do just that. Am I making myself clear here?"

"Yes, sir."

"Good. Oh, and forget about this whole thing. No cops, no nothing. Do what you are told, and I won't have to introduce you to the business end of Pearl here."

"You have my word, sir."

"Good, because I have your license number memorized."

Larry closed his eyes and rattled off the guy's license number. "So you can see I wouldn't have much trouble finding you. Now, you have a good day."

Larry walked over to his car, started it up, dropped it in gear, and floored it. With tires squealing and spewing smoke, Larry completed his U-turn. When finished, he had placed his car exactly where Tommy had instructed him to with all the skill of a stunt driver. Vic and everyone else in the café turned, staring out the windows at all the commotion that was being caused by Larry.

Suddenly, the bell above the front door rang as it announced the entrance of a patron. Vic, out of habit, looked toward the door to see who was coming in. As he did, he was looking eye-to-eye with none other than Uncle Tommy. Instantly recognizing him, Vic said, "Tommy, you old son of a gun, how on earth are you doing?"

Vic and Tommy walked toward each other, and Vic extended his hand for a shake, which Tommy reluctantly accepted. "So Tommy, what brings you to this neck of the woods?"

"Oh, I've got a cake to pick up for Larry. Today's his birthday, you know."

Vic responded, "I thought that was Larry I saw out there causing all that commotion a minute ago. You tell him happy birthday from old Victor."

Vic turned to Jessy, who owned the café, and asked, "Do you have a cake back there for my friend Tommy here?"

"You mean the one that says, 'Happy Birthday Pearl'?"

"That would be it," responded Tommy.

"Good," said Vic. "Jessy, you put that on my bill."

"Well, thanks Vic."

"No problem, Tommy. So how have you been, Tommy, really?"

"Really pretty good, Vic. Doctor says I need to squeeze a little more exercise into my day, so I try to walk a little each day. Must be old age creeping in."

"I'm doing the same," replied Vic. "I come down here, and then I walk back to my office."

"That's what I've been hearing," Tommy said. "You know, Vic, you really need to be more careful. It sounds to me like you are setting a pattern. You can't be too careful these days."

"Tommy, Tommy. Relax. It's only a short one and a half blocks back from here. Besides, I'm always packing my share of heat."

"Hey, I have an idea. Why don't I walk back to your office with you? And if you don't care, maybe we'll light the candles on the cake, and the three of us can have a little birthday celebration with Larry."

"That sounds good to me. Let me call the boys and tell them what's going on."

Tommy, with his free hand, grabbed Vic's right elbow firmly and said, "Here, Vic, hold out both of your hands and put your palms up." As Vic did this, Tommy placed the cake on them. "I wouldn't make that call right now if I were you. Let's get going. I've got a house call to make."

Now Vic knew this was no chance meeting. As they stepped out the door, Tommy reached into Vic's coat pocket and grabbed Vic's gun, and placed it in his own waistband. "Now let's walk. Oh, and Vic, do not try to run. It's hard on your joints, you know, and Larry gets real upset when he sees someone fleeing from me."

Vic turned his head and made eye contact with Crazy Larry as he sat behind the wheel of the car that was slowly following them. Larry waved at Vic with Pearl and then laid her on the dash so that Vic knew it was there, just in case Tommy needed him.

"So Vic," Tommy said, "just how is the cigarette business these days? Must not be too good. I haven't received any money from you for, what, six or seven months now? And I know at least three truckloads have passed through your hands in that time." Tommy slapped Vic hard on the back of the head. The slap jarred Vic's head and knocked his prized hat off his head and down to the sidewalk. Vic bent down to pick it up. Tommy stopped him and said, "Here, Vic old boy, let me get that for you. Crazy Larry might not like your movement."

Tommy stepped over in front of Vic and stepped purposely on the hat and ground it onto the sidewalk. Looking back at Larry and seeing that Larry had an eye on the situation, Tommy bent down and picked up Vic's smashed hat and put the now soiled, crumpled version back on Vic's head. Tommy pointed to the clownish-looking hat sitting on top of Vic's comb-over as he looked back at Larry. Larry smiled approvingly at Tommy, and Tommy smiled that wise guy smirk back at Larry as he shook his head from side to side.

Then Tommy turned his attention back to Vic and said, "Let's walk. What the hell were you thinking?" Tommy said to Vic. "Why have you decided to not pay me? Who do you think you are?"

"Tommy, I," Vic began.

Tommy interrupted. "Tommy, I what? I'm sorry? I screwed up. Oh, you screwed up, all right. Victor, Victor, Victor, what am I going to do with you?"

As they arrived at Vic's office, Tommy knew it would be vacant. He had taken care of that this morning. Vic's boys would soon wonder why their latest assignment had them hijacking an "empty" truck across town.

Tommy pulled Vic's gun out of his waistband and laid it on the brick ledge right near the front door. Tommy said, "Let me get that door for you."

Vic was shocked that the door was unlocked and that no one was there to help him. He reluctantly stepped through the door, knowing full well that he had no choice. Tommy let Vic pass by him, and then he followed right behind Vic. Before the door could swing closed, Crazy Larry had Vic's gun scooped up from the brick ledge and in his pocket as he scooted through the still closing door.

"First things first," Tommy stated. "Let's sing Happy Birthday and let Larry blow out the candles and open the gift I bought him."

Tommy was standing right behind Vic, and right behind the both of them was a watchful Larry. Tommy looked at Larry and said, "Now, Larry, haven't you forgotten something?"

"What? You mean Pearl? Nope." He patted his trusted sidekick through his coat and said, "She's right here, boss."

"No, not your .45. Your birthday present. Go out to the car and get it. Aren't you getting anxious to know what it is?"

"Anxious? Hell yeah. I'm like a little kid on Christmas Eve."

"Well, then go get it."

"Well, what about Vic?"

"Don't worry, my friend. I can carry on the conversation with Vic until you get back. Now, go already."

Larry pulled Vic's revolver out of his waistband and slipped it into Tommy's pocket, just in case. Then he turned and sped out the door, like a little kid would anxiously run down the stairs on Christmas morning.

Faster than you could say "foul ball," Larry was back, standing behind Tommy with his present in hand. "Boss, did you say something about blowing out candles, because if you did, does that mean you brought a cake?"

Tommy turned his attention to Vic. "Open up the box and let Larry see what's inside."

Vic opened the box and tilted it so that Larry could see it. "It's a birthday cake," Larry announced. "Tommy, I was beginning to think you forgot all about a cake." Tommy reached into his pocket and pulled out another wad of tissue, as he knew Larry's sensitive side would show up again. A now sniffling Larry grabbed the tissues and said, "Thanks, Tommy. Now, can I open my present?"

"Nope. You have to wait until you make a wish and blow out the candles. Let's see. Larry, find a place where we can set the cake."

Tommy looked around and eyed Vic's desk, which was piled high and wide with papers. "I think Vic's desk would do nicely. Larry, would you mind clearing off a little space?" Larry walked over and swiped his arm across the top of the desk, knocking all the papers onto the floor. "That will do nicely,

Larry. Don't you think, Vic?"

Vic nodded. You could read the concern and see the beads of sweat rolling down Victor's face.

"Vic, set the cake down right here," Tommy ordered, pointing at a spot. Tommy pulled up a tall stool and said, "Larry, this is your guest of honor seat. Oh, and Vic, you stay standing right where you are." Tommy walked around and sat in the chair at Vic's desk. Then he reached into his coat pocket. As he did, the concern intensified on Vic's face as he thought Tommy was reaching for the end-all weapon. But instead of a weapon, Tommy pulled out a few boxes of birthday candles and began placing the candles into the cake's icing. The room was silent.

As Tommy finished placing the last candle, he said, "All I need now is something to light them with." Opening Vic's drawers on his desk, Tommy said, "There has got to be something in here I could use. Oh, what's this, now? This looks like the perfect thing." Tommy pulled out a set of handwritten accounting records and started thumbing through them. "Hey, what's this entry all about? Cigarettes? That's a substantial amount. Wow! How come I don't see any payment for Uncle Tommy?"

Tommy ripped several pages out of the book and stuck them in his pocket. Then he ripped another set of pages out and rolled them into a long, tight roll. "Now, how am I going to afford these birthday parties for Larry if bums like you don't pay me what is rightfully mine?"

Vic started to speak, but Tommy silenced him with a hand signal. Tommy reached into his pocket, pulled out a lighter, and lit the end of the rolled paper. As the paper burned, he handed the roll to Vic. Vic looked at the burning paper, then at Tommy. Tommy pointed to the candles. Vic was concerned now not only about the information written on the accounting sheet but also the flame as well, as it burned lower and lower, getting closer and closer to the bare hand holding it.

"And Vic," Tommy said, "do not let that flame go out."

As Vic lit the 56 candles on the cake, he felt the heat and then the sheer pain as the paper burned into his bare hand. He could smell the stench of his smoking fingers. Beads of sweat were streaming from every exit in his body as he fought to suppress the scream that was begging to be let out.

Tommy spoke up. "Victor, Victor, Victor. I thought you knew better than to play with fire."

"Tommy, I'm sorry. I…"

Tommy interrupted. "It's time you and I sang Happy Birthday to Larry." Tommy sang, and Vic joined in. When they finished singing, Tommy said, "Now, Larry, make a wish and blow out those candles."

Larry looked up in thought, then turned his attention back to the flickering fires and commenced to blow them out.

"Now," Tommy said, "before we all have a piece of this cake, Larry, I would like for you to open your present."

Larry, without hesitation, grabbed the present and ripped the paper off. As he did, he saw what it was. "A baseball bat? Wow, Tommy. Thank you."

"Read the label, Larry."

As he did, he discovered that where the player's name normally would be written, it read, "Crazy Larry #1," in cursive. At the trademark, it said, "Pearl Slugger." Tommy handed Larry another batch of tissues. "Thanks, boss. You are the greatest." Larry walked over and gave Tommy a hug, all the while keeping one eye on Vic.

Tommy turned to Vic, "Now, Vic, you and I both know that this is Larry's birthday. And I only see one gift. I really think you should give him a present, too. This gift should be something that he really wants. I have an idea. Let's give him a chance to tell you just what he thinks that might be. Now, Larry, I don't want you to tell me what you just wished for. Besides, I'm pretty sure that I already know what it is."

Larry's facial expression turned from one filled with pleasure to a stern, steely look that seemed to say, "I'm going to send you to your maker." Then he turned to Vic, "what I want is for you to give Tommy every stinking penny you owe him. And I suggest you do it right now. Where do you keep your cash?"

Vic pointed to the closet and said, "There in the safe."

"Open it," demanded Larry.

Vic walked over and opened the safe using his unburned left hand. When the tumblers clicked and the door popped slightly open, Larry said, "Now, step away. It's my birthday, you know. If you're lucky, maybe you'll be around so that you can open it on your birthday."

As Larry looked into the safe, he saw several neatly stacked bundles of cash. They were all categorized under headings like Cars, Alcohol, Clothing, Beauty Supplies, etc. As he scanned the piles, he said, "Well, looky here," as he came to a large stack of cash labeled Cigarettes. "How thoughtful of you, Victor, to label everything for us. Come look at this, boss."

Larry stepped back out of the way with his bat in hand, all the while keeping a watchful eye on Vic. Tommy walked over to the safe. "Well, Vic, looks like a nice pile of lettuce under Cigarettes. The way I see it, all of this is rightfully mine. We'll just call it compounded interest."

Tommy stepped away from the safe and said, "Larry, grab a trashcan and empty it, and then bring it over here and fill it with our cigarette money."

"There's a trashcan under my desk. Let me get it for you," said Vic, as he moved.

Larry slammed his baseball bat down on the desk, nearly vibrating the cake off the top of it, and said, "Don't you move another muscle."

Larry reached under Vic's desk and grabbed the trashcan. As he tilted it over to empty its contents onto the floor, he felt something on the bottom. He turned it over to check out what it was and found a revolver duct-taped to the bottom of the can. Vic said, "Well, how on earth did that get there?"

Larry looked at him with a look that could have, and probably has, killed as he realized just why Vic wanted to be such a help when it came to the trash. His grip on the bat became intense, and he started toward Vic when he heard

Tommy. "Larry, bring that trashcan over here and fill it up with my money."

Larry walked over, grabbed the cigarette money, and filled up the bucket. "Now, grab a little from the automobile fund for yourself, Larry. I know I am speaking for Vic when I say that, as a birthday present from him, he wants you to go out and have a good time. Isn't that right, Vic?"

"Yeah," replied Vic. "Happy Birthday, Larry. Help yourself. Go out and enjoy yourself. Tommy, I'm sorry. It won't happen again."

"Victor," Tommy said, "what should I do with you? You think I'm weak? You think I don't have eyes around this town? You thought I would never make a house call again to anyone, let alone the mighty Victor? Well, what do you think now? Just what in the hell do you think now? A man should never go back on his word to me, never! You know what today is. As we all know by now, it's Larry's birthday. So, let's have some cake while I finish thinking this whole thing through."

As soon as Tommy had finished the word "cake," Larry pulled his six-inch switchblade out of his pocket and snapped open the blade. This move caused Vic to react with a quick step back. "Relax, Vic," Tommy said. "First, we have cake."

Larry was holding his knife over the very top of the cake, waiting for permission from Tommy. "So cut the cake already, Larry," Tommy stated. Larry cut several evenly proportioned slices of the cake and one double the size of the others. He placed three pieces of cake on napkins, one in front of Tommy, one in front of himself. These pieces for Tommy and himself were the same size. Then he grabbed the double sized piece and set it on a napkin in front of Vic. After he finished placing Vic's piece on the table, Tommy motioned for Larry to bend over toward him. As he did, Tommy whispered instructions into Larry's ear.

As Larry pulled away, Tommy said, "Victor, Larry and I are going to enjoy our cake now. When we are finished, I am going to step out of the room. Larry here is going to help you with your piece of cake, seeing as how your hand is burnt and all." With that said, Larry and Tommy toasted each other with their first forkfuls of cake.

When they finished their birthday treats, Tommy said, "Now, if you will excuse me," as he stood up and walked out of the room.

Larry pulled a partial roll of duct tape from his pocket and set it on the table. Then he pulled out a set of tight-fitting gloves and put them on. He pulled Vic's hands behind his back and duct-taped them together. Next, he reached down and picked up Vic's king-sized piece of cake and said, "Now open up there, Victor old boy."

As Vic opened his mouth, Larry shoved the whole piece of cake into Vic's mouth, much like a bride would do to a groom and a groom to a bride, only there was no look of love in Larry's eyes. As he smashed the cake into his mouth, some of the icing packed into the nostrils of Vic's nose. The caked jammed up his nose made it a little tough for Vic to breathe. Next, Larry reached down and tore off a piece of duct tape and methodically put it across Vic's mouth.

"Now, Vic, do not, and I mean do not, remove that tape until Tommy and I have been gone from here for five minutes." Vic was gasping for air and trying to blow the excess frosting out of his nostrils. But each time he exhaled, he took in an even deeper breath through his nose, which brought the icing right back in.

"Having a little bit of trouble breathing out of your nose there, Vic?" Larry asked. Larry walked over and grabbed Vic's expensive tan cashmere overcoat off the old wooden coat hanger that was sitting in the corner right by the front door. With the coat in hand, Larry headed back across the room to where Vic was, bending over along the way to pick up his new bat. Returning to the still gasping Vic, Larry reached up with the overcoat and held it up to Vic's nose as if it were a disposable tissue and said, "Now, blow."

Vic blew the biggest pieces of the icing into the expensive coat. "There. Is that better?" Larry asked Vic. Vic's red, fear-filled eyes seemed to roll up and down as they stayed fixed on Larry's birthday present, and he nodded yes. "Good," Larry said, as he reared back and crashed the baseball bat into the front of Vic's left kneecap with all of his might. You could hear the shattering noise echo off the old brick walls inside of Vic's office as Vic rolled toward his good knee in a concentrated effort to escape the pain and to brace himself. Larry reared back again, and this time struck Vic on his other knee with as much might as he could muster. Vic fell to the floor in a heap of frothing pain.

Larry knelt on one knee and whispered in Vic's ear, "You are lucky that Uncle Tommy didn't grant me my birthday wish." With that said, he dropped the bat to the ground. It bounced to rest right next to Vic's head.

Tommy stepped back into the room and said, "You know, I really do hate these house calls. Every time I go on one, someone ends up getting hurt. So Vic, I beg of you, do not ever give me a reason to do this again. Do I make myself clear, Victor old boy?"

Vic, grimacing through all the pain, looked up to Tommy and nodded yes.

"Good. Then let's get going, Larry. Consider yourself lucky this time, Vic. Be sure to tell the others how soft we are."

After Crazy Larry and Tommy reached the car and Larry closed Tommy's door, he once again tapped on the window two times with his knuckles. His superstitious action seemed to have worked once again. On the car ride back, it was business as usual. Looking into the rearview mirror at Tommy, Larry said, "Tommy, I almost forgot to tell you. Tommy Jr. called me early this morning. He wants me to take him around so that he can take some more pictures. Do you want me to do that again?"

"That boy sure does have a talent for shooting pictures, doesn't he?"

"He sure does, Tommy."

"You take him wherever he wants to go, but you make sure you keep a close eye on him."

"No problem, boss. I'll take care of him. And Tommy, thanks for a wonderful birthday."

"You're quite welcome, Larry."

After a short bit of silence, Larry said, "You know, boss, it was sure sad to see Duck look like that the other day at Runner's funeral."

"Yeah, it was, Larry. He really took that hard. It's bad enough to see your dad die, but to blame yourself. It's going to take some time. That's about the only thing that will help. He knows we are here if he needs us." Tommy reached into the box next to him and grabbed a couple of tissues that he handed to Larry.

"Thanks, Tommy," Larry said, as he wiped the tear from his cheek.

"Turn right up here," Tommy said. "We have to stop by Carl's and Mary's. They'll be expecting us. It's someone's birthday, you know."

CHAPTER 2

The sun turned the darkened alley—home of a group of homeless people into a new day. Generally, the first to rise was a tall, lanky man known as Speedo. Speedo enjoyed getting up before everyone else. It gave him great pleasure being the others' alarm clock. Speedo yawned, as his mind tried to get his eyes to focus in on this new crisp morning. Then he stretched and brought himself up to a sitting position. Suddenly remembering what day it was, he announced, "It's Thursday. Who's going with me down to the Vent for breakfast"? The Vent was short for St. Rose's convent, which was located just a short walk away.

"Count me in," responded Duck.

"Sounds good to me," replied a muffled B.F.D., as he spoke from beneath his tattered blanket. Chalk line, once again making a poor attempt at humor, asked, "Oh, is today Thursday? Let me check out my palm pilot". He looked at the palm of his hand. "Looks like I can squeeze a little chow into my hectic schedule."

"Clarice here. I wouldn't miss it. I hope she has some of that delicious nut bread that Carl and Mary make and donate to the convent."

"Tell Sister thanks, but I won't be able to be there this morning. I've got a meeting that I can't miss," said Cilus. With the group assembled, they headed out of the alley toward the Vent.

"So Cilus isn't going to breakfast again. Do you think he's afraid of catching a little religion?"

"Nope, he said he had another of one of his meetings to attend."

"Yeah, right. I swear one of these times I'm going to follow him."

Arriving at the back door of the Vent, Chalk line walked up and knocked on the door and then stepped back alongside the others. They wanted to make sure they were all visible when Sister looked out the peephole.

"Okay," Chalk Line said. "On the count of three, everyone assume the 'pitiful look on your face' routine. 1, 2, 3, faces up."

The back door of the vent swung open, and Sister Molly appeared at the door. She was wearing oven mitts. Standing there looking silently at the group of homeless, she scanned the faces. It's a test of her own memory to see whose name she could remember. Then she addressed them. "You poor, pitiful-looking souls. Get in here. Oh, and by the way, you really don't need to wear those 'poor me' expressions on your faces. I'd welcome you in anyway. Now, get in here before you let all the cold air in Brown County into my kitchen. I'm just about to take the first batch of muffins out of the oven."

Politely, but without standing too long in one spot, they filed into the kitchen. Noses turned into the air, taking in all the marvelous cooking aromas. Name tags on the table showed them where they were to sit. The name tags served a two-fold purpose. It would allow Sister to sit next to whomever she wanted. Her seat placement was more often than not influenced by the level of stench emanating from them on the last visit. She hated admitting this to herself, but she had to draw the line somewhere. The second reason is that it helped put a name with a face.

Sister Molly opened the oven and pulled out the batch of muffins. She loved the way the room seemed to light up, as her guests' eyes got wider and wider in anticipation of the warm treats. As the smell wafted under Clarice's nose, she said, "This must be what heaven smells like."

This brought a smile to Sister Molly's face. With the muffins piled high on a plate, Sister grabbed a long pair of silver tongs and placed one of the freshly baked treats on everyone's plate. "These might help warm you up a little while I finish breakfast."

There's was a second knock at the door. She set the remaining rolls in the center of the table and covered them with the excess cloth which lined the bottom of the basket. Sister walked over and looked through the peephole. Recognizing who it was, she opened the door. "Good morning, Carl."

"Good morning, Sister."

"Carl, you look kind of pale today. Are you feeling all right?"

Carl leaned in toward Sister and whispered. "It's Mary's driving. She's one of those who thinks the speed limit is for everyone else."

Seeing Mary at the driver's seat of their van, Sister called out, "Good morning, Mary."

Mary waved and responded, "We hope you all enjoy the Povotica."

"We always do," replied Sister. Carl handed Sister two fresh loaves.

"Thanks, Carl."

"You're welcome."

Then she turned to Mary and said, "Thanks, Mary. God bless you both."

Mary yelled out, "Come down to the store sometime! Carl and I will fix you a malt on the house."

"Thanks. I'll certainly take you up on that next chance I get."

Carl turned to leave. "Got to go now, Sister."

"Thanks again, you two." Mary, wanting to show off the sound of the new glass pack mufflers she had installed on the van, said, "Listen to this, Sister." She revved up the engine and let off. The sound of the muffler made Mary's smile fill that whole driver's seat window she was looking out of.

"Sounds mellow and mean," Sister replied, as she gave Mary two mitt-filled thumbs up. Sister Molly watched as Carl climbed into the passenger seat. And then he hung on for dear life. Mary again revved the engine, then she floored it, and they raced off into the sunset with Mary's temporarily free hand waving out the window.

Sister walked back in and placed the bread on the counter. Noticing an empty space, she inquired, "I guess Cilus isn't coming today."

"Nope, he said he had a meeting." They all shook their heads. She walked over and removed his folded name card in front of his seat. Fast Eddie reached down, picked up his roll, and put it in his mouth. Sister spotted him and stopped him dead in his tracks when she commanded, "Hold on there, Edward. Aren't you forgetting something?"

Eddie, with his mouth wide open ready to take a bite, paused, glanced around the table, and then he said, "Butter. Of course. Someone pass me that butter."

"No, not just butter. Anyone else care to guess?"

Clarice speaks. "A Thanksgiving prayer."

"Bingo. Now, put that back on your plate, and let's all bow our heads." They all bowed their heads. Even Fast Eddie bowed his head, although he never took his eyes off the muffin. Sister Molly said her prayer and concluded it by saying, "And please bless all of my friends gathered here at this table. Amen." They all repeated "Amen."

Sister Molly walked back over to the counter and retrieved a butter tray. Setting it down in front of Eddie, she stated, "And yes, you forgot the butter, too." Everyone was frozen silently in place, their eyes glancing down at the still steaming rolls, then up at Sister Molly's face. They were all waiting for the okay from her. Sister Molly walked back over to the large, old-fashioned gas stove. She was preparing to throw on the main course. She turned back to them. "Well, what are you waiting for? Dig in. Those muffins won't stay warm forever." Sister Molly knew she needed to keep this group in line, plus she also enjoyed the feeling of power a lot.

Turning back to the stove, she stated, "I'm fixing ham, eggs, and a hash brown casserole. Hope that's all right with you guys this morning. We are fresh out of pancake mix."

"Sounds good to me." "I'll say, I hope it tastes as good as it smells," Chalk Line stated. "I guess it will dew this morning. Get it? D-e-w, not d-u-e. Dew, as in morning dew. It is morning, you know."

"It's d-o, not d-u-e. Even with the right spelling, it's not very funny," Duck stated. Duck wound up and started to throw his muffin at Chalk Line. Then he realized what an idiot move that would be. Chalk Line, in his best Dirty Harry voice, stated, "Go ahead, make my day." He was disappointed Duck didn't throw the muffin at him. He would gladly have eaten it, too.

Clarice rolled her eyes. "Man, just give it up. Your attempts at humor, like your nickname, are borderline."

"Hey, I was just trying to make a joke." Still standing at the stove with her back to the group, Sister announced, "Six weeks from today, St. Rose's is going to be offering the G.E.D. testing. Do any of you have an interest in signing up for it? I just happen to have some application forms." Turning with a cast-iron skillet full of eggs and a spatula in her hand, Sister dished out the eggs. "Speedo, how about you?"

"Oh, no, not me. Someday maybe, for sure, I think. But not now. At least not this time."

"Duck?"

"Sister, I graduated from college."

"Really? Good for you. Then why....?"

Everyone signaled to her not to ask. "You see, Duck doesn't talk about his past." Sister got the hint and moved on.

"Then how about you, Chalk line?"

"No thanks. I'm happy right where I am in my life, but I'll have to admit I ain't too bad at spelling."

Clarice spoke up. "I would like to. But I don't think I could pass the test. I'm not good at reading, writing or arithmetic.

I think I'd be wasting my time." Wasting her time, Sister was thinking. Does she really think sleeping in an alley all day long is a better time management system? She wanted so badly to say this, but didn't. Instead, she walked into the other room and grabbed some books and an application form.

Laying the book on the empty chair next to Clarice, which was left vacant by Cilus' no-show, Molly said, "With me as your tutor, you will pass the test. Let's try it. What do you say?"

"You would work with me?"

"Absolutely."

"Well, I don't know."

Speedo interrupted and signaled for Sister to come over to him. Arriving next to Speedo, he signaled for her to bend over. He whispered in her ear, "You know she loves Povoticia. Offer her the bread." He used his head to silently point in the bread's direction. Sister looked at the loaves. Speedo tried to get her attention again and tugged on her sleeve. Sister turned back toward him; he motioned to her he had something else to say. She bent over and he whispered, "Give her both loaves and tell her she has to share."

Sister smiled, turned her attention back to Clarice. "Well, what do you think?"

"I just don't know."

Sister walked over and picked up the two loaves of bread. She turned and headed over to Clarice and handed them to her. "If you say yes, you can keep both of these."

Clarice, feeling the warmth that was still emanating from the bottom of the loaves, asked, "Do I have to share?"

Sister smiles, "They're yours to do with as you wish. What do you say?"

"Well, since you put it that way, okay."

"Good, we'll start right after breakfast while these guys clean up."

Hearing this, they all mumbled, "That's not fair. She should help, too. Why should we clean up her mess?"

"It's simple," Sister says. "If you want to sign up for the test, I'll excuse you from cleaning up. Otherwise, quit whining."

Clarice held up the bread and chimed in, "Do you want me to share?"

With breakfast done, Sister and Clarice walked into the study and sat at a conference table. The others were busy cleaning the table and washing the dishes.

Over the next five weeks, Sister and Clarice met twice a week in the study at the Vent. Usually in the evenings, around 6:30, just after Sister's daily work tasks had been completed, Clarice and Sister Molly met, growing closer and closer over this time. There were times of rebellion as the work got hard and Clarice wanted to quit. And there were also times of celebration as they pushed through the difficult assignments. The discussions that they would have after the assignments were completed brought a bond between them that neither one had felt in a long, long time. Sister, at Clarice's request, was glad to have Clarice show up early on Thursdays for a quiet cup of coffee. Then, together, Sister and Clarice would cook breakfast for the others. Clarice, feeling more confident about her present and future, had been talking lately about going to school to become a social worker, after she passed the test. It was no longer if she passed the test. It was when she passed it.

Sister was sitting this morning in anticipation of the arrival of Clarice and then the others. Clarice had not shown up for their early coffee. She wondered where she was. She was thinking how lucky she was to have been shown the direction her life's work would take her. Working with the homeless turned out to be her passion, her true calling in life. She offered up a silent prayer. "Thank you, God, for showing me my heart's true calling. I love assisting my homeless friends. And just maybe, You and I can make a difference in their lives."

The doorbell rang.

CHAPTER 3

Just about three blocks from Carl and Mary's restaurant, Deano Alonzo was sitting at this mother's '50s styled kitchen table, one of those that has the matching chairs with the red padded vinyl seats and curved backs trimmed in chrome. He was just about to finish the snack his mother had fixed. He kept glancing down at his watch as if he had an important meeting to get to. Deano got up from the table.

"Finish your milk."

"Oh Mom, I'm 18 years old. I'm not a baby anymore."

"You'll always be my baby, Deano." She walked over and gave him a kiss on the cheek. The smooch from his mom, unbeknownst to him, left the image of two rosy red lips on his face. This was her favorite color of lipstick. "Now, where did you say you were going tonight?"

"Out with Luke and Ken. They're a couple of my new friends from school."

"Hmmm, I don't think I know them."

"They're real good guys, mom."

"Well, if you say so. You know how I feel about Troy, Frankie and Joey; they're guys I don't like you hanging around with. It's nice to see you make some new friends. Just what and where does 'Out' mean?"

"I think we're going to go to the movies or something like that."

"That sounds fun. In that case, you're probably going to need a little cashola."

"Could I maybe get a little extra so that I can go down to Carl's for a burger, fries and malt, afterwards?"

"Oh, I don't know, we'll see. Did you clean your room and tighten that pipe with those pliers you borrowed from Tommy?"

"I'll clean my room when I get home. I've got the pliers right here in my pocket. Besides, like I said, I'm 18 not 3, and you don't have to tell me when chores need to be done and when my room needs cleaning anymore."

Deano's mom walked over to the cupboard where she kept a cookie jar filled with her grocery money. She counted out ten one-dollar bills, walked over and handed them to Deano. "I remember your father picking me up here when this used to be grandma's house, and we'd walk to the movies. Afterwards we'd go down to Carl's for a malt. You tell Carl I said hi." She reached out to hand Deano the dollar bills. He grabbed them and headed toward the door without saying a word. Saying thank you didn't even enter his mind.

Deano's mom noticed he left his jacket on the back of his chair. "Hold on, baby. You forgot your coat."

She walked over and picked it up. As she did, a nearly empty pack of cigarettes fell out of his pocket and onto the floor. "Come here, young man."

He walked from the screen door to where she was standing, saw the cigarettes lying on the floor, and thought to himself, "Oh shit, I'm in trouble now."

She pointed to the cigarettes and said, "Whose cigarettes are these? Son, are you smoking again?"

Deano replied, "Cigarettes? Where? Oh those, those aren't mine. Those are Frankie's or Joey's."

"Good. I didn't think you smoked anymore." She bent over and picked up the pack and put it back into his pocket. "I wonder if their mothers know they smoke. You are such a good boy, Deano."

Deano walked out the screen door and let the door slam against the frame as it bounced shut. She stood at the doorway and watched through the screen as Deano walked away, strutting right down the middle of the street, in a "get out of my way world, here I come manner". With a sigh of pride, she said to herself, "My little boy is growing up."

Joey Parma, Frankie Armattan, and Troy Mastersomn were standing on the corner of 1st and Main streets, waiting impatiently for Deano. Finally, Troy saw him coming up the street and said, "Here he comes," as Deano walked up to them. Troy looked at his watch and asked, "Where have you been, man?"

Deano said, "You are not going to believe this one." Frankie noticed the rosy-red lip prints on Deano's cheek and pointed it out to the others. The other guys, seeing this, gave out little snorts of laughter. Deano asked, "What's so funny?" They all gave that 'oh nothing, just something Troy said earlier about being afraid of lipstick.' Deano replied, "Lipstick! Troy, you're afraid of lipstick? Is there anything that you're not afraid of? Chill out, man." Troy said to Deano, "Yeah, and you should be afraid, too, very afraid. Of lipstick."

"Have you totally flipped out? Anyway, where was I? Oh, yeah." And Deano once again told his friends the story of the cigarettes falling out of his pockets and how sharp he was in talking his way out of that one. "I told her the cigarettes belonged to somebody else."

"She bought that?" Joey asked.

"Yep." He finished by telling them, "You know, guys, she really doesn't want her little Deano hanging around with the likes of you."

Troy said, "That's funny. My mom tells me the same thing about you guys."

Joey chimed in, "Mine too. You guys are a bad influence." They all four point at themselves and say in unison. "I'm the type of guy my mom told me not to hang around with." To them, this is funny.

Still laughing, Troy whispered to Joey, "Shouldn't we tell him about the lipstick?" Joey shook his head. Not yet. Once the laughter subsided, they began swapping tall stories, which always had a way of puffing up their tough guy images. The stories would grow taller and taller with every swig from whatever bottle of wine they could steal from Jake's liquor store, and each manly drag from their cigarettes swiped from Carl's place.

As the evening wore on, they became more and more full of their own pretend coolness. With every turn with the bottle and ring of smoke, they became a little bolder. Joey looked at his watch and said, "Hey guys, guess what time it is? It's just about time to deliver the 10 o'clock news to our waiting audience down at the Cardboard Hotel."

"You're right. Let's get going." They started walking toward the darkened alleyway ahead. Troy looked at Frankie and shrugged his shoulder and signaled in a way that asked, "Now should we tell him about the lipstick?" Frankie looked at the imprints and snorted out another laugh and shook his head and mouthed, "This is too good."

Deano said, "Okay, guys, what's so funny?"

"Nothing. Just Troy and his fear factor cracks me up sometimes."

CHAPTER 4

Down at the Cardboard hotel, the residents knew it was Tuesday night. And every man and woman knew they could be the headline story for tonight's news, and it scared the bee-jeebers out of them, but this was their home, and they weren't about to run and hide. This is where they lived, and they would not give in to a pack of hoods. Besides, it's the only part of town where they were not harassed by the local authorities. This is their home. This is where they have made their stand. Oh, they've had the discussions before, about whether they should just move. It would be safer and a lot easier on their old bones, but the decision always came around full circle to the same determined one. We'll make it. We always have.

They lay there, eyes half shut in their staked spots in the alley; some in cardboard boxes; some out in the open, covered by old rags or newspapers; some propped up against the wall of the old brick building. Some old faces and some new, all hoping that maybe they would be left alone this Tuesday evening.

As luck would have it this evening, Cilus, B.F.D., Chalk Line and Fast Eddie were down at the mission getting supplies and special goodies that were only handed out one time each year. Sister figured that there must have been a big crowd, because they were obviously running late and had not yet arrived back.

She couldn't help but worry about them. And somehow, as a group, they always felt more secure when more of them were present on Tuesdays. Soon they hear the meaningless faint mumble of words coming from an all too familiar source. As the voices grew louder and closer, you heard "shhhhh" as the patrons of the alley all pretended to be asleep, hoping that maybe they wouldn't be noticed and wouldn't be singled out for the "news and the weather"... As the pack of young men, all in an age range of 18 to 21, reached their destination, they stopped at the mouth of the alley, casting tall ominous shadows along the brick surface of the alleyway. None of them were tall, but their shadows made them look that way.

Troy suddenly remembered the lipstick and nudged Frankie. Frankie signaled for quiet and whispered, "Now is not the time. Don't even look at it, Frankie said."

"Well, good evening, ladies and gentlemen of the streets. Welcome to the ten o'clock news. Let's go to our reporter, Deano Alonzo, who has some breaking news for us, Deano."

Deano, speaking into the lit cigarette as if it was a microphone, said, "Thanks, Frankie. We are getting pieces of information regarding a big developing story that is taking place at this very hour. It seems the reports coming out of the alley say a group of bums are getting the crap kicked out of them. And you know what? No one gives a rat's ass. Is this apathy, or is it reality? We'll be right back with the full story."

They all laughed, and with that they continued walking into the alley and kicking people where they lay, pulling off the newspapers and old rags that they were using as covers just so they could see the fear in their eyes. Joey looking down at one of the faces asked, "What's a matter, old timer? Are you afraid that if I kick you in the face, it's going to mess up your handsome look? I don't think so. I can see you before, and you aren't pretty." He reared back his foot and kicked him in the face—"And now I can see you after, and I must say you look better with a little color in your face," as blood trickled out of the corner of his mouth and down across his bearded face.

"But to be honest, you look like ten miles of burnt gorilla crap either way."

Joey took a few steps further into the alley, spied another person hiding under the covers, and made a sneak attack. Quietly, he walked up next to the person lying on the ground. As he quickly pulled back his foot in order to gain momentum to kick the person in front of him, his heel accidentally struck a person who was lying right behind him. This first blow of the heel struck Molly right in the mouth. She gave out a moan and then she slipped into a state of semi-consciousness. Joey, hearing the noise, looked behind him, and saw what he realized was a golden opportunity for him, called out to the others. "Look guys, two for one."

He brought his foot back, striking the person behind him with the hard heel of his boot, and then kicked forward into the person in front of him. He did this over and over until he grew weary and decided he needed a new challenge. Unfortunately for Molly, the first blow that rendered her nearly unconscious left her without the ability to think clearly enough to move out of the way of the strikes. As Joey walked away, Molly regained her senses. The sharp pain coming from the front of her mouth caused her to reach up to locate its source. As she reached up to her face, she could feel warm blood flowing down her fingers, across the back of her hand and then on down her arm. It was coming from her mouth. Reaching into her mouth, she discovered that her front teeth were loose. She let out another moan from beneath the blankets.

Deano walked up and pulled the covers off the face of the moaning lump of humanity laying there and said, "Well, well, well, what do we have here, and what's your name?" She looked up at him with blood still pouring out of her mouth and slurred, "Molly." She reached and grabbed her loose teeth.

"Well, Molly, my name is Deano Alonzo." Pointing to each of his cronies, "He is Joey Parma; he's Frankie Amattan; he is Troy Mastersomn. Nice to meet you. Say, it looks like your gums are bleeding. Hmmmm. Open up. Let's see if we can figure out what your problem is in there." Molly refused.

Frankie walked over and stepped on her hand and wiggled his foot back and forth, pressing her hand down into the asphalt as if it was a cigarette butt he was snuffing out. Molly, feeling the pain, opened her mouth.

Deano said, "That's a good girl. Oh my, it looks like several of your front teeth are real loose. Can you tell me what kind of heel would do this to you?" He looked up at the others to see if they caught his pun. They just rolled their eyes at him. "You really should get those pulled as soon as possible. Hey, I've got an idea. Why don't I pull them all for you right now?"

He turned to Troy and said, "Hand me those pliers we brought with us."

Troy handed them to Deano. He took the pliers, and Molly tried to pull away. Deano grabbed her arm and said, "Looks like I'm going to need my dental assistants for this one. Ladies, if you would?"

Frankie, Joey, and Troy surrounded her. Deano pulled her up to a standing position. Joey and Frankie stood on each side of her, holding her arms so that she couldn't move. Troy walked around behind her and held her head still, and then turned his head away. As Deano started the pliers toward her mouth, they heard a voice, and they turned to see someone trying to get to his feet.

It was Bob Duckins, better known as the 'Duck', one of the residents at the Cardboard Hilton. Reaching his feet, he said, "Well, aren't we a bunch of real tough guys! Let me count. One, two, three—wow! Four really manly men and a pair of pliers against one nun. Molly, from the looks of these punks, I'd say that you have them right where you want them. Why don't you kiddies leave her alone and go on home to your mommies while you still can. And you, while you're there, tell your mommy to wipe off the lipstick next time."

Deano ran his hand down the side of his face and then looked at his hand. He saw smudges of the red lipstick on his fingertips. He turned and gave the meanest look to the others. They all pointed at Troy and said, "He didn't want us to tell you."

"We'll deal with this matter later." He tried to rub the rest off, but succeeded only in smearing it all over his cheek. Deano, still standing there with the pliers held up in a position just about to enter Molly's mouth, lowered the pliers. Deano, Joey, Frankie, and Troy spread out in the alley, looking toward the voice. They were temporarily distracted by a second figure that was now suddenly standing next to Deano and Molly.

"Take your hands off of her." It was Speedo, ominously standing there in his best karate striking pose. All 6 foot 5 inches of him weighing in at about 132 pounds, with his skullcap on. This will strike fear into the depths of their souls, he thought. He said again, "Take your hands off of her, or deal with this."

What Speedo hadn't noticed was that when he stood up, Frankie was standing right behind him. Frankie tapped Speedo on the shoulder. As Speedo turned around, Frankie clocked him right in the face. Speedo's legs buckled, and it was all he could do to maintain his consciousness. He tried to throw karate punches at Frankie, but he was not effective. He looked more like a guy trying to grab those little blue dots that you see after a camera flash goes off in front of your face than he did a Kung Fu force to be reckoned with. The fight to maintain his alert status was lost as he fell to the ground, out like a light.

Speaking of lights, just then Troy looked around as he thought he saw a flash of light, but he just shrugged it off as if he saw nothing. Then Deano turned his attention back to Duck and said, "Well, it seems like we've got ourselves one tough guy still standing. A hero. The white knight coming to the rescue of a damsel in distress. Maybe once was a Green Beret, or a Martial Art expert. From the looks of his face, I'd say more likely a punching bag for a boxer. What about it, tough guy? What were you before you started living on the streets?"

"Just leave her alone," Duck said in response.

"My guess is a punching bag - and I hope for your sake you can still take a punch." With that said, they surrounded him and commenced kicking the crap out of him. Duck yelled to Molly, "Run Molly. Get the hell out of here now! Go, go!"

But Molly didn't move. She was not about to abandon her friends. Finally, stumbling backward after taking all their punches, Duck - still weak from the earlier kicks he had received from the front end of Joey's boot - stumbled back and collapsed onto a collection of cardboard boxes. Blurry eyed and fading in and out of consciousness, Duck looked up at the group of young punks standing over him. He reached into his mouth and felt a loose tooth that he tried to pull loose and said, "Say, you wouldn't have a pair of pliers a fellow could borrow, would ya? Seems I've developed a loose tooth."

Then he heard a voice say, "Goodnight, tough guy." With one last kick to the midsection, Frankie knocked all the air from Duck's lungs. This time, Duck was out cold. Standing triumphantly over the now unconscious street person, they began to high five each other. They looked silently at the out-cold Bob Duckins. Frankie walked over to see if Speedo was still out, and as he approached, he saw something that he thought was funny.

"Hey, guys, come over here and look at this." As they all walked over and looked down at Speedo, still unconscious on the ground, they noticed that his hands and arms were still cocked in his karate fighting position, with his fingers spread out in a bear claw sort of way. They all got a good laugh out of that.

Then Deano picked up the pliers they had dropped to the ground during the struggle with Duck. Deano broke the silence as he called for his waiting patient. "Molly, where are you, girl? You didn't run away, did you? Sorry that your mean old dentist kept you in the waiting room all this time. You see, we had a couple of emergencies we had to deal with." They found her at her same location. She hadn't moved from where they had left her. They walked over and pulled her up to her feet. They all assumed the positions they had taken before they were interrupted. Troy saw another flash of light, and asked, "There, did you guys see that? It looked like a flash from a camera, didn't it?"

Joey berated Troy. "It's just headlights from a passing car. I swear, Troy, you are always so worried about everything. You're like an old woman. Relax, man, and just enjoy."

Deano forced the pliers into Molly's mouth and grabbed one of her teeth. With the tooth firmly in the pliers' grip, he rocked it back and forth. Finally, he heard it crack free, and he pulled it from her mouth. He let it drop to the ground. "Boy, that was in there pretty good." Molly was squirming, trying to turn her face away. The pain, though somewhat numbed by the shock of the whole situation, was still fierce. Speedo worked his way up to a crouching position, then to his feet, and he headed over to help Molly. Before he could take a second step, Joey walked over to him and smacked him with a hard right to the jaw. Once again, Speedo collapsed to the ground, unconscious.

Deano got back to the matter at hand. Again, he forced the pliers into her mouth and pulled a second tooth. Molly's eyes rolled back in her head. As she drifted toward unconsciousness, she said, "Lord, forgive these boys, for they know not what they do."

All went black for Molly as she collapsed limply into the arms of those who were restraining her. Deano asked if anyone else wanted to join in the fun. They all declined. Troy still couldn't look. Slapping her lightly on the face several times, Deano said, "Come back, girl, stay with me. We still have a couple to go. Hand me that cup of coffee over there." He tossed the now cold coffee into her face. Molly awakened.

"There you are. Did you miss me? Just two more to go, and then you are all done until your next visit. Hang in there, old girl. I'll try to get these next two at the same time." Deano grabbed two teeth with the pliers and worked them back and forth. As the teeth broke free, Molly let out a scream from the pain that echoed down the alley, and then she passed out.

Frankie said, "Hey, Deano, why don't you put those teeth under her pillow, and maybe the tooth fairy will come visit her." Frankie raised her head, and with the last two teeth still clasped in the pliers, Deano reached under, released his grip on the pliers and let the teeth fall. They lowered her head back to the ground. Joey kicked the other two teeth up next to her head.

Deano wiped the blood off the pliers in Molly's hair and then on her blanket. Deano said, "Shit, I ruined a perfectly good pair of pliers. Damn, these are the ones I borrowed from Uncle Tommy. Uncle Tommy would kill me if he saw these now."

He tossed them down the alleyway. This time, they all see a flash of light. Troy said, "See, I told you I saw a flash of light."

Joey said, "Lightning, that's all; it must be getting ready to rain." They all snickered. Deano, still talking about the pliers, acting as if it wasn't a big deal and wanting to show the guys how tough he was, said, "Screw Uncle Tommy. If he remembers I borrowed them and asks, I'll tell him I lost them. What is he going to do? I'm family."

Frankie got a devilish smile on his face and said, "And now the weather." With that said, he walked over to the still-unconscious Bob Duckins, unzipped his fly and said, "Looks like a 100% chance for rain in the area of the Cardboard Hotel." After saying that, he urinated on Bob Duckins. Duck didn't even flinch. He was one cold Duck. All the other guys moved around, urinating on different lumps of blankets that were covering the various residents.

When their bladders were emptied, Joey said, "Looks like the weather is clearing up." They all turned and walked away out of the alley, laughing, picking up their bottle of wine, passing it around, and feeling cool.

The other residents knew the storm was over for now. Thankful that they were spared tonight, they could now relax. As they did, the scared concerned looks on their faces turned to closed eyed, open mouth expressions of men and women escaping to sleep. Molly got up, swollen face and all, walked over to Duck, spread a newspaper over her unconscious friend, making sure it covered his entire body and whispered, "Thanks, Duck." Then she walked over to Speedo and did the same for him. "Thanks for your efforts, my old friend."

Molly then went back and sat down in her spot. As she ran her hand through her hair, she felt something stuck in it. With her finger, she pulled it out and brought it around to look at what it might be. It was one of her teeth. After gazing at it for a few seconds, she noticed her other three teeth on the ground. With her left hand, she swept the other teeth into a small pile and placed the one she was holding in her right hand next to them. She placed her stuffed gunny sack pillow over the nest of teeth, lowered her head, and slipped off to sleep.

As the young men were walking off, Troy asked, "Do you really think she was a nun?" They all say "Jeeezzz!"

Deano's comeback was, "Will you relax, Troy? They're a bunch of bums, that's all. Nobody gives a shit about them. And what on earth would an educated ex-nun be doing living in the alley with a colony of homeless losers? Somebody give me a cigarette?"

"Shit, there's only one left," Joey said.

"Well, don't just stand there worshiping it, light it up. I wonder how many of them pissed their pants from the inside tonight," asked Deano.

"I bet the tough guy and his skinny sidekick did," Frankie commented. "I bet they won't mess with us next time."

"Yeah, this is probably going to be the best night of sleep they have had in a while," boasted Joey.

"I'm not so sure they're going to appreciate waking up tomorrow morning," Troy added. "We beat them up pretty good."

"Frankie, give me a hit off that cigarette. Yeah, we all made impressions on them tonight. Heel impressions on the jaw, boot impressions on the back, elbow impressions on the rib cage."

They all laughed at Frankie's pun. "Hey, come on, pass me the cigarette before it's all gone", Troy demanded.

"Frankie, give it to Troy," ordered Deano. "But Troy, don't slobber all over it this time."

"Slobber, when have I ever done that?"

"When haven't you?" they all replied.

"Come on man, are you going to take a hit off that thing or watch it burn?" Joey asked.

Troy took his drag and handed it to Joey. Joey put it to his lips and immediately spat it out. The trajectory of the cigarette made it land on the back of Troy's neck. Troy started jumping around like a madman swatting at his neck, yelling, "Shit, shit! What the hell!"

Just as his neck stopped burning, he felt intense heat inside his shirt at about waist high. The cigarette had hit Troy in the neck, then slid down the inside of his shirt, and rested where it met his belt. Troy was now yelling like a baby and jumping around like a wild animal. He pulled his shirt out of his pants, and as he did, the cigarette fell to the pavement. Sparks seemed to fly from the still lit end of it as it bounced off the asphalt. Troy looked over his shoulder, trying to see the burn on his lower back, and he said to Joey, "Joey, you S.O.B., why did you flip the cigarette on me? I ought to kick your butt."

"Sorry. It was an accident. It was a spontaneous reaction. As soon as I put that slobber-ridden butt of the cigarette in my mouth, I gagged. I didn't aim it; it just happened."

Deano added, "You're lucky he didn't throw up on you. That's the last time we share a cigarette with you, Troy."

Troy responded, "Sorry, guys. Hey, let's go to C.C.'s and get us some cheeseburgers, some fries, and a malt. I'll buy this time." C.C's is what they called Cool Carl's Restaurant.

"Yeah, sounds good. I kind of worked up an appetite," Frankie replied.

Joey's tough-guy response was, "I barely worked up a sweat, but I've always got room for a chocolate malt, an order of curly Q fries, and one of C.C's world famous cheeseburgers."

Deano chimed in, "Can't be out too late. Mom will kick each side of my butt if I get home past 1:00. It's a school night, you know."

"Hey, remind me to pick up some more cigarettes when we get there. I heard C.C's is still running that '5-finger discount'."

"I can't believe Carl is so blind," Troy stated. "It's so easy to steal from him."

"Did you ever think that maybe we're so good at it?" replied Deano.

"I wonder what the Tooth Fairy will bring to Molly." Joey asked.

"Maybe a gift certificate to Carl's," was Troy's answer.

"Na," said Frankie, "they've already got one of those. It's called a dumpster."

CHAPTER 5

In the front section of Carl's store, there was a small area consisting of six 15 foot long two-sided counters which comprise a small convenience store display of groceries and sundries. In the corner there was a refrigerated cabinet housing milk, cheeses, cold soda and other chilled essentials for the neighbors to purchase on their way home.

Next to the refrigeration unit there was a freestanding freezer where some not so essential choices of frozen treats could be selected and purchased. When Carl and Mary first opened up their restaurant, some locals suggested they carry a few groceries. They took their advice, and ever since then Carl & Mary's has been a staple in this community, having to this day all the charm of a true old-fashioned neighborhood corner grocery store.

The back three quarters of the building was where Carl and Mary's pride and joy restaurant was located. People came from everywhere to feast on their famous cheeseburgers, Curly Q French fries, and what everyone swears were some of the best homemade malts in the universe. Mary always kept their business up to speed by making adjustments that the changing times often dictated. Two years ago she started placing "We will cater your event" posters around the building, and today it represents a good portion of their income. Their catering features ethnic foods like Povitica, Polish and blood sausages, German potato salads and, of course, some of Mary's famous surprise recipes.

When Mary wanted to cook, Carl carried her down to the kitchen, where she still reigned as Queen of all cooks. It is one of her great pleasures. Carl had rearranged the kitchen so that Mary could easily reach all of her cooking essentials from the wheelchair she is bound in ever since the automobile accident. Most of the time, Carl ran the place downstairs by himself. He was the short-order cook, the cashier, and the waiter. There never was much of a need for a waiter, however, since most of the folks who came in wanted to sit at the counter and visit with Carl. Carl J. Silva came over from the old country. He is a man who speaks his mind; a man with a rich, contagious sense of humor; a man with a heart of gold. If you found yourself down and out and needed a little grub stake or a plate of food, he'd be the first to offer, never expecting to be repaid - but most did. They didn't want to get on Mary's bad side.

It's been a long day, and it's not over yet. Carl is standing behind the counter cleaning up after the departure of his last group of customers. As he looked out through the full glass storefront window, he recognized Joey, Frankie, Deano and Troy walking slowly across the street, heading directly toward his restaurant. Instinctively, he closes the money drawer on his cash register and locked it. Sometimes money came up missing after a visit by these four—not to say they stole it, but it's better to be safe than sorry.

Carl reached under the counter and pulled out a huge pipe wrench he referred to as the equalizer. He turned to a painted exposed pipe that ran upstairs to his and Mary's apartment above the store and tapped three times on the pipe, using the handle of his equalizer. Then he placed it in a location easily reached back under the counter. Next, he grabbed a box of chalk, removed a piece of it and placed it on the holder tray at the bottom of the small chalkboard, which was attached by a nail to the back edge of the counter. On the small approximately one foot square writing space of the chalkboard, you could see several small squares with existing marks already on them. One square's heading read, "Cigarettes," one read "Magazines." One read "Combs," another "Condoms," another "Candy" and yet another "Miscellaneous." At the bottom, there was a slick space for writing remarks with a non-permanent marking pen. The slick space made it easy to wipe away the day's notes and be ready for useful comments next time.

Upstairs, his wife, Mary, instantly recognized the signal. She grabbed the wheelchair, which was next to the chair she was sitting in at the kitchen table. She lifted the side arm rest and slid herself from the chair over onto the seat of her wheelchair. Firmly in the seat, she pulled the raised arm rest handle back down in place. In her head she could hear Carl's voice saying, 'Now fasten your seat belt/stabilization harness as soon as you are in your chair,' so she does.

Now safely positioned in her chair, she unlocked her wheels and maneuvered her wheelchair over to her end of the pipe that ran down into the restaurant. She reached into a leather saddle bag type of pouch on the side of her chair and pulled out her pair of leather gloves, the kinds that are cut off at the fingers, and put them on her hands. Carl figured that the cutting off of the fingers of the gloves would improve her dexterity. Next, she pulled out a small pipe wrench from the same bag. As she pulled it out, you could see the label gun's adhesive raised letters stuck on the side of the handle. It read, "Mary's mini-E." With four taps on the pipe with the wrench, she acknowledged she had received Carl's signal. Then she gave three more quick taps on the pipe. This meant "I Love You".

Next, she moved herself to the storage area under the pull-down desk where her spy equipment was located. She lived for this. You see, Carl and Mary were old-fashioned, and they didn't see any need to purchase expensive surveillance cameras. Living right above your place of business had its advantages. What they did was drill several holes in the floor of their home, which was the ceiling of their store. From these holes, Mary could observe the customers throughout the store. Mary didn't have to be peeking down through the holes all the time. Carl didn't want her to work that hard, but when he needed her spy skills, he would signal her as he did this night.

Mary opened the door of the supply cabinet. Reaching in, she found the supplies that she would need for her mission. The first item she pulled out was a black stocking cap, which she put on. The next item she took out was her favorite 45 RPM record. She always played it in the background when she was on one of these missions. She placed the record in the two wire racks Carl had mounted on the left side of her wheelchair.

Next she removed from the cabinet a brass collapsible telescope that, when extended out, had a half circle curve to it, with the size of the extended telescope getting smaller and smaller. When it was fully extended, the small edge would fit easily into the various holes drilled into the floor. This made it easier for Mary to look into the holes from her wheelchair. She snapped the collapsed telescope onto the clips under the front of her chair's seat.

The next item to come out of the storage space was a chalkboard identical to Carl's. She attached it to the rotating arm that acted as a TV tray and held the board just slightly to her left. Closing the cabinet, Mary worked her way across the floor to the old record player. Retrieving the 45 from the side rack on her chair, she removed it from its sleeve and held it in her hand while she put the small plastic 45 record adapter on the turntable tower. With adapter in place, she placed the record on the turntable, switched the control to 45, then turned the second control to "on." As she lowered the arm onto the beginning of the record, she heard the scratchy sound of the first part of the record as the needle advanced toward the musical treasure. Even the goose bumps that had been dormant on her forearms sprang into action as the music filled the air. She hummed along as she continued her preparation.

On the back of Mary's chalkboard, Carl had installed a highly polished sheet of thin chrome. This served as Mary's field mirror when she was on a mission. Reaching once again into her leather bag at the side of her chair, Mary pulled out two small shoe polish canisters. On the front of one can it said black; on the other it says O.D. green. Mary opened both cans and set them on her lap. Positioning the mirror to easily see her face's reflection, Mary dipped her fingers into the green can first. With the skill of a Marine on the battlefield, Mary applied streaks of green across her face. Next, she dipped in the black can and fills in the blank strips on her face with black. Her camouflage disguise is nearly complete. The final touch was to put a solid black line under each eye to cut down on the glare.

As she gazed into the mirror at the finished product, she smiled back in a sign of approval while humming along with her theme song playing in the background. She was ready for action. Oops, almost forgot her army issued flashlight, the kind that is curved at the end and has a red lens cover over the bulb. She thought it looked cool, snapped onto her khaki shirt. Turning off the overhead light and turning on her flashlight, because of the red glow emanating from the flashlight, the room looked like the inside of a submarine as it ran silently in the ready mode. Piercing the red-colored light that filled the room were sticks of white light which streamed up from the holes drilled into the floor of their apartment. Mary rolled over to the hole that overlooks the front entrance. She unclipped the telescope from the bottom of her chair, extended it, and placed it into the hole. She checked to make sure her seat belt/harness was still fastened.

She recognized the four troublemakers: Troy, Deano, Frankie and Joey. Deano turned to Carl and said, "Hey, old man, how are things going?"

Carl responded with a watchful eye and said, "Boys." Troy walked over to the counter and ordered four chocolate malts, four orders of curly Q French fries and four cheeseburgers. The other three spread out to various locations around the six aisles of groceries. Deano grabbed two cartons of cigarettes and stuck them inside his coat. Mary made two marks under cigarettes on her chalkboard. Frankie walked over and grabbed a current top girly magazine from the very back of the stack of 6 identical magazines and stuck it down the front of his pants. Then he pulled his bulky sweater down over it in order to help conceal it. Mary made a mark under "magazine" and adds "girly".

As Mary rolled to another peephole in order to get a better view of what Frankie was doing, she observed him grabbing a hot rod magazine, and saw him stick it in the back of his pants where it will be covered by his coat. "I wish I had a camera," she said to herself.

Troy yelled at Frankie, "Do you want onions on yours?"

Frankie responded, "Sure, onions sound great."

Joey looked around from the secluded magazine rack area where he was shopping to see if any of his friends were looking. When he thought it was safe, he opened up a magazine to the middle section. He let out several fake coughs and then tore out the large multiple paged fold-out picture of the gorgeous blonde and put it in his pocket. Then he put the magazine back on the rack. He was more worried about his friends seeing him with his private stash he would view later when he was all alone in his room than he was Carl catching him. Besides, he was sure the fake, extended cough noise was sufficient to cover for the sound of pages being ripped out.

Mary said, "You little..." Then she put a note next to magazines. It read, "We'll have to throw that one out later; can't be selling damaged goods to our customers." She looked back in time to see him stick a second girly magazine into his coat. She made another mark. Mary again said to herself, "Sure wish I had that camera. I'll have Carl rig one up for the next mission. If I choose to accept it." Mary quietly tapped along with the beat to the theme song on the arms of her wheelchair.

Frankie walked up and sat down at the counter. Carl asked, "Why don't you boys ever take your coats off?"

Frankie just gave that 'I don't know' shrug of the shoulders. Seeing that Frankie had taken a seat at the counter, Mary rolled over to the hole that gave her the best view of Joey. Joey always went to the candy area second. If he was true to form, he would grab eight baseball card packages, the kind that included a stick of gum, eight packages of candy cigarettes to give to their little brothers, and four large candy bars. Mary marked down each item as Joey did as predicted. She really didn't have to worry too much about what Joey did, because Carl kept such good control of the inventory at the end of each day. Once he accounted for the day's sales, he could tell you exactly how many of each item they should have, so it was easy to keep track of the boys' "purchases." But Carl knew Mary needed something to do, and he loved the way she ate this spy stuff up.

Today, along with the cigarettes, Deano was all over the place, and Mary was busy above, rolling from hole to hole, trying to keep track of him. Today Deano grabbed four new butane lighters. On the side of the lighters there was a girl. She was designed so that when she was upright, she was in a dress, but when you tipped her to the side, the dress disappeared and she was shown in a two-piece bathing suit. Mary put four marks under "miscellaneous" and wrote G.L., which stood for girly lighters. At the bottom of the chalkboard, under remarks she wrote, "We're going to have to order another dozen girly lighters."

Deano stuck four packages of chewing tobacco in his pocket. Mary made the appropriate marks. His last grabs were four packs of gum, and four packages of rolled breath mints. They always thought the breath mint and gum would hide the smell of smoke and alcohol from their moms when they got home, and weren't smart enough to figure out that the smoke smell actually got into their clothes. They never did figure out how their mothers always knew they had been smoking. They just thought all moms had eyes in the back of their heads and that 'Sixth Sense thing' going on. Deano's pockets were full; with his work done, he headed toward the counter.

As Deano neared the counter, Carl steps through the swinging doors with the four plates of food. Carl put them down in front of the boys and walked back through the doors to get the malts. Carl said, "You boys have been coming in here a long time. Heck, I've known your moms since they were this big, coming in here with their boyfriends and your grandpas. So I tell you what. This one's on me, so eat up, boys."

Mary, seeing this, wrote in her remarks, "What in the world? Need to have a heart-to-heart with Carl about this free food crap." Carl was trying to instill a little guilt into their hearts. But it didn't work.

Frankie said, "It's about time. I was wondering when you were going to show some appreciation. Hey, where are the onions? I was supposed to have onions on mine."

Deano said to Carl, "Grab the ketchup while you're back there, old timer." Carl was tempted to grab them by the collar and pitch them right out that front door, but he couldn't. A deal is a deal. Upstairs, Mary marked four cheeseburgers, four curly Q's, four malts; then she wrote these letters- TANAGBK. Translation: "They all need a good butt kicking".

Troy told Carl, "Give me the rest of that malt." Troy had noticed that Carl hadn't poured all the malt out of the stainless steel mixing containers. "Wouldn't want you to waste it."

Frankie turned to say something to Deano. As he turned, Frankie's elbow caught Deano's malt cup and knocked it to the floor. As the cup hit the ground, the force of the impact sent malt flying back up into the air. Some of the malt splashed all over the front of the counter, the rest splashed back to the floor. Deano was mad. He stood and said, "You idiot. You spilled my malt. First Troy embarrassed me with that whole lipstick on my cheek fiasco, and now this." Deano looked down and noticed that he was standing right in the middle of the spilled malt on the floor. "I ought to kick both of your butts right here and right now."

Frankie tried to explain, "I'm sorry, Deano. It was an accident."

Troy began, "Deano, it wasn't..." but Frankie interrupted him and said, "Shut up, Troy."

Deano glanced at his watch. "Look what time it is. Let's get out of here."

Deano turned to Carl and said, "You owe me another free malt, old timer."

They all stood up to head out. Joey leaned back over and took one last sip of his malt. As they headed for the door, they were all leaving chocolate footprints all the way to the door. Deano turned to Carl when he reaches the door. "See you next week, old man… if you're still kicking."

Mary wrote "clean up" under miscellaneous. Watching through the hole overlooking the front door, Mary saw them leave the premises. She collapsed her telescope to its smallest form and snapped it into the clips under her chair. She went over to the window, pulled back the shade, and looked out to make sure they were leaving. As they walked away, she saw them handing each other cigarettes and candy. Convinced that they were gone for the night, she made her way over to the pull-down planning desk above the storage area, from which she had earlier retrieved her spy gear. Pulling down the desk as it rested on its side pins, she pulled out a record-keeping book which had the initials U.T. on the front of it. She opened the book and recorded what she has as the losses for the day. Finishing her entries, she placed the open book on her lap and maneuvered over to the kitchen table. She laid it on the table, opened to the page that displayed her notes. Knowing that Carl will have to walk around the store to see what else is not accounted for today, so that he can make the final entries.

Mary's attention now turned to the record player. She reached over and turned the player off. Grabbing a canister of moist towels from the cabinet, Mary pulled out a couple and wiped the camouflage off her face. Flipping the chalkboard over carefully, making sure she didn't accidentally erase any of her marks, she looked in the polished chrome mirror to make sure she got it all off. She had to look good for Carl, you know. Then she went over to the cupboard and took out a teapot and navigated over to the sink. Filling the teapot with water, she placed it on the front burner and set the setting to medium.

It was closing time, and Carl was just about finished walking around the store with his chalkboard. He locked the two deadbolts on the door, flipped the Open sign to Closed, and pulled down the shade. He turned to walk to the back of the store where the stairs were located that lead to their home above the store. As he ascended the stairs, he turned off the switch that shut off the lights in the store. Nearing the top of the stairs, he heard the tea pot whistling, as the water was reaching the serving point. That sound put a broad smile across his face as he anticipated another evening with Mary.

When he opened the door, Mary was pouring tea into his cup. Carl walks over to Mary and kisses her on the cheek and said, "So how's my little covert agent tonight? Any interest in going undercover with me this evening?"

"No, but I'm just fine. Thank you," she replied.

Carl said, "Thank you for my tea."

"You're welcome."

Carl raised his cup up and said, "Here's to my reason." After sips were taken, Mary said, "That was fun. But I have a question for you, Carl. Why on God's green earth would you offer free food to those worthless sacks of snake skins?"

Carl responded, "I got to thinking while I was cooking their orders. I thought maybe if we were extra nice to them, they would feel guilty about stealing from us."

"Carl, if they don't feel guilt and don't understand the word respect or know what's right and wrong by this time, you're certainly not going to teach them now."

"What was I thinking? From now on, Mary, I'll let you do the thinking."

Mary said, matter-of-factly, "Thank you."

Carl continued, "No more free food. Unless I—I mean we—okay, unless you decide I need to feed them a free knuckle sandwich. So what did you get?"

Mary rattled off from her list what the thugs had made off with. She said, "How about you?"

"Your notes match mine to a 'T', except for a cracked malt glass."

Mary again laments, "This just isn't right. If their hands are never caught in the cookie jar, how will they ever learn?"

Carl said, "You know it's taken care of. I gave my word to Tommy. Besides, they only come in four or five times a month, usually late on Tuesday Evenings." Carl made his final entries into the record-keeping book. Now it was Mary's turn to run the totals. Mary looked up and was reminded by the calendar that this was the last Tuesday of the month. As she finished rechecking the total, she showed the amount of this month's five-finger discount to Carl. He looked at the numbers and commented, "At least they're consistent."

As expected, the front door buzzer rang. Carl walked over to the window that overlooked the entry. As he pulled back the sheer lace curtain, he saw crazy Larry looking up and waving at him. Carl signaled he would be right down. Mary, still bothered by the inconsiderate actions of their visitors, said, "I don't care who they are. It's still not right." She handed the itemized list for the month to Carl.

Carl walks back downstairs and turned on the store lights. He walked to the freezer and picked up a package he had ready, and headed toward the door. As he unlocked and opened it, Carl greeted Crazy Larry, "Come on in, friend."

"Good Evening, Carl. How's Mary?"

"She's doing just great, thank you. Can I fix you a malt or something to eat?"

"Not tonight, no thank you. I've got to stop by Jake's liquor store, too. Then I've got to get right back to Uncle Tommy's. I hate to leave him alone too long."

"So how is Tommy?"

"He's great. He sends his best. He says he is appalled by the actions of his nephew and his buddies. But you know how he is about family and loyal friends. He told his sister he'd look after her little boy Deano, so how much this month?"

"According to Mary, it's about the same as last month. At least they are consistent." Carl handed the summarized list to Larry. Crazy Larry, in turn, handed Carl an envelope. "This ought to cover it."

"Thanks Larry, and tell Tommy thank you. I wonder if those boys will ever get it."

"Oh, I think they'll get theirs someday. I've got to get going."

"Here's some sausage for Tommy. Tell him Carl said to share with you."

"Thanks, Carl." Tommy appreciates this. He loves this stuff.

"See you later." They gave each other hugs. Crazy Larry turned and walked out the door. Carl pulled the door closed and locked it. Then he rolled down the shade again, turned and walked toward the back. With the envelope from Uncle Tommy in his hand, he headed back up the stairs, turning off the lights on the way up.

Entering their home, he walked over and handed the envelope to Mary. She headed over to the safe that they had installed in the wall. As she opened the door of the safe, she saw several of the same sized envelopes, all unopened. She put this one on top of the pile. No need to count what was in the envelope. It was from Tommy, and there always would be enough to cover the five-fingered discounts and then some. As she closed the door on the safe, she said, "I wonder if those kids will ever be held accountable. I wonder if they will ever amount to anything. Tommy won't always be able to bail them out, you know. Mark mine and Crazy Larry's words, they'll get theirs someday. What goes around comes around."

Carl, being a true friend to Tommy, said, "Tommy is just doing what his sister asked him to do. He wants Deano to have a chance to get a good start. He's trying, in the only way he knows, to help. He's afraid that if Deano gets thrown in jail now, there may not be any turning back."

Mary just shook her head and said, "Time will tell. Time will tell."

CHAPTER 6

As Deano, Frankie, Joey and Troy walked home from Carl's, a black cat ran in front of them and jumped into a metal trashcan. A startled Troy said, "Did you see that? It was a black cat."

Deano answered, "A black cat—so what?" Deano picked up a rock and threw it at the trashcan. His rock missed. They all picked up rocks, and one of them hit the trashcan, and that cat must have jumped straight up into the air a good six feet. Straight up into the air, right out of that trashcan. As all cats do, it landed on all fours on the pavement. The cat took off running, crossing right in front of them again. This time they were armed, and as the cat dashed across, Deano threw another rock and missed. Joey threw one that scooted past the running cat. It skipped up off the street surface and busted out the headlight of a parked car. The boys keep rapid-firing large, fist-sized chunks of rocks at the scurrying cat. Suddenly, the cat spun and fell to the ground as several of the large rocks struck it. At least one hit him right where his leg attached to the socket of the hip, and another struck at the bottom half of the cat's back right leg.

As the boys stood there silently, watching the fallen cat, they noticed it moved in an attempt to get off the ground. The crying cat struggled and managed to get back to its feet. It then turned and looked right at the four of them and let out a threatening, teeth-filled, angry hiss. It looked like something right out of a scary movie. With the cat now standing, you could clearly see that its back leg was broken. It turned and limped off as fast as its injured body would carry it. Frankie picked up another rock and threw it at him as the cat turned into the alley and disappeared.

"Come back here, you scaredy-cat," Joey yelled. "We'll teach you a little 'hiss-tory.'"

Troy didn't like this, and he spoke out. "Now we're asking for it. That was a black cat. It crossed our paths twice; heck, once is supposed to be bad luck. I don't want to know what twice means, but it can't be a good sign. Then we hit it with a rock. It even looked like we broke its leg. That's tempting fate - not to mention the fact that it's got to be illegal. People these days are serious about cruelty to animals."

Deano ran his hands through his hair and said, "I swear, Troy, you are the most paranoid person that I have ever known. You are more worried about that stupid black cat than you ever were about the bums in the alley. Besides, there are leash laws in Brown County, you know. Black cat, green cat, brown cat—it doesn't make any difference. It was just a stupid alley cat. Think about it, who will ever know that it was us who threw the rocks that hit it, anyway? Look around, there's nobody here!"

Then, from out of nowhere, they heard a voice say, "I wouldn't be so sure of that." A shadowy figure toppled over a metal trashcan on purpose with his foot. They all turned toward the sound and saw the still shadowy figure standing there in the darkness. They stood there silently in disbelief, just looking at the faceless figure. After what seemed like an eternity of silence, the figure spoke.

"What did that poor defenseless cat ever do to you girls? Let's see what you momma's boys can do against someone who's willing to fight back."

The figure opened his coat and removed something silver out of his pocket that glimmered like a knife's blade would if it were exposed to a beam of light in the darkness. He then started walking toward them. Troy, Deano, Frankie and Joey turned briefly to look at each other for support. When their eyes met, they could each see in the eyes of the others the same fear that they were feeling in the depths of their souls. That was all it took. The four of them turned and took off running for home, scared out of their wits. Troy was the fastest. As he led the pack down the street, he prayed to God, "Just let me get out of this, and I won't do anything bad ever again."

The shadowy figure stopped and watched the running herd of boys and said to himself, "You're a real bunch of tough hombres, huh!" Placing his silver transistor radio back in his coat pocket, he turned to help the cat. The injured cat tried with all its might to limp back home. She crawled under several fences and limped across a rooftop. She moaned as she lowered herself into a manhole that she knew was a shortcut. Finally reaching home, she came into the alley right up to where Sister Molly was sleeping and nudged her as if asking for help, then collapsed in total exhaustion.

Molly awakened and realized she has her hand on her cat. She said, "Princess, where have you been? Mommy missed you. What happened? Oh my goodness, you're hurt! What happened? Tell me what happened."

Molly looked up and standing above her was B.F.D. "She might not be able to tell you what happened, but I can. I saw the whole thing. It was our Tuesday night visitors. They hit your Princess with rocks. I left Cilus and the others at the Mission. It was getting late, and I wanted to get back here, it being Tuesday evening and all. Molly, I tried to stop them, but it was too late. I managed to put the fear of God in them, though. I tried, but I couldn't catch up with her, so I followed her. She was determined to get home to you, Molly."

Molly replied, "Thank you."

B.F.D. noticed Molly's teeth and mouth. "Molly, are you okay? What happened?"

"Never mind about me. Would you hurry and get me some rags so that I can tend to Princess? I'm also going to need something to make into a splint for her poor little broken leg."

Petting her cat, she said, "You're home now, baby. I'll take care of you."

B.F.D. returned with an old T-shirt and a couple of large wooden tongue depressors he found in the trash. He helped Molly rip the T-shirt into strips that they used to secure the splint in place. With the splint now in place, B.F.D. turned and walked away. Molly fell back to sleep with Princess in her arms. B.F.D. bent down and picked up his favorite blanket and walked back over to Molly and covered her up with it. Molly was sound asleep, and the cat was purring like she'd found her place in heaven. A smile came across Molly's face, exposing her bleeding gums, as she stirred and whispered, "God Bless you, my friend." B.F.D. walked back over to his place, laid down and covered himself with blankets, and drifted off to sleep. He stirred later as he heard the commotion of Cilus and the others returning from the Mission. He wanted to say something to them, but he figured it could wait till morning.

CHAPTER 7

The morning came as it always had, with the distant sound of barking dogs filling the misted breeze. The smell of bus fumes, accompanied by the rich roar of their mighty engines, erased the morning silence as they started and stopped along their designated routes. Bob Duckins raised his aching head up and felt throughout his body all the pain of last night. The visibility from his left eye was a mere sliver, since it was mostly swollen shut. His bones ached, but as he rose on his elbows and surveyed the area with his good eye and saw all of his friends, he realized they had survived.

At that moment, Cilus walked over to him and said, "Sorry we weren't here last night. There was a large line at the mission. Let me help you up; it's time for breakfast."

He bent down to help him up. "Are you okay, man?"

"Well, I've had better mornings, but I'm okay", responded Duck. Like migrating birds, they walked as a group down to the big green dumpster behind Cool Carl's. This dumpster always offered a good variety for breakfast, but with no guarantee of getting even one of the food groups—they knew they had to get there before the city trash disposal trucks did.

Duck, moving kind of slowly, grimaced from the pain caused by him moving his jaw back and forth as he made sure it still worked. Duck had no idea that what had happened to him last night, and what was about to happen to him this morning, would change his life and the lives of so many others. You see, Cool Carl's dumpster offered more than fuel for the body that morning… While taking his turn rummaging through the dumpster, Duck felt something hard and round under a clump of moist soiled paper napkins. He grabbed hold of it and pulled it out of the depths of the dumpster, and as he rolled back the soggy napkins and discarded the other trash that came out with it, he couldn't help but hope that he had found the mother lode. Hey, after what he went through last night, he figured he deserved it. Maybe it would be a whole piece of chicken, maybe a hunk of medium rare filet, not yet too rancid to eat. Just as his mind had his mouth salivating, he finished unwrapping his much anticipated edible treasure, and discovered it wasn't a triumphant food find at all. It was an old discarded golf ball. Disappointed, he began to toss it back into the dumpster when he noticed the ball had a large cut on it. Holding it at the end of his fingertips, he stared at the ball. As his mind drifted off in deep thought, in his head he heard a voice saying, "They call that a smile." As Duck looked up, he was seeing through the eyes of a little boy looking up at his dad, Runner Duckins. His dad said, "Yeah, when you don't hit the ball just right, sometimes you put a cut on the ball; they call that a smile. See how it curves up?" Runner was showing his son how the cut on the ball has a curve on it at the end, just like when you smile.

He continued, "Kind of funny, isn't it? A golf ball with a smile on it isn't much good for anything, but a smile on your face lights up my world every time. I love you, son."

Bob Duckins' dad Runner was the pro at the local country club, and the smiling golf ball story was one of Bob's first of many memories of him being with his dad on the golf course when Bob was eight years old. That summer, Bob's mother had run off with a member of the country club. It was hard, but through it all Duck's dad and he became best Buds. Duck respected his dad, and so did everyone else who knew him. He learned a lot about golf from his dad, and a lot about life as well. His dad's word was as good as gold. Little Bob Duckins grew into one heck of a golfer, and he owed it all, of course, to the hours upon hours of practice, the constant encouragement, and many helpful lessons given to him by his dad. His dad would tell him, "Duck, you are good enough to go pro if that's what you want. And if golf isn't your passion, then find out what is, and be the best you can be."

As it turned out, golf was Duck's passion, and he knew he would be good at it. His dad and golf were everything to Duck. Suddenly, a cold shiver shifted the daydream to another time and place. Duck suddenly was leading the pack, well on his way to winning a very prestigious collegiate tournament. As he was preparing to tee off on the 16th hole, his dad was there, as always, pacing nervously up and down the fairway. He was trying to act cool and calm on the outside for Duck's sake, but inside he was a complete nervous wreck, as everyone, including Duck, knew. Runner came over to offer some encouragement and swing advice to Duck. Then, as he often did to break the tension, Runner offered up a joke, and this time, it was a pretty good one. Duck had heard it before, but he loved this one.

As Runner reached the punch line, he stepped back and shook his head, as if to knock the cobwebs out. When he tried to speak, only mumbled words came out. He felt his chest with a look of 'something isn't right here' on his face, looked down, and then back up at Duck. He slurred the words, "No, not now." Right then, his eyes rolled back into his head and he collapsed to the ground. He hit the ground hard, offering no extension of arms or any attempt to break his fall. Duck rushed to hold him and yelled for someone to get a doctor.

"Dad! Oh my God! Hurry. Please hurry." As Duck held his dad in his arms, he heard the ambulance coming, but it was already too late.

The days leading up to the funeral were a daze. Many well-wishers told stories that brought comfort, but no relief from the guilt and the pain of loss. Closing the casket brought it all to a final realization, and soon the shock subsided into pure grief, and the guilt seemed to be the only truth. In his mind, Bob would play over and over the events of that fateful day. If only he hadn't played that day. In Bob's mind, he thought all this excitement over a silly game of golf caused the death of the one thing he treasured most - his dad. Feeling that he and golf were responsible for the death of his father, he walked away from golf and life as he knew it.

Suddenly, a voice interrupted his daydream. The first thing Duck saw was a half empty ketchup packet dangling in front of his face at the end of B.F.D.'s fingertips. B.F.D. said, "Here Duck, you might want some ketchup to dip that golf ball in the way you've been staring at it. It looks like you're really considering eating it. I can't imagine it would be any good without ketchup."

Duck looked up into the eyes of his smiling friend and he smiled, but for Duck, somehow it wasn't the same anymore. From that day forward, the smiling golf ball became Duck's constant companion, his gazing ball. He would constantly fidget with it while it was in his pocket, or toss it up in the air, or twirl it between his fingers, or bounce it off the ground. His thoughts turned to questioning why was he wasting his time. He wondered, "What would it be like to spend these hours doing something constructive with his life? In the same allotted time I can continue to sit here, day after day for hours on end, staring at a golf ball with a smile on its face, picking my butt, or I could step back into the world and spend those same hours doing something constructive, something I was meant to do, like playing golf."

Duck could feel the change. He realized it wasn't him or the game of golf that caused his dad's death. In fact, his dad wouldn't have had it any other way, his final breath being taken on a golf course after watching his son as he led the field in that tournament. Hopefully, he was proud of his son and what he had accomplished with his own life. But he couldn't help but hope that Runner wasn't watching him now.

CHAPTER 8

For the next few Wednesday mornings, Duck would wake up thinking, "Well, I've survived another Tuesday Night News Report from hell. But why in the hell am I doing this?" His mind drifted more and more, and he focused on what Wednesday mornings would be like if he had spent Tuesday evenings actually doing something meaningful with his life.

Duck held out his hand and looked at his grimy fingers and the dirty rags he wears as clothes hanging off his arm. He stood in front of a storefront window. Seeing his reflection, he scanned down the front of his wardrobe, and it hit him he was wasting his God-given talent. As his eyes focused, he peered through the glass. Instead of looking at his reflection, he noticed the store display of the pawnshop had an old set of golf clubs, and standing next to them was a used pair of golf shoes. At that moment, the name Anthony Bezmouskee popped into his head—an old friend and golf buddy from years back. He decided it was time to look him up and see if he was, in one way or another, still involved in the golf business.

"I'll try the library." Duck got up, feeling in his stomach the pain that's still lingering from the last "News and Weather" report, and headed toward the end of the alley. Reaching the end, he turned and said to his friends, "I won't be around for a while. I'm going to take a long overdue trip to see an old friend, but someday I'll be back. I won't forget about you guys."

With that said, Duck turned and headed out of the alley toward the Library. Upon reaching the library, he was received with the usual "Hey, you can't loiter here" look that he gets wherever he goes. Duck walked through the doors of the library and up to the information desk and said, "Excuse me. I'm trying to find a way of contacting an old friend."

The librarian, looking down while feeding information into her computer, replied, "Why, sir, just step over to"— She stopped in mid-sentence as she looked up and saw the appearance of the man to whom she was replying. "Sir, do you have a library card? If you don't, I'm going to have to ask you to leave right now."

"I'm just trying to find an old friend. His name is Anthony Bezmouskee. Could…."

The librarian interrupted, "If you have no card, you will have to leave right now." Duck replied, "Isn't this a public library? I mean…"

The librarian turned to her coworker and said, "Joan, could you call security, please?"

"Okay, okay. I'm leaving."

Duck was turning to leave when he heard a voice say, "Wait a minute. I'm sorry, but I couldn't help hearing your conversation. Why don't you give me the name of the person you're looking for and a few clues that might help me find her or him."

Surprised, Duck stated, "You'd do that for me?"

"Sure. Now, what's the name?"

"It's Anthony D. Bezmouskee. Golf - that's how I think you'll find him. The last time we spoke, he said he loved golf and that it was a part of his soul - that he would always be involved with it in one form or another for the rest of his days. As a matter of fact, we both used to swear that. And we knew that if, for some reason, we lost contact with each other, all we'd have to do was simply put the word out in the golf industry, and we'd be able to find one another."

"Are you sure about the spelling?"

The security guard from the library was now standing next to Duck, impatiently ready to escort him out the door.

"Oh, yeah, I'm sure about the spelling."

"Okay. You go on outside and wait for me by that red car out front." She pointed to her car, which you could see through the large glass windows of the library. Suddenly, she stopped and said, "No, wait. This is a public library. You come with me. Let's go find this Mr. Bezmouskee."

She signaled for the security guard to stand back and grabbed Duck by the arm. They turned and headed toward the computers and walked right past the cocked eye of the "not so happy" second security guard.

"First things first. Let's get you a library card." They walked up to the counter and said, "We'd like to get this gentleman a library card."

The librarian reluctantly began the process. "We'll need to see two pieces of identification." Duck reached into his pocket and pulled out an old chewed up cigar butt. "Well, I guess you can get my D.N.A. off this old cigar butt, can't you? I mean, that's all anybody talks about anymore - D.N.A. this, D.N.A. that."

Duck's new friendly helper put her hand on his shoulder and asked, "You don't have any form of identification, do you?"

Duck stuck out the old cigar butt. Smiling at him, she saw he had a sense of humor and said, "Put that away. Do you want to give them another excuse to kick you out of here?" She pointed at the No Smoking sign.

"Great. Now, I tell you what. I'll have them put you on my library card. That will make me responsible for your actions. I'm taking a risk, but what the hell—we all need to be extended a helping hand once in a while."

They had stepped away from the counter, and as they walked back up to the librarian, Duck's companion said, "Like I said, I would like to have my friend here, Mr."- she realized she didn't even know his name.

"Bob Duckins. Friends call me Duck."

She continued, "As I was saying, I want to have Mr. Duckins added to my library card."

In response, the librarian stated, "You know you will be taking full responsibility for this…" pausing, she said, "… gentleman, including late fees and his actions while he is at the library facilities?"

It was Duck's new friend's turn to interrupt by saying, "Hmmmm, I must have mumbled or stuttered or something, because I distinctly remember asking you to add Mr. Duckins to my library card. I don't remember asking for a lecture. Now, please be a good girl and print up his card."

The librarian looked up past the two of them and made eye contact with the head security guard who was closely monitoring Mr. Duckins' and his friend's actions. He was shaking his head 'no.'

The librarian turned back to Duck and his new friend and said, "I'm not sure we can do what you want. I'll have to check with my supervisor."

"Just a minute," said Duck's friend. She reached into her purse and pulled out a business card that she handed to the librarian. "I suggest you hand my card to your supervisor and remind her or him that this is a public library, and that I will take full responsibility for my friend here."

The librarian took the card and said that she would be right back. As she turned to walk away, the librarian glanced down to read her card, which read, "M.Y. Angel, Attorney at law, Angel, Marcus & Smith, Chartered."

A short while later, the librarian returned and apologized and began the process of issuing a card. "Sorry about the inconvenience. Would you mind spelling your name, sir?" No words were coming out of Duck's mouth. It's like he couldn't believe this was happening. The librarian said again, "Sir, your name."

"Oh, sure. That's Bob D-u-c-k-i-n-s. Bob Duckins."

"Sir, would you mind standing over by that blue backdrop? We need to get your photo to have it placed on the card."

Duck strolled over to the wall, turned around, and before the librarian could take the picture, Mya said, "Whoa, hold the phone." She walked over, took off his worn out golf hat. His hair looked like it had been under that hat forever. She reached up, and with her fingers, attempted to brush the matted mess into some semblance of a hairdo and said, "Now take the picture."

The librarian snapped the photo and said, "I'll have your card ready in a flash, maybe a flash and a half." She pushed a button, and within seconds, modern technology was printing out a personalized, laminated, Brown County library card. The librarian grabbed it from the machine and said, "Here's your card, Mr. Duckins."

Duck looked down and stared at the still warm library card with his photo on it. She handed it to him. He took it from her and said, "I have a library card!" With that said, he let out a loud, "Hot damn!"

The librarian looked at Miss Angel and said, "See what you got yourself into? Remember," Miss Angel said to Duck, "this is a library." She gave him the "finger over the mouth shhhhhh sign."

"Oh, sorry." He turned to address the entire library and said, "Sorry, everybody." Miss Angel just shook her head and smiled. The librarian stuck out some papers for her to sign, which he did. Duck leaned over the counter and whispered to the librarian, "Thank you very much."

Then he turned to his new friend and whispered, "And thank you very much, M.Y. Angel, attorney at law." He leaned over and gave her a kiss on the cheek. Duck noticed she looked a little taken aback that he took the liberty of kissing her on the cheek. "I am sorry about that, counselor." He extended his hand.

She shook his hand and said, "Friends call me Mya."

"Then Mya it is," Duck replied.

Then Mya said, "Now let's go see what we can find out about this friend of yours."

The two of them walked off toward the computers. All the while, Duck was looking down at his new treasure. Duck was thinking out loud and was saying, "I can't take my eyes off of it. I have a brand new, personalized, Brown County library card with my picture on it. Man, this is a definite step in the right direction. The Duck is back." He did a little dance.

As they passed by some folks standing at an old-fashioned, multi-drawered, index card cabinet, Duck said, "I'll show you my card if you show me yours." He held his card up and pointed to the name line. "That's my name right there, Bob Duckins. Capital Bob Duckins. But you, my new library friends, can call me Duck. I mean, Duck," he whispered.

Passing by a student sitting studiously in front of a computer, he put his hand on the young student's shoulder and said, "Yes, my new friend, you should be proud of the fact that you have a library card. You have one, don't you? Carry on, my friend, and keep up the good work. If you need the Duck, I'll be over there with my attorney."

On his way over to Mya, he passed a lady on a film machine and showed her his card as he passed by and said, as he pointed at his photo on the card, "That handsome devil is me, right there on the front of this Brown County library card. It's going to be a collector's item someday, because the Duck is coming back."

Mya had been sitting at the computers for quite a while, and she motioned for him to get over there. She was logging onto the internet. She pointed at the chair next to hers. "Sit down, Bob."

"Call me Duck."

"Okay. You said we are looking for Anthony. Is there a middle initial?"

"Yep. It's D. Anthony D. Bezmouskee."

She finished typing in the name. Mya had Duck check it out to see if the spelling was correct. Mya pointed and instructed Duck to push the "send" button. He reached over and pushed it. She asked him where he had last had contact with Anthony.

"It was in Manhattan."

Mya typed in "Manhattan, New York State."

Duck interrupted, "No—Manhattan, Kansas."

She corrected it to Manhattan, Kansas, and said, "Let's give this a try. Hmmm, still no such animal." Duck suggested trying "golf." She entered the keyword "golf." Duck reached over and hit 'enter.'

"Well, look at what we found," she stated. "Mr. Anthony D. Bezmouskee. It looks like, if it's him, he's now living in Duluth, Minnesota. And here's an address and a phone number." She jotted down the address and the phone number on the back of one of her cards.

Duck, looking at the number and the spelling of the name, said, "That's him, all right. I'd bet everything I own on it. Everything, that is, except for my new library card."

Duck continued, "Wow, that's it? I thought it would be much harder than this. You know, like one of those movies where the guy spends weeks, months, going from house to house, business to business - always getting the same answer, a silent shaking of the head 'no.' Then finally, after crawling completely across the Sahara Desert, when all hope seems to have disappeared, one last chance is taken. A wild shot, if you will. And voila - they find the person they are looking for. But this, it just seemed to happen so easily, like it was supposed to happen - maybe guided by some higher power of purpose. A few clicks of a button, and there he is, Anthony D. Bezmouskee. Chances are we hit pay dirt. I wonder what old Tony is up to these days. I wonder how many other fancy gizmos like this are out there that I have been missing. This is my first step toward coming back, and it's laminated, too. Look at that picture. I could be a wallet model, don't you think?"

To Mya, he said, "Thank you, thank you, thank you. Could I have one of your cards? Someday, I'll return this favor." She pointed at the card with Tony's address and phone number written on it that Duck was holding in his hand.

"Oh, yeah. Thanks again, counselor."

With that said, Duck bid Mya goodbye and turned to walk away. Armed with Tony's address, with the phone number written on the back of Mya's card, Duck walked toward the front door. His path took him right by the still-watchful security guard. As Duck walked by, he said to the guard, "I'll see you next time," and held up his library card for him to see. Then he said, "Oh, and when I come back next time, you can call me Mr. Duckins."

Totally out of character for patrons of a library, as Duck reached the door and put his hand out to push the door open, he heard one person start clapping. Then the whole library, except for a few, broke out in applause. "Good luck, Duck. We'll see you here next time."

Duck smiled, stopped at the door, turned back to acknowledge them, tipped his golf cap, and walked out the door. The look on Mya's face was one of confusion. She brought herself back to the task at hand and said to herself, "Now, why in the heck did I come in here?" She paused. "Oh, yeah." She turned back and smiled at the man that she figured she would never see again. As she watched him, she could see he was looking at her card as he walked down the sidewalk past the windows of the library. She saw him showing it to the meter maid. Mya was thinking to herself, "I have no idea why I did what I did, but you know what? It just felt right," and back to work she went.

Duck walked back to the Cardboard Hotel to contemplate his next move. Arriving at the alley, Speedo comments, "Hey Duck, I thought you were out of here."

"I've got to figure out my plan of action," Duck replied. "I'll most likely be leaving first thing in the morning. You haven't rented out my space yet, have you, Molly?"

Molly chimed in. "Duck, you do know this is Tuesday, don't you?"

Duck was concentrating on his plan of action and answered, "Tuesday night. Okay. Thanks, Molly." He was not really thinking of the consequences of it being Tuesday night because of the deep thought he was in, planning his next move.

"What will I say when I catch up with Tony? 'Hey, Tony Baby, this is Duck. Tony, Tony, it's me, Bob Duckins. Tony, remember me? It's Duck.' Lord, what if he doesn't remember me at all? I got it. I'll write him a letter. Now, that makes sense. 'Dear Tony, blah, blah, blah. Sincerely, Bob Duckins. Let me know what you think. My address is Cardboard box #3'. Jeez, I don't even have a return address."

Duck laughed, as he pictured in his mind the postman coming by saying, "Registered letter for Box #3." Or, he thought, 'Maybe I'll make a cardboard mailbox and hang it next to my box. I can just see myself. I wrote him a letter, and he hasn't written me back. Why? Why? Why? Doesn't he remember me? Maybe he does but won't write me back because I'm the person who he still owes 20 bucks to. Maybe he knows what happened to me, what I have become, and doesn't want to be associated with me. Or does he still feel inferior to my straight and long drives? And all the while, it would simply be because there is no return address to give him. This calls for other options. I'll have to either call him or take a road trip. Either way, I will have to retrieve my small stash of cash from a place where even I fear to go. The dreaded bottom of my only pair of socks, lying flat, pressed between the bottom of my foot and my sock. I hope they haven't rotted away. It's been a while since I've checked on them. Man, I have worn this same unwashed pair of socks for the past several years. Those two Ben Franklins have been in there so long, I bet even old Ben has gotten athlete's foot. Maybe I'll hop a train, go on up to Duluth and just pop in on him. Or maybe I'll take a bus. That's it, I'll take a bus. The bus depot is two blocks away from here. It's perfect.'

Finally realizing what Molly had said earlier, Duck said, "Shit, did Molly say this is Tuesday night? I'm out of here." This, he thought, is as good a time as any to hit the road. "See you guys. Good luck with the 'Ten O'clock News'".

Dick grabbed a blanket and left the alley, looking determined. He walked out of the alley armed with Tony's address written on the back of his attorney's card. Duck noticed the silhouette of the thugs coming to the alley to deliver the 'Ten O'clock News'. As he walked away down the street, he decided to pick up the pace. It seems he had left just in time. He quickly turned away to not make eye contact with them, hoping that maybe they wouldn't see him.

Deano spotted Duck walking out of the alley. "Hey, it's our tough guy."

Joey yelled, "Where you going? Didn't you remember we have a standing date every Tuesday night?"

"Come back here," said Frankie. "We brought along something to help you sleep better tonight, and we think you'll really get a boot out of it."

"Maybe he's heading down to Carl's to get us something to eat," Deano added.

Frankie called out to Duck, "Remember, I take onions on my cheeseburgers."

Deano snickered, "What a chickenshit."

They noticed Troy wasn't saying a word; he was just surveying the area as if he were looking for something.

Joey asked Troy, "What's up with you, man?"

They all walked over to him and bent over to look on the same trajectory as he was. Troy announced, "That cat. You know, that black cat? I thought I saw it out of the corner of my eye."

They were all standing behind Troy. Deano tapped the others on the shoulder and put his finger across his lips to let them know he wanted them to stay quiet. Then Deano pointed at himself and silently mouthed, "Watch this."

Suddenly, Deano interrupted the silence with a loud, "Shit, there it is!" Troy jumped just about as high as that cat did coming out of the metal trashcan the other night.

"Real funny," said Troy. The others were laughing uncontrollably. Deano walked up and put his hand on Troy's shoulder and said, "You're still worried about that stupid cat. Hell, man, that thing probably died that night from that rock you hit him with. You really have to learn to relax and enjoy. After all, we're only kids once."

Realizing what Deano had just said, Troy responded, "The rock I hit him with? I didn't. And how do you know my rock was the one that hit him? I mean, you guys threw rocks, too."

Deano interrupted. "I just know these things."

"Oh, shit," Troy said, "what about the guy/gal shadow—whatever it was that saw us? He might be around here, too."

Duck's no dummy. He increased the pace of his walk to almost a run toward the bus depot. Frankie yelled at him, "You better hurry off, hero."

Joey reached down and picked up a rock and said, "Here, Troy. You're a good aim with rocks. Get him while he's still in your range."

Troy just let the rock slip out of his hand and fall to the pavement. Then he said, "I didn't hit that cat, did I?" Deano looked at his watch and said, "Hey, we're five minutes late for the news broadcast." They turned and headed back toward the alley.

CHAPTER 9

With a sigh of relief, Duck reached the bus depot. As Duck entered the bus stop, he walked right up to the counter and said, "Excuse me, sir. Does your bus line go to Duluth?"

The clerk, after inspecting Duck's appearance, said, "Say what?" He just knew Duck was wasting his time.

Duck repeated, "Does your bus go to Duluth?"

Sarcastically, the clerk said, "You mean Duluth as in Duluth, Minnesota?"

"Well, of course I mean Duluth as in Minnesota."

"Well, of course we go to Duluth, Minnesota, but it's not free."

"Did I ask for free? How much is it for a one-way ticket to Duluth?"

"Let me look it up." He scanned through his rate chart book and saw that the price for a one-way ticket was $75. Wanting to make sure this street guy wouldn't travel on their bus, he doubled the price and said, "Looks like that fare would be $150 for a one-way ticket."

Duck looked around and didn't see 8,000 people waiting to get on the bus that takes you to Minnesota or any other of the 43 stops it makes along the way getting there. Duck said, "Twelve."

"What do you mean, twelve?" said the clerk.

Duck continued, "As I looked around, I saw maybe twelve people waiting for your 100-seat bus. I think you're trying to overcharge me. I'll tell you what, I'll give you fifty bucks."

"Fifty! You have got to be kidding me."

"Fifty," Duck repeated. "And why don't you go talk to that funny-looking man? You know, the one who has been looking out from around the corner at me ever since I walked in here. He's got to be your boss. If he's not, you need to know that there is some sort of pervert behind you, watching our every move. Now, be a good boy and go tell him my offer."

"Very well. I'll be right back."

The ticket agent disappeared around the same corner where the man had been observing them. A few seconds later, the sound of laughter came from around the same corner. Then the balding ticket agent came back around the corner with a smug grin planted on his face.

"My boss says if you can produce sixty-eight cash, we will sell you a one-way ticket to Duluth."

Duck, seeing his opportunity to return some of the sarcasm, said, "You mean Duluth as in Duluth, Minnesota? So you're saying that you won't accept my personal check?"

The clerk just shook his head, folded his arms, and rolled his eyes. Duck looked at him with that 'well, you've got me now' look. The old 'deer in the headlights' look. The clerk shook his head with that, 'I knew you were wasting my time' look on his face when Duck said, "Sold!"

The clerk's mouth flew open. Duck turned, leaned his back against the counter, raised up one of his worn out brown and white saddle oxford golf shoes, and rested it across his knee. "These used to have spikes on the bottom, but I wore them off long ago on the back streets of Brown County," he said to the waiting clerk. "Such a shame," Duck continued. "I used to get such better traction in the snow and ice with the spikes. It will be just a second. I've got to get into my piggies bank."

Looking and seeing no one else in line, Duck says, "You can go ahead and help the person behind me if you want. But

I guess you can't, because there is no one else in line." Duck cocked his head away from what he figured was going to be a butt awful smell. He removed his right shoe, and he was right—it was bad. He took off his moist sock, and much to his chagrin, there was no money. "Where are you hiding my money, my little piggies?" He looked between his toes. And then he stuck his hand up into the sock in order to search for his money.

The clerk was now standing far away after smelling the aroma. He now knew for sure that this guy couldn't afford the ticket. Duck turned back to the agent, pointed at his other shoe and said, "What an idiot - it's in the other sock. Just one more second, please."

Duck reached down and took off his other shoe. This time he could almost see the yellow wavy cartoon lines indicating a foul odor emanating from his socks. Off came the other sock, and then Duck reached down in there and felt around for the money. He knows he had two $100 bills in there. Duck grabbed both socks and tossed them onto his shoulders. The clerk backed out of the way as he attempted to dodge the sock's path as they swung aromatically around to their resting place.

Peeling the one hundred dollar bills apart was no easy task. Both bills stuck together. They were moist and had taken on the shape of Duck's foot. After Duck had successfully pulled the bills apart, he grabbed one and tried to hand it to the ticket agent. The clerk turned his head in utter disgust and said, "You don't expect me to grab that, do you?"

Just then, the boss came out from around the corner and said, "We're going to need to see some form of I.D."

Duck thought, 'Hmmmm. Oh, yes, the library card!' He handed them his cash and said, "This is my cash." Then he handed them his library card and said, "And this - my bus depot friends - is my I.D. Be careful with it. Someday it's going to be worth a lot of money." Then he pulled out M.Y. Angel's card and says, "And this is my lawyer's card. Do you have any other questions?"

Both the clerk and his boss just stood there. They knew they had met their match. However, they doubted that he really had an attorney. "You probably found the card on the street," they said. Bob Duckins interrupted, "My ticket and change, please. And can I get a couple dollars' worth of quarters? I may need to make a phone call. You never know."

CHAPTER 10

The Bus trip to Duluth was quite comfortable, although no one wanted to sit by him—wonder why. As Duck watched the passing scenery, his mind drifted back to some of the happy times back at the alley. He was wondering if this was a good idea. Living on the streets wasn't so bad, and his friends had taught him a lot about life. In a way, they were like 3-year-old kids. Their real personalities were out there. They were not afraid to say what was on their minds. Sure, there were the stormy Mondays and the Tuesday evening 'Weather Reports', but there were many fond memories as well, like the time Chalk Line was talking about how tough his week had been so far. Speedo in response said, "You know, I've been thinking. You seem to be tired and cranky a lot. I'm wondering if your problem is that you are not getting enough rest at night. I'll bet it's your mattress."

Fast Eddie chimed right in as if it was scripted and said, "Yeah, I think you are supposed to rotate your mattress every so often. If you don't, I hear it sags or something like that."

Then Chalk Line said, "You guys are so stupid. How on earth do you expect me to rotate a brick mattress? What a couple of idiots you guys are! How would bricks sag?" The funny part is that he spent the rest of the night and most of the next day digging up his bricks one by one. Then he would rotate each one of them and then wedge them back into their sand base. He tried to retrace the chalk line around himself, but he didn't do a very good job. Still, he swore up and down that he was resting better.

Duck snorted out a loud laugh. Then he realized the other two people on the bus were staring at him, and he said, "Sorry. I was just thinking about some of the good times with my old friends."

Then his thoughts were warmed as he remembered standing around the fire that he had built in the barrel with Sister Molly as they talked about everything under the sun. How about that damn blues harp that B.F.D. found! You would have thought after three years he'd at least be able to play 'Mary Had a Little Lamb' or some other tune fairly well, but he never did. Oh, at times he moved you with his music, all right. He would move you to throw a few insults or an empty milk carton at him. Or occasionally, it would get so bad that it would move you right out of the alley.

Fast Eddie. Oh, Fast Eddie. He was always bending over and getting into that sprinter's starting position, as if he was about to start the biggest championship race of all time. One time, while he was in his stance, Molly snuck up behind him with a paper sack she had blown full of air. Molly popped that sack right behind him. I must say, Eddie took off faster than anything I'd ever seen around here. He ran right out of the alley and halfway down the block before he came to his senses and stopped. That was hilarious. Come to think of it, that was the only time I had seen him actually run. Most of the time, he'd stand straight up from his starting position, move his arms as if he was running, and then he'd start mumbling something about the events he was experiencing in his imagined competition. Usually he wouldn't be standing there long before he would be breathing heavily, and then he'd say something like, 'That's enough exercise for one day. I better sit and rest a while. I don't want to overdo it and end up pulling something.' The disgusting part of this is he would do all of this while dressed only in his now brownish-yellow tight underwear and a pair of his old track shoes. He swore those weren't skid marks. After his workout, he'd always walk up to someone and say, as he turned and flexed his calf muscle, "This is what a runner's calf looks like. Quite impressive, isn't it? Do you want to touch it?" No one ever did.

We even had our own sheriff's department. If someone came in from another alley and they overextended their welcome, we would have our legal counsel, B.F.D., serve them with a subpoena signed by Cilus. Come to think of it, I saw Fast Eddie run one other time. Three dogs chased him back into the alley one night. Apparently, he was eating their food. Duck laughed out loud again. He looked around the bus. This time, no one paid attention. Duck thought to himself, 'No, this is the right thing. I owe it to my dad and myself.'

Leaning his head against the window, Duck nodded off to sleep. When he got off the bus in Duluth, even after eating some vending machine food at several of the stops along the way, Duck still had one $100 bill, the $2.00 worth of quarters, and $12.50 in cash. He would have had a little more, but as he was getting off the bus, he tipped the driver five bucks. A bum tipping him five bucks. I didn't see anyone else give him a penny. You should have seen the look on the driver's face.

Duck was thinking, 'Okay. I'm here. I better get to work finding Tony.' Duck approached a passerby and asked, "Say, sir, can you tell me where this address is?" He showed him the paper.

"Sure, pal. Actually, you're not very far from there. That's in the old business district. Just go up there past that first stop light, take the second right, and you're there."

Duck had that feeling all over again that this was supposed to happen, some sort of divine intervention or something— but no desert to crawl across. The address was right down the street. In a little less than a half hour, Duck reached what he thought was the address. He stopped to double check that the address on the building was written on Mya's card. Then he said to himself, "Ladies and gentlemen, clear your cards. We have a bingo. Well, I'll be. Here it is—and it makes sense—got to be Tony. Look at that big green 1967 Cadillac convertible with personalized tags that read 'A D Bezmo.' Jeez, some things never change."

Duck took a deep breath and grabbed the door handle. He paused as he said to himself, "Well, here I am. My hand is on the door handle now, and it's shaking a little. Correction. It's shaking so much it sounds like someone is rattling a chain. Okay, Duck," he said to himself, "Calm down. Everything is going to be all right."

He tried to turn the knob. It was locked. Shit! Duck cupped his hand and tried to look in the door's window. Unable to see much, he took a step back and noticed a three by five card taped on the door. Written on it was a message. It said, "Anthony D. Bezmouskee, Sports Agent. Be back in 10, Baby."

Okay. Does this mean ten minutes from now, or was it back in ten minutes three weeks ago when he left for vacation? Hey, he can't be too far; his Caddy is still here. Is this too good or what? Tony's a sports agent. Might as well pull up a hunk of sidewalk and get some rest while I wait.

Leaning back as if he was settling into his favorite chair in front of the T.V., Duck leaned back against the old brick building, and he did what had become his favorite outdoor event, people watching. Watching the different packages people came in seemed to lull him to sleep, and that's what happened this time - or it might have been that he was exhausted from the trip.

The next thing Duck remembered was a pair of white shoes with buckles on the sides and attached to the bottom of a lime green leisure suit attacking him. He could hear a voice telling him to "get the hell away from here, you're scaring off business." Waking up like that, he didn't at first know where he was. The first thing he thought was, "Oh, crap, it's Tuesday. I better get out of here before they start the 'Weather Report'."

As his eyes focused, he was facing a backing-away lime green leisure suit. It was Tony, no doubt about it. "Tony, it's me—Duck."

Tony questioned, "What did you say?"

"Tony, it's Duck."

"You're shitting me!"

"Nope. And thank goodness you're not pissing on me."

"What?"

"Long story," Duck said.

Tony asked, "Where on earth have you been? And look at you."

Duck gestured at Tony's outfit and said, "Look at you—nice! Hey, where's your disco ball?"

"Still a wise guy, huh, Duck? Jeez, some things never change. Come in."

Tony unlocked the door. "I lost total touch with you, man."

Duck picked right up as old friends do and said, "From the looks of you, that's not all you've lost touch with." Duck continued, "Unless I've lost all track of time, it's the year 2000. Let me look. Yep, the year 2000. Says that right here on my library card. So why do you still dress like this?"

Tony didn't like anyone poking fun at how he dresses and snapped back, "Lay off of me. It's how I dress. It's me. It's my calling card—my image. I don't want to be like all those other sports agents. I want to stand out, you know, be different. You, of all people, should know that. You and I have always gone to the beat of a different drummer. Look at you, Duck. You look bad, man. Have you played any golf lately?"

"It's been awhile. We don't get many invitations to golf tournaments down on the street. So Tony, how come you're an agent and not playing yourself?"

"Long story, so I'll just give you the short version. You know I never have had the 'it,' like you did, man. You had the 'it.' You had the long game, the short game, the looks—well, you used to have the looks. This was my way of staying close to the game. Remember, I told you I'd always be involved in golf. But to be honest with you, things are not working out quite as well as I had thought they would. In the last ten years, I've represented nothing but minor league players. You know, not even 'close but no cigar' type of guys. Mostly baseball and hockey also-rans. It's funny, but I always knew someday you'd come walking in that door and say, 'Tony, how about being my agent?' It's still not too late. What do you say, Duck? I've still got plenty of contacts on the tour. All I would have to do is make a few calls."

Duck shook his head negatively, thinking, "How odd is this that this is unfolding like it is?"

Tony responded to what he thought was a "no" answer from the Duck and asked, "Why not? Is it the suit? You'll get used to it, I swear."

"No, no - the very reason I came here was to see if you would help me get back into golf, and I can't believe the chain of events that has led me here. Let's do this—you be my agent, and I'll give my best."

"The reason you haven't heard from me is that after my dad died, I completely dropped out of the mainstream. I wasn't drinking, I wasn't on dope, I just dropped out and was living on the streets. And then one day I found my smile again." Duck pulled his golf ball out of his pocket and handed it to Tony. "That ball, along with a few good ass-kickings, made me start thinking 'what if' and 'why not.' It's a long, long story. Someday I'll tell it all to you. It's strange, but I knew I had to come see you, so here I am. I had no idea you were now an agent. This is perfect. I need your help. What do you say?"

Tony wiped the ear-to-ear grin off his face and said, "First things first. About my fee—I want 15% lifetime."

Duck had already thought about that and said, "I'll give you 20%, plus 15% of the endorsements. Deal?"

"Deal!" With a handshake, the two old friends sealed the deal. Tony, not wanting to waste any more time, said, "Now, let's go and hit some balls."

Still tired from the trip, Duck said, "Now?"

"Now!" Tony replied. "I've been keeping something safe for you, Duck. Like I said, somehow I knew this day would come. I had to sell my own clubs when things got tough." Tony went into the back room and brought out the very set of clubs that

Duck used in college. It was the set his dad had given him. It was the set he was using on that day his dad died. Tony asked if Duck recognized them. "I didn't have the heart to sell these; besides, like I told you, I knew you'd be back." He handed the clubs to Duck, and Duck just stared at them.

Then he said, "I thought I'd never see these clubs again. In fact, for years, I didn't think I ever wanted to see them again. Man, this feels right. Thank you, Tony. Now, let's go hit some balls."

With tears in his eyes, Duck got up and gave Tony a big hug.

Tony curled his nose and said, "Duck, no offense, old buddy, and it's great to see you and all, but you could use a bath in the worst way. But let's go to the range first." Tony ran to the back room and got a couple of days' worth of newspapers. He stopped Duck from getting into the car. He stepped in front of him and spread newspapers on the passenger seat for Duck to sit on and said, "Again, no offense; just until we reintroduce you to a shower."

The two drove off, doing a lot of catching up along the way to the driving range. What a sight they were—Tony in his lime green leisure suit topped off with a bright orange shirt, and Duck looking ever so much like the former homeless man he was.

Side by side riding down the road in a Green 1967 Cadillac convertible, Tony asked, "Got an extra cigarette?"

"I don't smoke anymore," Duck replied.

At the driving range, all went well. Duck said, "Tony, it's like it was yesterday; like I never left. And with every swing, I swear I can hear the encouraging words of my dad. I can feel his presence standing right behind me saying, 'Attaboy. Now try this.' I can feel his warm breath on my neck as if I was eight, and he was leaning over me with his hands on my hands as we both gripped the golf club, saying, 'This is the feeling. Did you feel that? That's what you call hitting the sweet spot.' Man,

Tony - this," Duck said as he looked out over the golf course, "this is what I was made for."

Duck grabbed a few more range balls and walked up to the tee, placed a ball down, and sent it far and straight. Tony said, "OOOOOHH ... you crunched that one. Nice hit. Okay!"

Tony painted another scenario and said, "This time you've got a tree in front of you about 75 yards. I'd say in order to reach the green, you'll have to slice around the tree. Now, let's see the shot."

Duck hit what would have been a perfect shot. As they watched the ball he hit purposely slice to the right, Tony said, "That's a good little Ducky. Nice shot."

Duck smacked another one even further. "Cha-ching, baby. Looking good," was Tony's reaction.

Tony grabbed a pencil and pretended it was a microphone and announced, "This just in. P.G.A. players everywhere are bowing to the great Duck-meister."

Duck hit another one even further, right down the heart. Tony lamented, "Missed you, baby; move over all of you pros."

Duck duffed one. "Had your head up your ass on that one, didn't you, Duck old boy? But that's okay; just get it out of your system now."

Duck rested the driver on his shoulder and turned to Tony and said, "What a sight we must be, a bum driving golf balls being cheered on by a friend in what has to be one of the two remaining lime green leisure suits in existence. I just had a scary thought. What if there really were only two lime green leisure suits left in the universe? That would mean you own both of them."

"Just hit the ball," replied Tony. Duck hit his last shot. Tony put the golf bag over his shoulder and said, "Okay. Shower time. Let's go. Stay on the papers. Good Ducky. You did good out there, man. I can't believe it. After all this time, you've still got it. It's your gift, man. Now, it's not going to be easy. Hell, nothing is if it's worth having. It's really good to see you back, Duck."

"It's good to see you, too, Tony." Silence fell as the miles passed by the windows of the Cadillac. Tony broke the silence. "So tell me, Duck, what happened? Why did you just up and quit?"

"Like I said, it was my dad's death. For years, I thought I—and golf—were responsible for his death. I lost the dream."

"Duck, you should have called me." Tony continued, "I tried to reach you, Duck, but nobody knew where you were. Several of my letters came back 'Return to Sender—Not at this Address.' Hell, Duck, the last time I talked to you was at the funeral."

"Sorry, Tony. I wasn't thinking; had my head up my ass. But never again, my friend. You have my word. Never again."

"Is that to be considered a promise?"

"That, my friend, is a promise!" Duck extended his hand to Tony, and again they sealed the deal with a handshake.

"I live at the office," Tony told Duck. "There's a pull-down couch in the living room, which will be yours until we can do better. That is, if that would be okay with you?"

"Sounds good to me," replied Duck.

"I think I'll start making some calls first thing in the morning. It's time to collect on some IOUs." As they arrived back at the office, Tony pulled his car over to the curb, put it in park, and activated the switch that closed the top of the convertible. With the top up, he really got a whiff of his friend's unwashed body.

"Duck, my boy, it's time to get you reacquainted with the shower."

Tony marched Duck right to the shower. On their way, Tony bent over and pulled out a trash bag from under the kitchen counter and handed it to Duck. "Duck, when you step into the shower, I want you to place all your clothes into this trash bag, and while you're at it, say goodbye to them, because they, my friend, are history."

"But, Tony, I don't have anything to wear."

"Don't worry. I'll take care of that, Ducky boy. I'll find something you can slip into tonight. In the morning, we'll go do some shopping. I've got a friend who owns a clothing store. We'll go see her." Tony went into his room and pulled out of the closet an old green robe and said, "This will do for tonight." He walked back into the bathroom, hung it on the door and said, "Duck, when you get out, put on this robe. It will have to do for this evening."

After Duck got out of the shower, he and Tony sat at the kitchenette table reminiscing while they watched golf on T.V. It wasn't long before Tony said, "Duck, did you know that Jonesy Standlovich ended up winning that tournament?"

Duck, looking at the tv, said "Now, why on earth would you use a 2-iron from there?"

"Duck," Tony repeated, "did you even hear what I said?"

"Yeah, something about a tournament."

"What I said was, did you know that Jonesy ended up winning that tournament the day your dad died?"

"What was that about, my dad? Okay. Now you have my attention. What did you really want to tell me?" Tony walked over and turned off the television.

"Just what I said. Jonesy took home the trophy that day, boasting that he sent you off with your tail between your legs." Now it was sinking in.

"You have got to be yanking my chain, right?"

Tony just shook his head. "Why, that sorry excuse for a human being, let alone golfer, couldn't beat me if I had one hand tied behind my back. Tail between my legs. Why, that no good..."

"Well, Duck, that day a lot of things changed for old Jonesy boy," Tony continued. "He used the high emotions caused by your dad's sudden passing to his personal advantage, and boy, did he milk it for all that he could. He even announced after winning that he was dedicating the victory to one of his best friends and mentor, Runner Duckins."

"He actually had the gall to say that? Why, that no good... Tony, my dad couldn't stand Jonesy and all of his 'me-isms.'"

"From the winner's podium, he went on to tell everyone that he owed a lot to your dad."

"Yeah," Duck replied, "like $45,000 that Dad cosigned for that inconsiderate loser's college fund after his own dad refused. And to this day, he never has offered to pay it back. He told everyone he was on a full-ride scholarship. My dad died without Jonesy ever paying that back. My God, he must have turned over in his grave when he heard all of this. You know, Tony, he is the only guy that I ever heard my dad speak negatively about, unless you count his comments regarding those green leisure suits of yours."

"Very funny. Anyway, the press and the public ate up his speech. And today, well, Duck, today he's quite powerful in the pro ranks. A lot of doors opened for him that day, and he took full advantage. Heck Duck, somehow, he even managed to capture his share of victories. I ran into him a while back at a fundraiser for the fight against cancer. Funny thing is, he asked about you. He said something else that... on second thought, never mind. It doesn't really matter now."

"What did he say, Tony? Don't start something with me and not finish it." Tony just smiled. "What's that stupid looking condescending smirk of a smile all about?" Duck asked.

"Oh, it just seemed funny hearing that statement come out of your mouth."

"What is that supposed to mean?"

"Nothing. It's water under the bridge now that you're back."

"Okay. Tell me what he said, Tony."

"What he said was that he knows for a fact that he would have kicked your tail, even if your old man hadn't croaked. He said that you quitting that tournament was a weak, cowardly, easy way out of a losing situation you had yourself in. Then, as he walked away with his group of kiss-up buddies, he turned and said, 'Tony, you and I both know that Duck was scared of me. That's the real reason he quit that day.' Can you believe that arrogant sack of crap?"

Duck leaned back in his folding chair as he let it all settle in, and then he abruptly stood up and flipped over the card table where he was sitting and said, "Where is that son of a bitch? Tony, you tell me right now where I can find him. I swear that when I find him, I'm going to drive your green Cadillac right up his pompous ass."

Tony said, "Now, hold on, Duck. Let me finish." Tony bent over and lifted the folding table, which was lying on its side. He reached down to pick up some of the papers that had scattered across the room. Tony said, "Now, sit back down and listen to me. I have a plan. While all of this was happening, in my mind's eye, I saw an opportunity for the future. That day when he was saying all of that at the fundraiser, I stuck up for you. I told him you could beat him two out of three rounds anytime, anywhere, anyplace. He laughed at me. Then he said, 'I tell you what. If you ever see that sorry-ass loser, tell him I'll play him head-to-head. Hell,' Jonesy said, 'I'll put my money where my mouth is. Two out of three rounds. Duck beating me ain't ever going to happen. No way, no how. I'll take that bet any day, any time. My schedule permitting, of course.'"

"And then he said he'd put up $2 million if you would put up $45,000, and that when he won, he'd take that $45,000 and pay off the debt that you think he owes Runner. He told me to tell you that if I ever saw you again. So I told him, 'Oh, I'll see him someday. And when I do, we'll take you up on that bet. That is, as long as you follow through on your word.'"

"So then Jonesy fanned his hand around the room, pointing to all the people who were listening, and said, 'In front of all of these witnesses, you have my word.'"

"His word—right. Tony, his word isn't worth shit," replied Duck.

"I know. That's why I had him sign this."

Tony walked over to a small safe, dialed in the numbers, opened the door, and pulled out a napkin. He walked over to Duck and handed it to him. On the napkin, Tony had written the details of the bet and had it signed by Jonesy Standlovich and four witnesses.

"Hey, what's this?" Duck noticed Tony's signature. It said, 'Tony D. Bezmouskee, Sports Agent for the Duck.'

"Oh, that," Tony said. "I knew you'd be back, and I knew you would come begging me to be your representative."

"Kind of sure of yourself, weren't you?"

"What can I say?" replied Tony. "You're here, aren't you? Now, shut up and let me finish. I say we take him up on the bet. He's making so much money now. Who knows, maybe we can even get the deal sweetened. His ego is Paul Bunyan-ish these days; I think it's time we cut him down to size. I think it's a sure bet. Two out of three is easy for us. And getting him to put up a couple of mill to our forty-five grand, I don't think we can go wrong."

Duck stood up and paced around, saying, "Do you really think that would be to our benefit? Well, maybe you're right. Those are quite good odds for us. In fact, I think the whole idea sounds really swell, or maybe even keen, or peachy."

Tony thought he recognized Duck's wind-up right before he was about to slam someone with a sarcastic comment. "So Anthony, have you given any thought to where in the hell we are going to get this $45,000?"

"Don't you worry about the money. That, my friend, is my department. I mean, we've got a few other old friends that might want a piece of this. We beat him two out of three, and we are on the fast track back. Hell, we may even get some tv action out of this. You kick his ass, we get a cool two million."

"What if we lose?" Duck asked.

"Then we build us a duplex cardboard box, and we both move back into your old neighborhood. Can't you just see it now? It will be like David against Goliath. So what do you think, Duck?"

"Forget about the duplex. We aren't going to lose. I was just teasing you, Tony. The way I see it, the odds are against him. It's three against one."

"Three against one. What are you talking about?"

"Three—you, me, and my dad—against one sorry, loud-mouthed also-ran. One thing, though, I want him to put up two million, and I want him to pay off the $45,000 plus interest."

"So if I can get this all worked out, are you in, Duck?"

"Absolutely, with both feet. I'm in hook, slice, and driver!"

"I knew you would say that. I'll make the call in the morning. Now I need to get some sleep."

CHAPTER 11

The next morning, Duck was awakened by the sound of Tony on the phone. "Anthony D. Bezmouskee. He knows who I am. Just make sure you give him this message. Tell him Tony and Duck would like to talk with him. Thanks. Bye."

Duck walked into the room naked, wearing only his old golf hat. Tony looked up after jotting a few notes in his appointment book, and seeing Duck standing there naked, he turned his head in disgust. "For God's sake, man, put some clothes on."

It was then that Duck realized he was standing in front of the storefront window naked, staring eye-to-eye with a couple of women passing by on their way to work. Duck looked down, then back up, tipped his hat, said, "Ladies," then turned and headed back through the doorway leading to Tony's living quarters. Back on the sidewalk, the ladies tried to act nonchalant as they watched him retreat.

"Duck, you're going to get us arrested if you pull that stunt again."

"Sorry, Tony. Old habits, they're tough to break. So did you get a hold of Standlovich?"

"I left him a message. It could be awhile before we hear back."

"So what's on the agenda today, Anthony old pal?"

"We need to get you a new wardrobe, so we'll head to the Mall to my friend's clothing store." Tony walks over to his closet, opened it and grabbed a few articles of clothing. He handed them to Duck and said, "Put these on for now."

Duck took the clothes from Tony and said, "You've got to be kidding."

"No, I am not kidding. Put them on. I'm going out to put the top down on the Caddy. I expect you to be fully dressed and ready to go when I come back in."

"Okay. If you insist." Fully dressed in the clothes Tony gave him to wear, Duck stepped back through the doorway in the partition leading from the living area. As he did, Tony, now finished putting the top down on the Caddy, walked back in, carrying the boot cover. Seeing Duck, he said, "Hey, you clean up real nice."

Tony put the cover over the counter, reached down and opened a cabinet door and removed a large rectangular bag that carried one of those original '60s mobile phones and headed back out to the car. "Just pull the door shut behind you—it'll lock on its own—and come on. We've got things to do."

Duck paused at the door, took a deep breath, and stepped out onto the pavement. Passersby stared and choked back laughter. One teenager driving by shouted out, "Hey, guys, can I go with you to the costume party?" What a sight he was. Duck treated the twenty-five feet to the curb where the Cadillac was parked as his own personal fashion runway. He thought it was exactly what Speedo would want him to do. He was wearing one of Tony's lime green leisure suits with an orange frilly shirt.

As if the color and design weren't bad enough, Duck was a good 6 inches taller than Tony, so the sleeves rested a quarter of the way up his arm. The coat had some definite stress points at the seams, and the lime green trousers looked like a pair of capris. The only things that fit right were his old golf hat and shoes.

Reaching the end of his personal runway, Duck stopped, did a model's twirl, took three more steps, walked to the passenger side of the car, tipped his hat to the gawking crowd, opened the door, and stepped into the Caddy. Sitting next to Tony, he said, "Do you think I can keep these clothes?"

Tony just shook his head and said, "You always have been a showman. But don't ever make fun of my suits."

Tony reached down and pulled out the huge old cell phone and dialed. "Yeah, this is Tony. We'll be there in about twenty minutes; see you then." Tony hung up the phone and looked over at Duck. Duck was looking in the rearview mirror at his outfit. He glanced down and grabbed the sleeve of his jacket with his fingers and moved his arm over next to Tony's matching lime green sleeve and said, "Look, we're twins." He laid his head on Tony's shoulder and said, "I always wanted to be just like you, and now all my dreams have come true."

Tony pushed his head off his shoulder and drove off. Duck patted his pocket and noticed something was missing. He startled Tony by saying, "Stop the car! Stop the car!"

Tony pulled over and stopped. "What's wrong, Duck?"

"Just give me the keys to your place. I forgot something, and I'm not going any further without it."

"Okay." Tony reached down and shut off the engine, pulled the keys out and handed them to Duck.

"My smile. I forgot my smile."

"Your what?"

"I'll be right back. Wait here." Duck got out and headed back to Tony's place. It wasn't a very far walk since they had barely gotten a block and a half away when Duck realized he forgot his smile. Tony turned to watch his old pal heading back, shaking his head and mumbling to himself, 'He forgot his smile? What's up with that?'

Duck entered the apartment, reached into the pants pocket of his old pants that were lying in a plastic bag next to the fold-down couch. He pulled out his lucky golf ball with a smile on it. "There you are, my little friend. I almost drove off without you. Oh, and sorry about this green suit." Duck tossed the ball into the air, grabbed it, and put it in his pocket.

When he got back to the Caddy, Tony asked, "You forgot your smile?" Duck reached in his pocket, pulled out the ball, opened the door, sat down next to Tony, and showed him the ball with the cut on it. "My smile. It's my lucky ball."

"Oh, your smile." Duck handed the keys back to Tony, and they drove off. They passed a guy at a bus stop who commented, "I didn't know this was St. Patty's day."

"You know, Tony, all I really need now are some of those clown shoes."

"Real funny, Duck. What kind of name is Duck, anyway? Why don't you just go barefoot and show off your webbed feet?"

Arriving at the mall parking lot, Tony said, "Hey, grab that card out of the glove box, will you?" Duck reached down, opened the glove compartment, and pulled out a card.

"Do you mean this one? Hey, it's one of those handicap parking things!"

"I know what it is. Just hang it over the mirror."

"Is there something I need to know, Tony? Is there something wrong, man? Tell me what it is."

Tony replied, "I'm a golfer, aren't I? All golfers have a handicap. Now, put it on the mirror." Duck shook his head and put it on the mirror. "Ah, this will do nicely." Tony pulled into a handicapped parking space and shut off the engine. Duck asked if he wanted to put the top up, but he said, "Not this time. We won't be in here long."

Looking in the mirror, Duck said, "You know, Tony, I kind of like this suit. I can see why you wear them."

"Well, don't get too attached to it, and for God's sake, don't spill anything on it, don't put anything in the pockets that might disgust me later, and don't rip out the seams."

"Okay, okay, man. Tony, you really need to let go a little. They're just funky old lime green out-of-date leisure suits, for crying out loud."

Tony stopped dead in his tracks and turned and looked at Duck with a mean look, a look someone might have on their face if their mother was just insulted. They stood there silently looking at each other, Tony with his mean look, and Duck with his 'Oh, shit, I've never seen this look from Tony before' look on his. Duck broke the ice by saying, "But you—you look fabulous in that color. You make that suit look, you know— leisurely, the way it was meant to look. You're stylin'. Good job dressing yourself, Tony, old boy… sorry, man."

Tony just turned and walked through the entrance of the mall. Duck followed behind, and as Duck entered, a couple exiting stopped to gawk at Tony and Duck in their matching suits. Duck grabbed his lapels and said to the couple, "Don't even think about buying clothes from this mall. The salesman told me this was the only one of its type." Then he turned to follow Tony.

The couple turned toward each other and laughed, then turned and exited. Duck yelled at Tony, "Wait up, honey!" and broke into a trot to catch up. As he did, Duck heard a rip coming from the crotch area of his pants. He reached down and discovered that's exactly where it came from. Tony stopped, and Duck suddenly was standing there next to him. Tony looked at Duck and smiled; then he put his arm around Duck and said, "I still say it's good to have you back."

Duck replied, "Yeah, yeah, it's good to be back." Then he bent over and showed Tony the rip in the pants and said, "Are you still glad I'm back?"

"You ripped my—I thought I told you—yeah, I'm still glad you're back. Lilly can fix that."

Entering the door to Lilly's sporting goods store, Tony stopped at the cashier. "Hey, Dot, is Lilly around?"

"She's in the back room, Tony. She told me to send you on back." They walked through the store toward the back room. Tony looked back and noticed that Duck had stopped at a rack of expensive sweaters. He was standing there looking into the mirror as he held up one of the sweaters to see how it would look on him. Tony turned and walked back to Duck, reached over and grabbed the sweater and said, "Too expensive. Come with me."

"But I look good in it, Tony." Tony put it back on the rack and said, "Just shut up and follow me."

Arriving at the back room door, Tony stopped and knocked and said, "Lilly, are you in there?"

"Tony, is that you?"

"It's me and my friend Duck."

"Good. Come on in." As they entered, Lilly walked up to them, gave Tony a big hug, then stepped back and extended her hand. "And you must be Duck."

"That's me," replied Duck. "I decided not to wear my feathers today."

"Pleased to meet you. Come over here, you two. I'll show you what I have laid out." On two long folding tables, there were several complete sports outfits. "Seven outfits," Lilly said, "one for each day of the week, just like you ordered, Tony. Some of these you can mix and match to stretch them out even further. I got as close to the sizes you wanted as I could, Tony. Pants 36–32, and extra large shirts. You can try them on if you want."

"No, that won't be necessary. Thanks Lilly."

"No problem."

With Tony's help, Lilly put all but one outfit into Lil's Sporting Goods shopping bags. Tony turned to Duck and said, "I want you to wear this one out of the store; and hang my suit on this." He handed Duck an expensive, highly polished wood hanger. Duck grabbed the hanger and set it down on the large folding chair.

"Oh, and Lilly, if I leave these here, will you fix this?" He turned Duck so that she could see the rip. Lilly said, "Sure, Tony, no problem."

Duck unbuttoned his pants and started to get undressed right where he was standing. Seeing this, Tony said, "Whoa, hold on—not right here."

Lilly interrupted. "Oh, it's okay. Just let me shut the door." She walked over and shut the door, but stayed inside the room. "It's okay now." Tony looked at her. "Oh, I have to stay with you for, uh, insurance purposes. You know."

Duck shamelessly dropped his pants and took off his shirt. A big smile crossed Lilly's face, and she murmured, "Lilly likes," and began to daydream.

"Lil? Lilly?" Tony said, trying to get her attention. "Uh, we'll be leaving now, Lilly. Thanks for your help."

"No problem, Tony. Thank you for your help," she said, smiling.

Carrying the sacks filled with clothes, Tony and Duck started heading out of the store, but Duck caught a glimpse of himself in the mirror on the way out and stopped to admire his new look. Tony had to pull on his arm to get him to move. "Come on, Romeo."

"Hey, Tony, don't you think we should stop and pay for this stuff? Walking out without paying is still stealing, isn't it?"

"Not now," Tony replied. "Lilly and I have a deal worked out."

"What kind of deal?"

"Things like tickets to the Masters and other tournaments, product endorsements, personal appearances by a top golf pro. And there may even be a deal on a line of sports clothing soon."

Duck stopped. "Wow, now I am impressed. Do you really have those kinds of connections?"

"Well, not yet, but we will soon, son. We will soon."

"Oh, you mean 'us' as in you and I will have those kinds of connections."

"Yep. Lilly's banking on you to play well. If you do, she wins."

Seeing his reflection in a storefront window, Duck said, "I look good, don't I?"

Tony just rolled his eyes.

"Not that I didn't look good in my—I mean your—old limey, but I mean, I look gooooood in this stuff! I wish the guys on the street could see me now. Hey, maybe I should go back and retake my library card photo now."

"Yeah, yeah, you look good. So come on, already."

Duck and Tony walked back to the convertible, opened the trunk, and threw the new clothes on top of the set of golf clubs in the trunk. As Duck was closing the trunk and Tony was starting up the car, a mischievous grin came across Duck's face. As he walked past the right rear tire, he rubbed his hand across it. Then he jumped over the closed door and landed in the front seat. Duck turned to Tony and said, "Man, I've wanted to do that ever since I was a little kid and saw a guy do that on TV."

Tony just continued looking straight ahead and said, "Don't ever do that again." He put the car into gear and drove off.

After a few minutes of quiet, Duck said, "So what now, my lime green agent?"

"Open the glove box and grab the appointment book that's in there." Duck grabbed the book and set it in his lap.

"Well, open it up and read it."

Duck opened the book and saw that Tony had the next thirty days all planned out. Personal trainer, 5:00 a.m. to 6:30 a.m. Putting clock, 7:00 a.m. to 8:00 a.m. Driving range, 8:05 a.m. to 9:30 a.m. Tee time, 9:45 a.m. Thirty-six holes of golf every day.

As Duck turned the pages, each day had the same schedule. The only difference was that he would play a different golf course each day.

Duck looked at Tony and said, "You have got to be shitting me. Tony, I don't need all this. I'm ready to compete right now."

"Duck, if you want me to be your agent, let me be your agent. You're out of shape and practice. You'll listen to me, and we'll do it my way and adhere to my schedule. End of story."

"So, when do we start?"

"Look at your schedule, Ducky boy. What date does it show?"

"It says the 1st."

"That's right. And when is the 1st?"

"The 1st is tomorrow morning? Why do we have to start this so soon?"

"Don't question me, Duck. You and I both know I'm right. And if we want to do this, we have to do it right. We have to be prepared. If we jump too early from the nest, we're not going to enjoy the fall."

"But Tony, isn't this going to get expensive?"

"All I can say, Duck, is that a lot of people have faith in us, and I pulled in a lot of favors for this."

Duck interjected, "Not to mention personal appearances, product endorsements, etc."

"Oh, I mentioned it, all right. As a matter of fact, they are all counting on it. Besides, Duck, you know you need the added pressure. Some day when you need to make that fifteen-foot putt to win, you'll be thinking, 'I'll get this for all of those who had faith in me and are counting on me.' And you know what? With their help, you will sink that putt."

"Man, Tony, you sure set this entire thing up in a hurry."

"Like I said, Duck, I knew you'd be back, and I wanted to be ready. I've been laying the foundation for this for years."

Realizing what a great friend he had in Tony, Duck reached over and put his hand on Tony's shoulder and said, "Thanks, Tony. Let's do this."

When he took his hand off Tony's shoulder, he saw he had left a dirty hand print on his suit. "Shit," he said, and tried to wipe it off, but he only made it worse. Tony looked up into the mirror and saw the smudge. He glared at Duck with a look of hate in his eyes. Duck, once again startled by the angry look, said, "Sorry, man, I didn't mean to."

Tony just silently stared straight ahead through the windshield the rest of the way back home. Pulling up in front of the building, Tony put the car in park, then, still staring straight out the front window of the Caddy, broke the silence and said, "Duck, you've got to show some respect for my suits. They're as much a part of me as my mouth, eyes, and hands."

Duck's reply was, "So what's for dinner? Can we go get a limeade? Some key lime pie? And then later tonight maybe we could go out into the limelight?" Tony was somewhere between breaking into laughter and making a lunge toward Ducks neck. He remained quietly staring out the windshield.

"Tony, come on, man. I'm just kibitzing with you. I'm sorry, okay?"

Still no reply from Tony. Duck was getting worried when Tony—still looking straight ahead—said, "This time, Duck, you have definitely crossed the lime." At first what Tony said went right over Duck's head, and he thought, "Shit, he must really be mad at me this time."

Tony said, "Don't you get it? 'Crossed the Lime'? Lime, Duck, not 'line.'"

As it sank in, Duck looked at Tony and Tony looked at Duck, and they both cracked huge smiles and let out chuckles. Then Tony said, "But don't think you won't be getting a cleaning bill for this someday. Come on, I've got a frozen pizza in the freezer. We'll throw it in the oven, sit back and watch a little of the Golf Channel, then we'll hit the hay early. You have to be at the gym by 4:50, ready to go. And I have to get you to the gym, come back here, take a shower, read the paper, take my morning constitutional, all before 6:30 when I will be back to pick you up to take you to the golf course."

After finishing the pizza and relaxing for a while watching TV, Tony looked at the clock. "It's nine o'clock. Time to turn in." As Tony shut off the lights and climbed into bed, he said, "Good night, Duck."

"Good night, Tony boy." After a few seconds of quiet, as if they had rehearsed it, they both at the same time said, "Good night, John Boy."

Duck drifted off to sleep. In his dreams, he was suddenly confronted by a huge screeching golf ball rolling right at him. It startled him enough that he opened his eyes. When he opened his eyes, he realized it was only a dream, but then he realized he could still hear that screeching golf ball. "What the..." as he looked toward the direction of the noise, he saw the red, room-illuminating, flashing light combined with the worst screeching noise that he had ever heard coming from what must have been the most annoying alarm clock known to man. "Tony, you S.O.B."

Tony was standing in the doorway. "Now, Duck, if I were you, I wouldn't call your best friend an S.O.B." Tony reached over and hit the snooze button.

Duck, still groggy with sleep, said, "Okay. Then how about son of a tomato, son of a father, son of a whatever. I don't know. It's early. How about this? You can be a son of whatever you want, as long as you leave me alone. It's too early for this." Duck rolled over and saw what time it was and said, "I take that back. It's at least an hour before early."

"Here's a cup of wake-me-up." Tony set a cup of coffee down on the nightstand just out of Duck's reach. Duck mumbled, "Just five more minutes, please, honey. I had a rough night last night."

Tony reached down and cranked the volume on the alarm clock up even more, then turned and walked out of the room. A few more clicks of the clock, and boom! The alarm activated again. "Tony, you son of a ditch digger."

Tony, sitting in the other room with the paper in his hand, smiled as he turned the page. Duck sat up on the side of the bed, put his hands over his face, and began rubbing his face. He stretched, then reached over and grabbed his cup of coffee, brought himself to his feet and shuffled out to the front room where Tony was sitting, leaving the alarm clock blaring. Before he reached the door, Tony yelled, "Duck, turn that damn thing off!"

Duck turned and headed back to the alarm clock, reached down, and yanked the plug out of the wall. Thinking how nice the noiseless room was, he lay back down. From the other room, he heard, "Duck, don't you even think about getting back in that bed."

Duck then turned once again and headed toward Tony's voice. Tony was still sitting at the table reading the sports page of the morning paper. He looked up just in time to see a naked Duck walking toward him. He was scratching himself with one hand and holding a cup of coffee in the other. Duck walked across the room over to the coffeepot and poured himself a little more coffee. Then he walked over and plopped down on one of the chairs at the table. Tony broke the silence. "Duck, I think you forgot something again."

"What, Tony? You're like an old woman. What now?"

"Oh, nothing, outside of the fact that at this precise moment, you are probably putting skidmarks on my chair. For Pete's sake, Duck, go put some clothes on."

"What? Oh, okay." Duck reached over, put his hand in the bowl, and grabbed out a couple of sugar cubes. Then he got up, cup in hand, and headed back through the door, scratching his bare butt.

Tony looked at the sugar container that Duck had just put his hand in. He picked it up, walked over to the trashcan, and threw the whole thing away.

From the other room, Tony heard, "I'm not exactly a morning person anymore, you know. We didn't have to get up this or any other early on the street, ever."

"Hurry up, Duck. We've got to get to the gym. I laid out some shorts, socks, and some tennis shoes for you to wear. Now, get them on. Fritz will be waiting for us at the gym."

"Fritz," replied Duck. "Sounds kind of German-ish."

"It is German-ish," replied Tony. "Let me put it to you this way. 'Schnell, schnell!' You don't 'vont' to be late. Fritz 'vould' not like this."

Duck was now in the bathroom putting on the workout clothes Tony had laid out for him. Mumbling to himself, he said, "Fritz! Now, what in the hell am I doing getting dressed and voluntarily going to meet someone named 'Fritz' at 4 o'clock in the frickin' morning? Am I nuts? Hey, I have these running shoes in my hand. This would be a good time to put them on and take off running back to my pals on the streets."

Duck reached down to pick up a pair of socks and put them on. He looked at them and yelled, "Hey, Tony, I think Lilly gave us a pair of used socks."

"No, she didn't. They're a pair of mine."

"Yours? How come they're not green, then? Actually, they look a little green-ish moldy-ish around the edges."

"Just shut up and put them on, wise guy."

"This is great. I'm putting on a pair of Tony's old socks. I always thought he had ugly feet. Now, this is sick. I'm putting my feet in the same garage where he has kept those ugly feet parked for Lord knows how many years."

"Come on, Duck. We've got to get going."

"Okay, Herr Commandant." As Duck reached down to put his tennis shoes on, he noticed his golf ball rolling back to the opening of the shoe. Tony had put the ball in the shoe as a reminder to Duck of his reason for doing all of this. He turned the shoe upside down and let the ball with the smile fall into his hand. As he looked down at it, his head was once again filled with memories.

Tony broke the silence as he said, "That ball and those memories dancing in your mind right now are your reason. Don't ever forget that. Now, get those shoes on, and let's get going."

CHAPTER 12

Arriving at the gym, Tony and Duck proceed through the doors. As they did, several huge guys and shapely women walked by them, heading to their next station of weights or cardio equipment or out the door to work. In Duck's mind, Fritz had to be some huge guy or gal with bulging muscles and, of course, a deep Australian accent. Tony walked over to the counter.

"Hi. I'm Tony Bezmouskee, and this is Bob Duckins; everyone calls him Duck. We're here to see Fritz."

"I'll need an I.D. from each of you."

Tony showed the person at the counter his driver's license, and Duck whipped out his library card. Pointing at it, he said, "That's me right there."

The person at the counter got on the microphone and announced, "Fritz, you have clients waiting." Then he turned and said, "You'll find a water cooler just through those doors in front of you. Wait at the water cooler for Fritz. He'll meet you there."

Tony and Duck headed through the second set of doors that lead from the reception area to the actual workout area. Sure enough, there was a water cooler; and as instructed, they stood by it waiting for Fritz. Duck looked at every large sculpted person who walked by, thinking, "This is him," or "This must be her. Is this him? Is this her? Shit, I hope she's not him," he said to himself. From behind him, he heard a voice say, "Hey, Tony, how are you doing?"

"Good, Fritz. How are you?"

"I couldn't be better, thank you." Duck took a deep breath, grimaced, and then turned with his hand extended and said, "My name is Du..." He didn't see anybody.

Then he heard a voice that said, "You must be Duck. You kind of look like a golfer."

Duck looked down toward the voice, and there stood a well-sculpted little person. Fritz extended his hand. "Hi. I'm Fritz." With a look of shock on his face, Duck reached down to shake Fritz's hand. Not that Duck had anything against men who were small in stature. Hell, living on the streets for as long as he did left him without a single judgmental bone in his body. The look was from the fact that Fritz wasn't quite what he was expecting.

But Fritz had seen this look before, and in his mind, it was an insult. He broke the awkward pause first by saying, "I'm three foot nine and one-half inches tall. Now that you know that, do you have any other questions?" Duck shook his head no. Then Fritz continued. "Respect, Mr. Duckins, is earned through action, not words or physical display. You better hope you can earn mine."

While still shaking Duck's hand, Fritz said, "What if I told you I could kick your ass right here and right now if I wanted to? Would you believe me? Well, would you, Mr. Duckins?"

Duck, always a wise guy, said, "Kick my ass? Uh, no, I don't think you could kick my ass. I'm sorry, but have you looked in a mirror lately? You might be able to jump up and touch my ass, but kick it? No way."

Fritz reached down and touched a pressure point on the side of Duck's foot, and as he did, a great deal of pain shot through Duck's foot. As Duck reached down to grab his foot, Fritz slapped him across the face, lightly but firmly.

"I had you, Mr. Duckins. I played you, and if I had really wanted to, I could have laid you out cold. Never disrespect my stature."

"But I didn't mean to. I..."

"What I just showed you, Ducky boy, was just one thing I'm going to teach you. But you have to be willing to listen to me. Do I now have your attention, Mr. Duckins?"

"Yeah, you do."

"Mr. Duckins, when I address you, I expect to hear a reply of 'Yes, sir.' Do I make myself clear?"

Duck looked toward Tony and shrugged his shoulders and asked, "What's up with this guy?"

"I think he feels you showed him disrespect." Tony turned his head away and tried with all his might to suppress his laughter. Fritz kicked the side of Duck's foot, and Duck yelled in pain.

Fritz repeated, "Do I have your attention?"

"Yeah, yeah—you've got it."

Fritz cupped his hand around his ear and said, "Pardon me?"

Duck replied, "Yes, sir!"

"Good. Now, let's get to work." Fritz turned to Tony and said he just might be a fast learner, after all. "We'll see you in an hour and a half." Tony turned and left.

Duck followed Fritz through the gym, much like a new recruit would follow his drill sergeant on his first day of boot camp. Fritz stopped at a set of scales and said, "Let's see what you weigh." Duck stepped on the scales. "Not bad, but you need some work. We've wasted enough time. Now, step off the scale, and let's get to work."

As Duck followed Fritz, some people he passed said things like, "Good luck, rookie. Prepare to be sore."

Fritz turned to Duck. "So, Mr. Duckins, have you ever been serious about getting in shape before?"

"It's 'Duck.' And no, I never have. And I really don't think I need to now."

"Well, I disagree. If you want to compete, you have to have endurance. You need to develop a physical as well as an inner strength. That's why Tony hired me. If you follow the instructions and consistently stick with the routines that I am going to lay out for you, you will be competing at a level that you didn't know was possible. I'll be honest with you, Mr. Duckins, if you're just going to waste my time, then I want you to head for the door right now. How about it? Are you willing to commit?"

"This was all Tony's idea, you know." Thinking that he was mumbling to himself, Duck said, "I suppose Fritz vouldn't like me saying no."

"What's that?"

"Oh, nothing, sir. Yeah, yeah, I'm ready. Even I have to admit that I have taken the easy way out far too many times. But you have got to call me 'Duck,' not Mr. Duckins."

"Good. Now, Duck, I want you to stand right over there directly across from me. This will be our first stop this morning and every morning henceforth. Here we will do ten minutes of loosening up. I will be your mirror. Just follow me and do as I do."

Fritz pulled out two golf clubs from behind a chair and showed Duck how to get loose properly by using a golf club. "When you are about to play a round of golf, I want you to use this exercise before you even think about swinging a club."

"Hey, where's your Australian accent?"

"Where's my, what kind of accent?"

"Tony told me you had a deep German accent."

"Well, we both know how Tony is. And speaking of Tony, Duck, I have to tell you all that stuff earlier this morning—that was Tony's choice. He told me to give you the 'number one' with regard to our introductory meeting so that I would get your respect."

"Well, one thing about Tony," Duck said, "as much as I hate to admit it, he's usually right. And by golly, you have my attention."

"Good. You probably don't remember me, but I used to watch you play a lot in college. You made it look easy. I always wondered what it would feel like to be in front of a gallery, competing on a golf course. Enough dillydallying. Let's get to work."

Over the next thirty days, Duck and Fritz became good friends. As Duck's game grew stronger and stronger, he knew he owed his progress to Fritz and Tony, and he wasn't about to forget it. After thirty days came and went, Duck, Tony, and Fritz continued the workout program indefinitely. Duck could feel the hard work beginning to pay off. Now, all he needed was a chance to play.

About three weeks into the second month of training, Tony picked up Duck and Fritz after a workout. "I got a call back today. It seems a lot of folks have somehow heard that the Duck is back."

Duck responded, "Could it have been the 10,000 photos of my mug that you sent out across the country to all the major and not-so-major news sources?"

"Well, that might have had a little to do with it. Anyhow, do you want to hear about the call I got or not?"

"Well, yeah, I—we do—don't we, Fritz?"

"We sure would."

"Well, then shut up and listen. After I dropped you off this morning at Fritz's, I came home, had my cup of coffee, sat on the throne, took a shower, and right as I was stepping out of the shower, the phone rang. So I put a towel around my waist and walked into my room to answer it, and—guys, I swear this is true—even before I picked up the phone, I knew who it was."

"As I answered, a voice on the other end said, 'Tony, it's been a long time. Any idea who this is?'"

"Immediately I replied, 'Yeah, Jonesy Standlovich. I knew you'd be calling.'"

"'So how have you been, Tony?' he asked me."

"I said, 'Good. And you?'"

"And of course, he said, 'On top of the world. Hey, Tony, I've been hearing that Duck has resurfaced. Is there any truth to the rumor?'"

"I said, 'It's more than a rumor; it's a fact. And he's on a mission.'"

"Then he said, 'What do you say we get together for lunch sometime—you, me, and the Duck—for old times' sake?' But then he said, 'Oh, and Tony, what's this I've been hearing about a supposed bet I made with you? You've got to help me stop that rumor right in its tracks, Tony old buddy.'"

"I said, 'Jonesy, hang on one minute.' I put the phone down on the dresser. Then I walked over to my closet, pulled out one of my lime green leisure suits and a frilly orange shirt, and put them on. Hey, it wouldn't be right if I wasn't properly dressed. 'I'll be right there,' I yelled at him as I adjusted my collar in the mirror. Hey, he made us wait. I figured it was his turn to go on hold. I grabbed my white shoes and a pair of white socks, picked up the phone and said, 'Just one more minute there, Jonesy.' As I rested the phone on my shoulder, I could hear him blow cigar smoke into the mouthpiece of the phone. He's not used to people making him wait. I sat on the edge of the bed and put on my shoes and socks. Now I was ready for business."

"'So, are you still there?' I asked."

"He impatiently replied, 'Yes, I'm still here.'"

"Guys, I had been waiting a long time to play out this next scene, so I told him, 'Jonesy, come on, old buddy, you and I both know that it's not a lie.' And then I reminded him about that napkin he signed that night at the fundraiser for cancer research and the fact that three of his buddies and yours truly all signed it as witnesses. 'You know, the one where you said you would put up $2 million to our $45,000 - and that part where you said that you would beat Duck two out of three games anywhere, anytime, anyplace. Well, I have in my possession a copy of that napkin. The original signed and witnessed copy of your so-called bet is being delivered to our attorney via registered mail as we speak. And I'm thinking lunch would be good, say, next Thursday at 11:30 at Cow Mickey's?'"

"Jonesy told me he had to check his calendar. Well, I waited as he checked, 'so Thursday it is,' he announced. Then Jonesy asked if I minded if he brought along a few friends. I said we didn't mind at all. In fact, I suggested he might want to bring along his attorney, because ours was going to be there."

"So now what?" Duck asked.

"We meet him for lunch. Duck, I already know the way I want this to go. We'll back him into a corner and let him think this was all his idea. Oh, and don't be surprised if a certain old friend of mine—who just happens to be a reporter—is coincidentally there somewhere. He's been dying to get his teeth into an exclusive story for years, and I think we're about to give it to him."

"So Duck, how have the workouts been going? Do you think they're helping you?"

"Absolutely. Fritz is a great motivator and a really good guy. And Tony, did you know Fritz is also a caddy?"

Acting surprised, Tony said, "No way. What a stroke of luck." Tony continued, "Of course I know he is a caddy! And I'll tell you what, Duck, he is the best-kept secret around. He knows the game; he studies it. You see, Ducky my friend, it's all part of my plan."

"So Tony, about this meeting—are we really going to have a lawyer there to represent us?"

"Yep. It's mostly set; just waiting for a final confirmation from our legal department."

"Now, don't take this wrong, Tony, and don't think that I'm ungrateful, but we already have an attorney."

Just as Duck had finished saying that, Tony's 1960-style phone rang. "Hold that thought, Duck." Answering the phone, he said, "Yeah, this is Tony. So Thursday will work for you? Great. What time should we be at the airport to pick you up? Super. We'll see you at 9:00 at Gate B. Yeah, I'm looking forward to meeting you face-to-face, too. Who? Oh, Duck.

Yeah, he's right here. Just a minute. Duck, our attorney wants to speak to you."

"Hello, this is Bob Duckins—anybody there?"

A voice on the other end said, "So, Duck, have you been to the library lately? I guess I'll be seeing you Thursday for lunch—that is, if it's okay with you."

Speechless, Duck lowers the phone from his ear and stares with amazement at Tony. "So talk, Duck. That thing charges me by the minute." Tony grabbed the phone away from Duck and said, "He'll be okay—but I think this is a first. Right now, he's totally speechless. We'll see you at the airport."

Duck shook his head in amazement. He reached over and put his hand on Tony's shoulder and said, "You're the best. Thanks."

Tony looked in the rearview mirror after Duck had removed his hand and noticed another smudge on the shoulder of his leisure suit. "Why do I even try?"

"Sorry, Tony. I guess I forgot or got excited or something like that."

"Duck, I want you to sit back and take notice of how I'm reacting to your latest assault on my wardrobe. Inside, I'm yelling loudly at you. But outside I'm calm and collected. I want you to remember this, because I know what you've been thinking. You're thinking, 'When I meet up with Jonesy Standlovich, I'm going to kick his ass right in front of God and everybody.' Well, Duck, you cannot do that. You can kick his ass on the golf course with your clubs, but a physical attack on him would ruin it all. Am I making myself clear here? There's an old saying, Duck. It goes like this: 'Eat shit and take the money.' That's what we have to do. Trust me on this. All you have to do is be polite, amiable, smile a lot, and let me and Mya do the talking. Are you listening to me, Duck?"

Duck just sat there quietly, tapping on the door's armrest with his fingers.

"Duck, did you hear me?"

"I heard you. It's just that sometimes I wish you weren't so damn good at reading my mind."

"Duck, we have worked too long and hard for this opportunity; we can't blow it now."

"Yeah, yeah, I heard you. You're the boss, Tony."

"Okay, Duck. Our attorney Mya is flying in on Thursday morning. We'll to pick her up at 9:00 a.m. She'll only be here until about 6:30 that evening when her return flight is scheduled to leave. She had to rearrange her schedule in order to make the luncheon. I don't know what you did to deserve this, but this woman is definitely in your corner. Do you know she is paying her own way here and back home?"

Not another word was said the rest of the way home, and for that matter, nothing was said for the rest of the evening. Only pleasant 'good nights', as they both retired early. Thursday morning rolled around quicker than anyone expected. Duck got up early and hopped into the shower. When Tony got up, he found Duck was already dressed in one of the outfits they had gotten from Lilly's. He was sitting at the kitchen table.

"Duck, aren't you going to work out this morning?"

"No, I need you to drop me off somewhere. I need to do some thinking. Oh, and don't worry about calling Fritz. I told him I wouldn't be in today."

Duck and Tony climbed into Tony's Cadillac. Tony was on his way to the airport to pick up Mya. He knew where he was headed, and he would have thought that Duck would have wanted to come along with him. Tony said to Duck, "So, where do you want me to drop you off?"

"I'd like you to take me to the library, please. I don't think they're open yet, but that's okay. I can wait out front until they do. I'll do some people-watching."

"Okay, Ducky boy, the library it is." Arriving at the library, Duck got out, shut the door and said, "When you come back, would you send our attorney in to get me? She'll know where to find me."

Tony drove off. Duck walked up to the door and read the 'Open and Closed' times printed on the door. The library opens in one hour, he said to himself. He looked around and found the perfect chunk of concrete sidewalk to sit down on. This, he thought, was a great vantage point to watch the people as they passed by. There wasn't much foot traffic passing by at this hour. It was just like old times. He wondered how everybody back at the alley was doing. He wondered if they still were getting the 'Tuesday Night Weather Reports'. He wondered how Sister was doing. What a saint! He heard the security guard unlocking the entry doors to the library, so he got on his feet.

CHAPTER 13

Entering the doors of the library, he looked around until he saw the computers, and that's where he headed. Plugging into the internet, he looked up old newspaper articles. He found several articles about his dad, including one on the day that he died. Out of his pocket, he pulled out a folded up piece of paper. As he unfolded it, his eyes filled with tears as he saw the memorial card that he had saved from his dad's funeral. Brushing his fingers across his dad's cheek in the photo, he then read on down to the date. It read August 25, 1989.

He returned his focus to the computer, typed in the name of his home town gazette, and hit enter. Duck reached into his pocket and pulled out his library card and set it on the tiny front ledge of the screen created where the outside of the casing of the computer cradles up against the computer screen. He clicked on the home page of the Gazette ad then scrolled down to "dates." He typed in August 25, 1989, and hit enter.

The article jumped right off the page at him. It read, "Local golf pro Runner Duckins died in his son's arms at the collegiate golf tournament. Contender Bob 'Duck' Duckins was disqualified when he failed to complete the last three holes of the tournament. All players in the tournament except one had agreed to postpone the rest of the tournament. Jonesy

Standlovich, the eventual winner of the tournament, fought tooth and nail and threatened lawsuits if the last three holes weren't finished, stating he had to strike while his irons were hot. Tournament play was resumed and finished that day."

Scrolling further down the article, Duck found something that made his blood boil. A reporter nicknamed 'Scoops' asked Jonesy why he insisted on finishing the round today, considering the tragic circumstances. Jonesy's reply was, "I did it for Runner." He went on to tell a story. "It was the summer of my sophomore year in college, and I had just completed shooting what had to be the worst round of golf in my life. I was worried about losing my scholarship. Runner was there for me. He came up and took me aside and gave me some advice. He said, 'Jonesy, golf is a game of ups and downs; you have to stay focused, no matter what. You're going to have bad days, but you have to keep your head up and charge on. You can't let anything distract you or your game. And you always, always, no matter what, you always finish what you start.'"

"That's bullshit," Duck whispered to himself. "My dad never spoke more than one or two words to Jonesy after he danced around, paying him back for that college loan. The only words he would have spoken would have been either yes or no, mostly no."

Reading on in the article, that same reporter asked Jonesy a tough question. "Isn't the real truth of the matter that your only real competition in the tournament was Duck, and with him out of the way, you stood to win?"

"That's the farthest thing from the truth," Jonesy replied. "I was only two strokes down with three holes to play. I had him right where I wanted him. He should have listened to his own father. There were only three holes left. The man was dead. What would three more holes have hurt?" The photo in the paper showed him holding the trophy triumphantly in the air.

Reading this and seeing that picture infuriated Duck even more, and the more he read, the more he steamed until he reached a boiling point. He stood up, pointed at the screen and yelled, "You are one sorry sack of shit!" From behind him, he heard, "Well, I see you still don't have that whole being quiet at the library thing down yet." Duck turned around and came face to face with Mya.

Mya said, "I guess you can take the boy out of the alley, but you can't take the alley out of the boy. Come here, you." They stepped toward each other and embraced.

"Thanks for coming," Duck said.

"I had to come. You're my client, remember?"

After a few more moments of silent hugs, Duck turned, grabbed another chair, and set it to his right in front of the computer. Pointing at the chair, he said, "Sit down. There's something I want you to read." Duck scrolled back to the top of the article. "Read this."

Mya read the article from start to finish. As she reached the end, she stood straight up, knocking her chair to the ground. She pointed at the screen and yelled, "You son of a bitch, you're going to be hearing from this lawyer soon!"

Duck stood, too. "Shhhh. You're in a library, you know."

"Oh, yeah," she said. "Sorry. Like Duck, like lawyer, I guess. You know I was representing you with that whole yelling thing, don't you?" Then she turned to the few people who were in the library at that hour and apologized, then sat back down. "So, this is your story?"

"Yep, at least up until now." Duck reached out and grabbed his library card off of the computer and handed it to Mya. "Would you mind keeping this in a safe place? It's going to be worth something someday, you know."

They both got up and walked toward Tony, who was waiting for them out front. As Duck walked past the security guard on his way out, he pointed at Mya and said. "Tourette's. She'll be okay once we get her outside and into the fresh air."

"So, did you have a good flight, Mya?" Duck asked.

"Yes, I did."

"Good. Now, I want you to keep track of your receipts. I'll pay you back one day soon." Arriving at the car, Duck opened the door for Mya and let her in. Tony just shook his head. He knew what was coming. Duck stepped toward the back of the car, reached down and rubbed his hand across the dirty tire. He placed his clean hand on the side of the car in order to jump into the back seat, but this time his tennis shoe hit the side of the car, throwing him off balance enough that he awkwardly fell into the back seat where he landed face first. When he finally untangled himself, he saw Tony and Mya laughing in the front seat.

"Did you have a good trip?" Mya asked.

Tony chimed in, "Yeah, I had a great summer. How was your fall, Ducky boy?"

"That's right. Go ahead and make your little jokes and laugh at this fallen Duck. I can handle it." He rubbed his hands together, making sure both hands had a chance to accumulate some of the tire soot. Then he reached up and put his hands on the shoulders of Tony and Mya. "You know what? I'd be laughing at me, too. I love you guys. You make me feel so warm and fuzzy."

Tony instantly knew what Duck had done. Mya looked over at Tony's shoulder and said, "Duck, look what you've done to Tony's nice green suit." Tony reached up and turned the rearview mirror toward Mya so she could see the similar smudge on her beige suit and said, "Join the club, Mya."

"Oh, let me rub it off," said Duck, showing Mya the palms of his hands. Tony looked at Mya and said, "He thinks he's cute."

"Stop the car!" said Mya. Tony said, "We don't have time. We're on a tight schedule, and we're also on a two-lane bridge."

"I don't care. Stop the damn car now!" Tony did as he was told. He pulled over and stopped the car. Immediately, cars back up behind them on the two-lane bridge.

Mya grabbed the handle, opened the door, and stepped out onto the bridge. She reached over and slammed the car door hard. Tony grimaced at her treatment of his pride and joy Caddy and said, "Hey, easy on my car." Mya just gave him a dirty look. Tony put his hands up—"Sorry."

She turned her attention back to Duck. She opened the door and slammed it again. Tony started to object, but thought better. Mya stared directly into Duck's eyes and said, "Did you hear that sound, Duck, the sound of that door slamming shut? That's the sound of what will be your ex-attorney if you ever disrespect me again. The door will shut, and it will never reopen. Have I made myself clear?" Duck mumbles to himself, "Why is everyone always trying to teach me a lesson?"

"What was that?" Mya asked.

"Yes, yes, you have made yourself perfectly clear. It was just a joke."

"There is a time and a place for jokes. Right now," Mya continued, "we are playing like we are serious adults." She looked at Duck, folded her arms, turned her back to the car, and strolled a short distance to the edge of the bridge. She stood there looking out through the web of cables that offered support for the old, gray steel bridge's structure.

Duck leaned up to the front seat and whispered, "What is she doing, Tony?" Tony whispered back, "Tell her you're sorry and that it will never happen again, you birdbrain."

Duck rolled down the window and yelled, "Really, Mya, I'm sorry. It won't happen again."

"Do I have your word on that?"

Tony could see in the rearview mirror that Duck was displaying his crossed fingers for him to see. He just shook his head.

"Yep, you have my word," Duck fibbed, "and Tony is my witness."

"And how about Tony?" she asked.

"I guess," Duck replied.

Mya opened the door and climbed back in, and Duck slumped down in the seat and quietly looked out the window the rest of the way. Mya had accomplished what Tony had told her needed to be done. She had let Duck know who was in charge here. Tony was afraid of what Duck might physically do to Jonesy, and he knew he needed an ally to help keep him in check.

Just on the other side of the bridge, they came to Fritz's home, where Tony pulled over and honked his horn. After Fritz came out and the introductions were made, they were soon back on the road.

As they pulled up to Cow Mickey's Restaurant, they saw a black limousine had already pulled up to the door of the restaurant, and they watched as four members of Jonesy's entourage piled out of it followed by the big man himself, with his fine cigar in his mouth. All five of them quickly disappeared into the short, dark green canvas tunnel leading to the front door of Cow Mickey's. Just the sight of Jonesy got Duck's blood boiling again.

Tony looked into the rearview mirror at Duck and said, "Remember, congenial and cordial. You let Mya and me do most of the talking. Getting angry and doing something stupid won't do anybody any good."

Tony parked his baby in the back of the parking lot across three spaces, taking no chance of getting his door dinged. Reaching the entrance to the restaurant, Mya grabbed Tony and Duck's hands, and Tony grabbed Fritz's hand in a show of unity. As they entered the door, Mya was all business. Duck realized he was holding his breath.

The maitre'd greeted them. "May I help you?"

"Yes. I'm Mya. This is Tony Bezmouskee, Fritz, and Bob Duckins. We're here to have lunch with Jonesy Standlovich."

"Yes. Mr. Standlovich is expecting you. Right this way, please."

They were led to a back area of the restaurant that was less crowded; an area of the restaurant where it was thought Jonesy's celebrity status wouldn't affect his lunch meeting. As they reached their table, they noticed Jonesy and his cronies already had cocktails.

Jonesy looked up and said, "Ducky, come here, my boy. How are you doing? Can I get you a drink?" Never getting up from his seat, he reached back over his shoulder to shake Duck's hand.

"I'm good," replied Duck. "And you?" It was all he could do to keep from adding, "you sack of shit," but he took Tony's advice and opted for the shorter, more congenial version.

"On top of the world, Ducky, my boy, on top of the world. What's this I hear about you living on the streets, man? You should have come and talked to me. I would have gotten you help."

"Actually, Jonesy, I learned more from my friends on the street than I ever would have through counseling. It just took a lot longer. Jonesy, you know Tony."

"Well, of course I do. How's it going, Tony?"

"Just fine, Jonesy. Thanks for asking."

"This is our friend and colleague, Fritz."

"Hey there, little guy, how you doin'? Come here and sit on my lap," said Jonesy, patting his thigh. This got a round of laughs from his buddies, but Duck just bent down and whispered something in Jonesy's ear. Tony cringed as he thought about what Duck could say, but whatever it was, Jonesy got right up and shook Fritz's hand. "It's a pleasure to meet you, Fritz."

"And last, but definitely not least, this is our attorney, Mya."

"How you doing, sis?" was Jonesy's reply. "She's a pretty little thing, isn't she, boys? Now, you can come sit on old Jonesy's lap anytime you want. Hey, are you looking for some work? Dave here could always use a good looking little filly like you at his firm. Isn't that right, Dave? Hell, I could keep you both busy, just keeping me out of trouble."

"By the way, this is Dave Labinsky, my main attorney. This here is Porter Agnesh, Jade Spellbunde, and Maurice Antone. They kind of all protect me in their own way. Sit down, sit down. Take a load off. I took the liberty of ordering lunch for us all."

Not one to dance around a subject for very long, Jonesy said, "So what's with this napkin?"

Tony stood back up. "Actually, I have met three of your buddies here before at a fundraiser for cancer research, and I think maybe you all might just recognize your signatures on this napkin." Tony had several copies of the napkin and walked around the table, distributing them all. "The original," Tony said, "is in a safe deposit box under the control of our attorney here."

"S-o-o-o," Mya said, as she reached down and picked up her hard-shelled, rectangular briefcase and set it on the table in front of her. She opened it up and withdrew an envelope. From the envelope, she pulled out an 8 ½ x 11 sheet of paper with typing on it and handed it to Jonesy's attorney, Dave.

"As you can verify by reading your copy, this is a letter from our banker verifying the deposit of the $45,000 required in order to hold up our end of the agreement." Mya scribbled something else on a piece of paper and handed it to Dave. On it, she had written, "While you're contemplating the matters at hand, you also might want to think about advising your client about some of the protocol regarding sexual harassment lawsuits."

Dave had been fearing this for a long time. Up to this point, Jonesy had got away with talking to women any way he liked because of his celebrity status. Dave, after reading the letter, looked up at her, trying not to show the fear in his heart. He turned and whispered something into Jonesy's ear, to which Jonesy scoffed. "Does this little lady know who she's talking to? Maybe she needs a good old spanking from Jonesy boy."

Duck and Tony immediately looked at each other with their mouths hanging open. They shut their mouths and wondered where on earth she had come up with the $45,000. Fritz just sat back with his hands folded across his ripped stomach and smiled, just taking in the show.

Jonesy's attorney spoke first. "So you have signatures on a napkin. So what? This would never stand up in court. You and I both know that."

"I thought you might find a way to not perform on a binding contract," she said, "so I brought along a little bit of something else. I thought you might try to say this wasn't binding." She reached into her briefcase and pulled out a stack of papers. She pulled one off the pile and read it. "Casey v. Nash, $2 million awarded, written on a red shop rag with a felt-tip pen." She laid it down as the start of a new pile and picked up another.

"Rone v. MacDougal's Hardware, contract written on a torn seed sack, 1.1 mil awarded." She laid it on the new stack. "Mason v. Malone, contract written on the bill of a baseball cap, $500,000 awarded." She placed the papers on top of the original stack and slid them all across the table to Jonesy's attorney. "And these, counselor, are more cases that I'm sure would serve as proof to any judge and jury that our contract is legal beyond any shadow of a doubt.

Unbeknownst to everyone seated at the table except Tony, sitting right next to them with a tape recorder, a cell phone camera, and his trusty 35mm camera was an old friend of Tony's, Scoop, a reporter. He was taking in every moment and had no soft spot in his heart for Jonesy Standlovich. He had witnessed Jonesy's ugly, behind-the-scenes rise to the top first-hand.

After he finished talking with his attorney, Jonesy spoke up. "So Runner Duckins' little boy wants to step up and play with the big boys. What do you think, Dave?"

"Well, honestly, from the case history she brought along, there seems to be substantial proof of the validity of such contracts being held up in a court of law. It's up to you. I'll fight it all the way if you want me to, but as your counsel…" Jonesy interrupted. "Yeah, yeah, as my counsel, you're going to tell me I have made myself a deal. Well, what do you guys think?" All his friends just shrugged in the fashion of 'yes men.' "Whatever you think, Jonesy."

"I tell you what I think. I think we should kick this little Ducky's ass all over the golf course once again. Let's do this. I just hope he doesn't quit in the middle again." In anger, Duck started to stand up and retaliate, but Mya's look made him sit right back down. She said, "There is one other matter. We want you to pay an additional $45,000 plus interest and penalties to your alma mater in order to pay off the student loan that Runner signed off on for you."

"That's not part of this! I won't agree to that. Besides, I was on a full ride scholarship. Everyone knows that. I won't agree to that unless you have a signed napkin, a signed golf cart, or some other weird signed thing proving that I owe the money." He looked at his buddies and let loose with that annoying laugh of his. Jonesy turned to Mya and said, "Little lady, all that you have is the word of a dead man and this ex-bum here."

Mya could see the anger boiling up inside of Mount Saint Duck, so she walked over and stood behind Duck and put her hands on his shoulders to prevent him from jumping out of his seat and flying across the table at Jonesy. She bent down and whispered in Duck's ear. "Remember. Eat shit and take the money."

She walked back over and sat down once again. Then she said, "Agree to our terms, and there will be no sexual harassment lawsuit." Jonesy's attorney grabbed his client's arm and whispered in his ear the benefits of her offer. Jonesy continued, "Well, it's a moot point, anyway. When I kick your little duck ass, I won't have to pay anything, so it doesn't matter. Here are my terms: no press. When I win, no more talk about this bogus student-loan deal. My attorney will supply a letter to your counsel stating that the $2 million worth of funds are on deposit."

"Uh, that's $2,045,000 plus penalties and interest, Jonesy boy," said Duck.

"Oh, right. $2,045,000 plus Runner's interest and penalties," replied Jonesy. "We agree to meet and play a round of golf quietly, like every other Joe does on a Saturday morning. We want to keep this out of the press. I wouldn't want your humiliating defeat to be printed in all the papers once again. We'll play 54 continuous holes on the same day, come rain or shine."

Mya busily captured the terms on her laptop, pressed the print button, and out popped the legal document. Duck just shook his head at the wonders of modern technology and said, "That is so cool. And it's in duplicate. Whatever happened to carbon paper?"

She slid the agreement over to Dave, Jonesy's attorney. "This will make it official." Dave said, "Well, wait a minute. I thought your napkin made it all official. We don't need to sign anything else." He slid the paper back to Mya.

"So what about the $45,000 plus interest?" Mya asked.

"Well, you'll just have to take our word on that. We agree it's part of this." Mya tore up the agreement, which also referenced the sexual harassment settlement, and said, "Fine. We'll let the napkin and the gentlemen's agreement stand on their own merits."

"Well, about the sexual harassment issue?" asked Dave. "We'll need something in writing about that."

"Well, I guess you'll just have to take my word on that," said Mya as she dropped the pieces of the document into her briefcase, which she then snapped shut and placed next to her on the floor.

Jonesy looked at Duck and said, "Let's you and I settle this the old-fashioned way, with a handshake." For the first time, Jonesy and Duck stood up. As Duck got up, he stuck his left hand into the pile of strawberry jam he had stockpiled on his saucer as he fidgeted during the negotiations. He then walked toward Jonesy to seal the deal. Scoop, the reporter, grabbed his 35mm and walked around to get in position so he wouldn't miss this photo op.

Duck reached up and put his left hand on the shoulder of the $5,000 sports jacket that Jonesy was wearing over his blue Polo shirt. Then they shook hands to seal the deal while Scoop snapped a series of photos. When Duck removed his hand from Jonesy's shoulder, he had left a perfect strawberry jam hand print on Jonesy's jacket.

Jonesy, seeing the flashes and hearing the shutter click several times, looked toward the source and saw Scoop. "Shit," he said.

Scoop said, "No, Jonesy, it's 'cheese,' when you have your picture taken. You say 'cheese,' not 'shit.' Say cheese!" He snapped yet another picture, which, when viewed later, showed the shock and anger on Jonesy's face and a dark, messy substance spread all over the shoulder of Jonesy's sports coat.

"What are you doing here?" Jonesy asks Scoop.

"Hey, it's a public restaurant. And, man, does your voice carry in here."

Jonesy walked over, plopped down in his chair, and said, "Where in the hell is my food?"

As they walked out of the restaurant, Tony asked Duck, "Okay, Duck, just what did you whisper in Jonesy's ear?"

"Yeah," Mya said. "You scared me there for a second. I thought you were going to blow the whole thing. Just what did you say to him?"

"Oh. I just gave him a quick history lesson about Fritz. I let him know Fritz could kick his pompous butt anywhere, anytime, even with one hand tied behind his back."

He turned to Fritz. "And then I told him about the three men you hospitalized in self defense during that bar fight."

"Well, thanks, Duck," Fritz replied, "but actually, there were four."

CHAPTER 14

The next morning, as Jonesy was reading his morning paper, he saw the headline, "Golf Match of the Century."

The article continued, "Jonesy Standlovich vs. Bob 'The Duck' Duckins. 54 holes." The story reminded readers of the event surrounding the last time these two met, including the sudden death of Runner. The caption below the photo in the article read, "The deal was sealed with the handshake shown here. The only thing left is to set the date. Stay tuned, sports fans. I'll update you when I have more."

Jonesy slammed the paper down, picked up his phone, and speed-dialed Tony. "I thought we agreed that there would be no press."

"Hey, those were your words, not ours. Besides, who knew Scoop would be there? What were the chances?"

Jonesy, still steaming, said, "I'll settle this once and for all right where it started—on the golf course. I want a time and place set immediately." Tony jumped at the opportunity. "How about June 9? I have a tee-time reserved for 9 a.m. We'll play at the Brown County municipal course, the same place our tournament was played, and we'll start and finish on hole 16, the hole you said Duck quit on. How's that for immediate?"

"Done. I'll clear my calendar," Jonesy said. "Oh, and tell your boy that he owes me five grand for the jacket that he ruined with that ridiculous strawberry jam stunt." With that, he hung up.

The next morning, Scoop's column read, "Jonesy vs. Duck is set for June 9, 9 a.m., at none other than the same golf course where all of this started. Looks like this reporter will be making a road trip. I'll keep you posted. This is going to get interesting."

That morning at Fritz's, while loosening up, Duck said, "Fritz, would you consider working with me as my caddy? The pay won't be great at first, but eventually you'll do more than all right."

"Hmmmm. Me be your caddy? Well, of course I'll be your caddy. You need me, Duck. Together we are going to kick some serious boo-tay! But didn't you know Tony had signed me up a month ago? I guess he knew we would hit it off. But he said I have to wear lime green caddy overalls with matching socks, tee shirt, and hat. Do I really have to wear that stuff, Duck?"

"Hey, Tony's the boss. What he says goes." Duck just shook his head at another one of Tony's prearranged plans unfolding perfectly in front of his eyes. "Hey, why don't you go to the golf course with us today?"

"I guess you didn't know that, either. Tony already told me that from today on, I'm your shadow on the golf course. He told me I'm to be your own personal golf mentor."

Tony was right again, Duck soon realized. Fritz was a true student of the game, and his insights were a perfect fit for Duck's game. The more rounds they played together, the more comfortable they became with each other. Even the conversations at the morning workouts began to center on the previous and the upcoming days of golf.

On the way to the golf course one morning, Tony announced Mya had called to say she received the $2,045,000 verification of funds from Jonesy's attorney. "So we are now official, boys. Next Tuesday, we get to put this whole thing to rest and get on with Plan B, which, incidentally, includes making a sizeable deposit into our operating account."

Instantly, Fritz's wheels started turning. "I'll get the weather forecasts. It's an early morning round, so we'll have to deal with the dew. I'm betting it will be raining on his parade."

CHAPTER 15

On the morning of the golf match with Jonesy, Duck woke up early from a dream in which he was eight years old, and standing over him, showing him how to hit the ball correctly, was his dad, Runner. In the dream, Runner told him, "I want you to lose the first round of golf today. Make it close, mind you. It's Jonesy's ego. He just can't let it go. I have it from a good source that if he wins the first round, he'll up the ante. Then you can charge back and kick his legs right out from under him."

Duck's head was dancing with the vivid memory of the dream; he rolled over and looked at the clock. It was 2:45 a.m. He immediately got up and walked over to Tony's room and said, "Get up, Tony, and call Mya and Fritz. Tell them we'll be by to get them at 3:50."

Tony said, "Do what?" He rolled over and looked at the clock. "Do you know what time it is, Duck?"

"Tony, just do this for me, please. Come on, man, let's get going."

Tony wiped the sleep from his eyes, reached over, and grabbed the phone and speed-dialed Mya. She answered on the first ring.

Tony explained, "Duck wants to get going early, and we'll be by at 3:50."

Her reply was, "Good. I've been up all night and just stepped out of the shower when the phone rang. I'll be ready."

The next call was to Fritz, and he answered the phone with a voice laden with sleep. "Fritz, this is Tony."

"Tony, do you have any idea what time it is, man?"

"Yeah, I know, but the Duck wants me to pick everybody up by 3:50. He wants to get out there early."

"If that's what he wants, I'll be ready."

"See you in a little bit, Fritz."

"Hey, that wasn't cool. Did you call me 'little bit'?"

"As in shortly; not too long." Realizing none of this was sounding right, Tony said, "Just be ready," and hung up.

Sitting in the car at the golf course drinking cups of coffee quietly, Tony said to Duck, "Are you all right, man?"

"Tony, I couldn't be better. I have a hunch, that's all, and I wanted to run it by you guys. Here's the deal. I want to lose the first round today."

"You what?"

"I want to lose the first round today."

"You mean on purpose?" Fritz said.

Tony said, "You can't do that."

"Well, why can't I? It's all part of the hunch that came to me in my dream last night. Think about it. If he wins the first round, he'll be so full of himself that he will up the ante. I can hear it now. The first words out of his mouth, after he lights his cigar and gloats, will be, 'Come here, Ducky boy, what do you say we make this interesting, like—oh, I don't know, maybe double or nothing.' He'll do it, I know he will."

"Just how do you know this?" asked Mya.

"My dad told me this morning in that dream."

"Your dad told you this morning in a dream?" Tony asked. "So you want to risk everything on a dream. Duck, you are beginning to scare me."

Fritz chimed in, "I don't know, Tony. I think he's right about Jonesy. He will want to increase the bet. I'd wager my gym on it, and I know Duck can take him, especially with me, as his caddy."

Mya spoke up. "Of course, I'll deny that we ever had this conversation, but I think it's a brilliant idea. Not sure if it's legal, and I don't want to know, but I think it will work."

"Hey, I'm the one with $45,000 invested in this venture. I say it's worth a try. My money, as we know, is on Duck, and I say we go with his hunch."

Tony gave in. "Okay. I don't like it. It's risky, but what do you say we at least keep the game close?"

"Then it's settled." They all joined their coffee cups together in the middle of the Caddy for a toast. "Here's to our futures," was the toast that Fritz had them raise.

The sun was turning the pre-morning darkness into light. "Now, let's go hit some golf balls." Dave and Mya exchanged notarized copies of the Verification of Funds. "It's now 8:45—time for a little golf," said Tony. "Let's flip a coin to see who tees off first."

"Hold on there, boys." Jonesy said as he handed Tony a wooden nickel. And then he said, "If you don't mind, let's use this for the toss."

"We don't mind," replied Tony. "Duck, do you call heads or tails?" Duck was standing there staring at the tree that was planted in honor of his dad in an area near where Runner took his last breath. "Duck—heads or tails?"

"What? Oh, heads. We'll call heads." Tony flipped the coin into the air, and when the wooden coin landed, it showed 'tails'.

"Looks like I win," boasted Jonesy, "and you know what? I elect to let your boy go first. And here, Tony," he reached down to pick up the wooden coin, he said "You keep this." As Jonesy took a drag of his large cigar, he said, "I can't believe you took that from me. Didn't your mother ever tell you not to take any wooden nickels?" Jonesy was laughing the loud, forced, 'look at me' laugh he had. And his buddies were fake-laughing right along with him.

Tony walked over to Duck. "Well, Ducky boy, you're up first." Duck was still staring. Tony put his hand on Duck's shoulder. "Duck, you're up."

"What? Oh, you must have won the flip."

"Nope, he did, but he wants you to go first."

"Okay, Fritz, would you hand me my driver, please?"

"Gladly. This one dog-legs to the left just the other side of the furthest evergreen."

"Thanks, Fritz." Duck stepped up to the tee box, planted his golf ball and tee, took a couple of practice swings and then hit one of the prettiest drives you have ever seen. He started his golf ball out to the right side of the fairway, and played it to hook—and it did just that, as it disappeared over the crest of the hill.

Jonesy stepped up on the tee box and said, "Not a bad shot for an old lame Duck." Then he planted his ball and took his practice swings, then hit an equally beautiful shot. The first hole went to Duck. Holes 2, 3, 4, and 5 were push holes. Hole number 6 was a short par three, which had them hitting across a small pond. Jonesy put his shot on the green about 25 feet from the pin.

Duck stepped up to the ball and turned and looked at Fritz. Duck started his backswing, and as he came down on the ball, he hit it fat, and it landed in the water. Acting as if he was extremely frustrated, Duck yelled at Fritz, "Just give me another ball."

Fritz said, "What are you doing? Why don't you go up to the drop area and play your third shot from there?"

"No, I can do just as well from right here. I'll take my third shot from right here."

"You're the boss." Fritz handed Duck another golf ball. Duck dropped the ball over his shoulder. It hit the ground and settled on top of a clump of grass. Duck set up his shot. As he hit the ball, he somehow again hit the ball fat, and it also landed in the water. Duck was acting real mad. "How stupid is this?" he said. "Shooting a 5—and not even on the green yet—on a par 3."

He hit his fifth shot, and it landed on the green about 20 feet from the pin. "Now, why didn't I do that the first time?" Duck ended up 2, putting for a 7. Jonesy rolled his second shot to within a foot of the cup. He stroked the easy short putt right in the heart of the cup, giving him a par 3. This hole put Jonesy up by 4 strokes. The closest Duck got through the remainder of the first 18 was 3 behind Jonesy—and that's how the first round finished, with Jonesy on top as the winner.

Mya and Dave compared score cards and confirmed the victory for Jonesy. Jonesy, with a towel draped around his neck, walked over to where Duck was standing with Tony, Mya and Fritz, and said, "Well, Duck, it looks like this old game is perhaps a little too tough for you. Maybe it's time for you to stick your head back into the sand. You know, you might as well head back to the streets now. After all, I only need to win one of the two remaining rounds, which will officially put all these questions and rumors to bed once and for all. What do you think, guys?" Jonesy said to his band of yes men. "The rookie played all right, but will he ever beat the master? Do you still feel cocky, Ducky boy? I know I do. And you know what? This feels good, rubbing your nose in it once again."

Duck responded, "One bad hole—one stinking bad hole cost me this round, but it won't happen again. Are you sure you can afford to lose $2,000,000?"

"I tell you what, Duck. If, by some fluke or a miracle, you come back and win this thing, I'll pay you 4 million—and I'll never miss it."

"Let me get this straight. You just upped the ante to your 4 million—to our 45 G's?"

"That's right." Mya sat in her golf cart and hit "print" on her laptop. Out came a document from her portable printer stating the wager was increased from 2 million to 4 million. She walked over to Jonesy's attorney and handed him the document to review.

Dave called over to Jonesy, "Hey, you don't have to do this. Are you sure you want to do this?"

"Hell, yes! Were you asleep at the wheel? Didn't you see how bad I beat him? He doesn't have a chance, unless Runner comes back out of the big golf course in the sky and helps him."

Dave walked over to Jonesy. "Well, if you're sure, sign here." Jonesy grabbed the pen and signed it. Mya and Dave also signed as witnesses to his signature. Jonesy grabbed his driver and headed for the T box. "Let's get this thing over with. Somebody hand me a ball."

"Just hold on a second," Duck said, as he walked over to Jonesy and whispered something in his ear.

Jonesy said, "Do what?" Duck repeated it. Then Jonesy shrugged his shoulders, looked at his caddy, and then he looked at Fritz and said, "Why not?"

"Good," said Duck. Then he turned and looked at Fritz and gave him the okay signal. Fritz extended his arms and said, "What?"

Jonesy hit his drive. Again, he played this dogleg perfectly. Duck stepped up and hit one just about 10 yards farther and just as pretty. Like a bell sounding in a prize fight, round two was on.

Fritz asked, "Just what did you say to him?"

"I told him that when we got to the third round, I wanted the caddies to play the first hole head-to-head."

"Man, are you kidding me? That's awesome. Thanks, Duck. I won't let you down."

Duck charged through the second round of golf and beat Jonesy by three strokes. "Jonesy and his caddy are looking a bit tired. 4 million! We can do a lot of good with that money, and it's only 18 holes away," stated Duck. "Let's finish this. You're up, my friend."

Fritz reached into Duck's bag and pulled out his custom-made driver. As word spread around the golf course regarding the match between the famous Jonesy Standlovich and Duck, the crowd grew. With almost everybody owning a cell phone, calls went out to friends and family to come out and watch this. And of course there was Scoop, the reporter, taking every bit of this in for his morning column. By the time the third round was to start, the crowd had grown to the size of a good professional event. Suddenly, Scoop wasn't the only reporter on the scene, but that was okay. He had the earlier rounds all to himself, and he was guaranteed an exclusive interview with Duck, whether he won or lost.

"Count them," Fritz said. "Five, six, seven—no, eight television cameras. This is too good. What a way to make my debut."

"Go on, Fritz, let's get going." As Fritz headed toward the tee box, it was as if the world were in slow motion. As he looked from one side to the other, he could see the large crowd staring at him. 'So this is how it feels', he thought to himself. 'I was born for this.' And a huge, confident smile came across his face as they watched him send a beautiful first shot right down the middle of the fairway. The crowd was staring in a kind of quiet disbelief. Fritz tipped his hat to all sides of the gallery, and as he did, the applause erupted. And it wasn't just a polite golf clap. It was a loud clap, as if a grand slam had just been hit. After relishing the applause for a few minutes, Fritz raised his arm and signaled for the crowd to quiet down, and they followed his instructions immediately. Fritz stepped off the tee box.

Jonesy's caddy stepped up and hit a beautiful shot about 30 yards farther than Fritz had. Duck turned to Fritz and said, "Well done, my friend."

"Thank you, boss. It was sweet, wasn't it?" Fritz then pointed to the set of golf clubs and said, "I'll be needing those."

Duck looked at the bag, smiled, and said, "Gladly." He picked up the bag of clubs. It was his turn to caddy for Fritz.

Seeing this, Jonesy's caddy looked down at his clubs, then up to Jonesy. Jonesy snapped, "Don't even ask." So Jonesy's caddy picked up the clubs and walked alongside Fritz and Duck up the fairway to their balls. Meanwhile, Jonesy hitched a ride with Dave in his golf cart. Reaching his first shot, Fritz asked, "Duck, what should I hit?"

"If I were you, I would hit a fairway wood."

"Then a fairway wood it is." Fritz smacked his second shot, and it landed about 90 yards from the green. His third shot landed just short of the green and rolled up onto the green and stopped about 18 feet from the pin. "Nice shot" were the first words out of the mouth of Jonesy's caddy as they walked the 30 yards further to his ball. Jonesy's caddy, Ray, also hit a beautiful second shot, and his ball rested about 20 yards from the green. His third shot landed a little past the cup, then back-spun, and finally stopped about three feet from the cup.

"Wow! What a nice shot," Fritz commented to Ray. When they arrived at the green, Ray started to mark his ball. Fritz said, "Go ahead and putt out if you want." So Ray did. He lined up and sunk his short putt. Fritz, with his putter in hand, eyed the green and noticed a slight break to the left. Since Ray had sunk his putt, the pressure was on Fritz to make this shot. After studying his ball's imagined path one more time, Fritz stood over the ball and hit it. As the ball rolled toward the right side of the cup, you could sense that it had enough distance. Fritz turned his back on the ball, grabbed his hat and extended his hands into the air, just like a prizefighter would after winning the bout. He began to jump and shout, "Yes, yes, yes," over and over. Then he pumped his fists back up into the air again. The ball broke left and rolled to the very edge of the cup, and as if right on cue, the ball hung there for a split second before dropping into the hole. At that point, all that could be heard was the lone celebration being carried on by Fritz. It was as if the visiting team had just won the World Series in the 9th inning at your home field. The only sound you heard was Fritz.

As the ball fell into the cup, the looks on the faces of those watching seemed to say, "Can you believe this?" After realizing what a great, confident shot they had just witnessed, the onlookers broke into a loud clapping frenzy, accented with several, "You are the man's." Fritz decided to milk this for all that he could. He walked down the line of cheering fans, pointing and saying, "No, no, you are the man." Right then and there, this group became known as "Duck and Fritz's flock." As Fritz walked off the green, Duck said to him, "You heard a voice, didn't you?"

"Yes! How did you know?"

Fritz continued, "Duck, I knew it was going in when I stroked it. The voice in my head said, 'Start celebrating—this one is going in.' It was the strangest thing. And I tell you what! It was like someone was standing over me with his hands on my club, too. I could actually feel the warmth of his breath on my neck. He gave me permission to gloat, so I did."

"That," Duck said, "was my dad. He told me in a dream that he would be here. Good job, Fritz. You are the man."

"Thanks, Duck. That was fun. Now, get out there and finish this thing."

"Splendid idea, Fritzy my boy." They gave each other high fives. With Ray and Fritz playing a push hole, Duck retained the honors. Duck started to walk up to the tee box with his arm around Fritz. "You know what, Fritz? I feel like I could play all day long. I feel strong, and I owe it all to you and your conditioning program. Thank you, my friend."

The second hole, Number 17, ended in a tie, but on the third hole, Number 18, Duck went up by one. After that, he never looked back. As they teed up on Number 15, the final hole, it was all over but the shouting. It was here that Runner's spirit decided to have some fun with old Jonesy. The fact that he was about to lose to Duck and have to fork over four million wasn't even the worst part for Jonesy. The worst part was that his ego was getting stepped on and he was coming unraveled. He berated his caddy by saying, "You're the worst caddy ever! You couldn't even beat that little person on one stinking hole! You're done after this round. I'm getting me a new caddy and a new lawyer. All of you guys suck! Look at what you got me into.

I've carried all of you money-leaching dumb-asses for these years. Why are you trying to ruin my career? Answer this for me—why in the hell should I keep you losers on my payroll?"

Dave, the lawyer, spoke. "Hmmm, let me see. Who tried to keep you from doing this? Could it have been me? Who saved your ass down in Tijuana when you were in trouble with the Federales? Who landed you the Fourthsmith Clothing sponsorship? You know what? You can shove this job up your ass. I will be your lawyer for one more hole, up to the time you fork over the four mil you owe. After that, you're on your own."

Ray turned and walked over and stood next to Dave and said, "I'm done. I've had enough. I'm tired of you and the slug trail you leave behind you. You can carry your own clubs the rest of the way." Jonesy took a puff off his cigar; then he turned to his cronies and said, "Who needs these losers?" He grabbed a club out of his bag and headed for his ball.

Duck had already hit yet another beautiful shot. He was tired of waiting on Jonesy. Standing over his ball, Jonesy began his backswing when he heard a voice that said, "A bit of misdirected anger there, Jonesy, don't you think?" Jonesy stopped his swing and said, "Who said that? Did you guys hear that?" They all looked at each other, then shook their heads no.

Thinking that maybe he heard nothing, Jonesy once again got prepared to take his shot. Then Runner said, "He did the right thing that day, you know. I don't think you have ever done the right thing in your entire life." Jonesy stopped mid-backswing and said, "There it is again. Did you hear it?" His friends exchanged glances, their expressions suggesting they thought he was losing his mind. Looking away, he addressed the ball again and started his backswing. As he started his downswing to hit the ball, he heard, "I wouldn't hit this club if I were you. You better stop your swing."

He continued down on the ball and hit it. The ball shot off to the right and into the woods, where it rattled off of several of the trees, much the way a pinball would do off of a machine's bumpers. "Someone's going to pay for this!" shouted Jonesy. Tony, who had been fairly quiet throughout these rounds of golf, said, "Yeah, you're right, Jonesy, someone is about to pay. And I'd say that someone is you—to the tune of four million."

"That's $4,045,000 plus interest," Mya added. Duck finished that hole with a par 5. Jonesy managed a 7. He made a couple of nice comeback shots but fell way short. Mya and Dave verified the scores on all three rounds of golf. Clearly, Duck won the last two rounds.

Dave had Jonesy sign a check for $4,047,946.38, made out to Duck. Dave handed the check to Mya. He then hit "print" on his computer and grabbed the piece of paper as it came out of his portable printer, signed it, walked over to Jonesy and handed it to him, saying, "And this will serve as my immediate resignation."

Scoop's columns for the next few weeks were filled with stories he got from witnessing and capturing this match on paper and film. Fifty-four columns, to be exact. He stretched each of the holes into a day's worth of column. Jonesy never, ever regained the prominence he once enjoyed and was sued a couple of years later by a lady claiming sexual harassment. The case is still pending.

On the other hand, Duck's career, handled expertly by his sports agent, Tony, his exquisite personal trainer/caddy, Fritz, along with the solid legal advice from his Attorney, M.Y. Angel, soared to the top. Tony continued to be an absolutely fantastic sports agent and treasured friend. He got Duck back in the position to get his P.G.A. card, and Duck did the rest, making the cut into many tournaments, in which he won his share - including twice winning the Masters. Tony also landed several nice endorsements. Lil's line of "The Duck" sportswear rewarded both Lilly and Duck's group handsomely. It didn't hurt that Fritz agreed to carry her sportswear at all of his gyms. Tony had earned enough money that he could afford to buy several Cadillac Dealerships, as well as a leisure suit factory or two, and still had plenty of cash left over. But you know what? Today, he still wears the same lime green suit and still drives his old Green Cadillac convertible. However, he did splurge and bought two more bright orange shirts.

Fritz's notoriety grew from the legendary golf hole played in the David vs. Goliath match between Duck and Standlovich. His face plastered on TV screens across the country helped advertise Fritz's workout facilities, and at present, he has fifty facilities franchised across the country. Through it all, they remained the best of friends.

CHAPTER 16

The offer that Tony and Duck made to Mya at the beginning, which included a base salary plus a percentage, netted her back many times over her initial $45,000 investment. The partnership continued to flourish, with Tony digging up deals; Mya approving them and making sure all the t's were crossed and the i's dotted; Fritz caddying and keeping Duck in shape; and Duck doing what he does best on the golf course.

But Duck still had some old business that needed tending to. Between him, Tony, Mya, and Fritz, they established a home where those on the streets could come for help. They contributed a substantial amount of money from their newly formed Duck's Run charitable organization. Combined, Tony, Duck, Mya and Fritz had some big plans that they wanted to get to work on. But first they had those old issues that they wanted to deal with.

They agreed, at Duck's suggestion, to send a messenger to the cardboard hotel and ask if the residents would be so kind as to give an old friend some of their time. Duck told Mya and Tony, "We have to contact my old friends to see if we can arrange a meeting with them. This has to be done right in order to preserve their dignity. We'll send them a letter requesting a meeting."

Mya agreed. "I'll draft a letter and send it off in the morning." But Duck said, "No, I need to handwrite this one personally. Then we can send a courier down there to hand-deliver it. They'll like that. There will be an option for them to have the messenger wait for their reply or have him come back, at a time of their choice, for their decision."

Duck pulled out some stationery with his letterhead on it and wrote his letter, addressing it to all his friends in care of Sister Molly. It read:

'Dear friends:

Well, I won't waste a lot of time with words. I am writing this letter to you, hoping you will give me and my new friends a little of your time so that we can discuss some old unsettled issues with you, like the 10 o'clock news and the Tuesday Evening Weather Reports. And I have another idea that we want to run by you.

We're available any time, so please make the time and date convenient for you.

Always your friend,

Duck'

"Tony, would you mind getting a courier to deliver this? Be sure to give him the instructions about how they can reply."

"Well, that's not such a good idea!" Tony replied.

Duck was confused and more than a little surprised by Tony's response. "You don't think—what have we been talking about? I thought we agreed."

"I mean the courier. I think I should deliver this. I'd like the opportunity to meet your old friends, Duck."

"You know, Tony, thanks, but I think they might feel better if we had a uniformed courier bring it to them."

"Whatever you think. You know this one better than I do. I'll get right on it." Tony delivered the letter to a courier service and gave them the instructions, along with a detailed list of the best times to show up so they would most likely catch most of them at home.

The courier balked at delivering a package to that area let alone early in the morning, but when Tony gave him the first half of the nice tip, he would receive for his work, with the other one-half due when he returned with their reply, he jumped at the opportunity.

Early the next morning, at 4:30, a rather timid voice was heard at the entrance to the alley. The courier knocked on one of the brick building's front walls with his open palm, saying, "Excuse me, is anyone in there?" No reply. "Good morning! Is there a Sister Molly that lives here?"

A little afraid to respond, but even more afraid not to, Molly stepped out into the alleyway entrance and said, "I'm Molly. How can I help you?"

"Good morning. I have a letter here for all of you, and I was told to deliver it to you and ask if you would read it to the others."

Molly took the letter, and seeing "Bob 'Duck' Duckins" on the envelope, she hurried to open it. She read the letter along with the instructions and said, "We'll have our answer at 4:30 a.m. tomorrow. Please come back then."

After Molly read the letter out loud to everyone in the alley, they decided that Saturday morning at 3:33 would be the perfect time to meet with their old friend.

The courier came back at 4:30 the next morning as instructed. "Sister Molly, are you in there?"

"Yes. Please come in, young man." He entered the alley without apprehension. "Good morning, Sister. Mr. Duckins wanted me to tell you that if you have decided to meet with them, they will be here at your appointed time."

"Then we will look forward to meeting Mr. Duckins at 3:33 a.m. this Saturday." Sister Molly handed the courier the reply letter.

As the courier delivered the letter back to Tony, Tony handed over the balance of the tip as promised and took the letter to Duck. Duck opened it and shook his head. "They want us there at 3:33 on Saturday."

Mya said, "Perfect. That will give me time to file those 1099's, grab some lunch, then meet you there at about 3:15 or so."

"Hey, that's good for us, too," said Fritz. "Duck will have time to get in an early workout tomorrow. Hey, Tony, why don't you come work out with us? Looks to me like you've been eating a little too good lately."

"Sorry, guys. That's 3:33 a.m.," Duck replied. "That's this Saturday, and we can't be late. We'll all meet here at 3:00. We'll need plenty of bagels, Povitica, coffee, and juice."

"And don't forget about Fritz's new power bars," added Fritz.

"Oh, 3:33 a.m.," Mya said as she rolled her eyes. I'll get all that stuff at CC's. Saturday rolled around, and Bob, Mya, Tony, and Fritz were in Tony's Cadillac with a large box of bagels, four loaves of Povitica, all the fixings, and several big thermoses filled with coffee and juice in the back.

As the car's headlights shined across the alleyway, Duck said, "You know, I'm nervous. Here I play golf on TV in front of a gazillion people, and I'm nervous. This is just like when I came to see you, Tony. Okay. Just remember, we use their coffee cups. They won't mind us bringing coffee and all this stuff from Carl and Mary's, but they will take offense if we think we're too good to drink out of their cups. Besides, it never killed me."

Fritz, always a positive thinker, was looking forward to the whole situation, but Tony and Mya weren't so sure. Arriving at the alleyway's entrance, Duck, Mya, Fritz, and Tony stepped out of the car and leaned against it as they waited for someone to emerge from the alley. Then they saw a figure step out of the shadows of the alley and into the light. The light was coming from the old brick buildings' store fronts and neon lighting of the signs hanging in and around their windows.

Duck recognized the figure was Cilus. Cilus greeted them. "Right on time, too. We like that. So how you been, Duck? Want a cup of coffee?" Cilus extended his hand and offered Duck a cup.

"Sure do. That sounds great to me. I haven't had a good cup of coffee since I left here." Duck could tell that Cilus was pleased, and that he had passed the test. He wasn't too good to take a cup of their coffee from them in one of their cups. After taking the cup from Cilus, the two shook hands. As Duck took another swig of coffee, he said, "I hate to be rude, but do you have a couple extra cups of coffee for my friends?"

After giving Duck an I-can't-believe-I-heard-what-you-just-said look, Tony, Fritz, and Mya tried with everything they had to look happy about this offer. "Well, sure," said Cilus. "Wait here a minute and I'll get them a cup." Fritz was now not too sure about this whole coffee thing. He walked up to Duck and said, "Are we really going to have to drink their coffee?"

"Yes, Fritz. You're going to have to trust me on this one. You'll live through it." A few minutes later, Cilus came back out with three of the dirtiest cups you have ever laid eyes on. He walked over to Tony, Mya, and Fritz and handed them their coffee.

"Here you go!"

They all three forced out a "thank you" and managed a smile. Cilus stood and watched them take a sip and decided these friends of Duck's must be all right.

"Can we come in?" asked Duck.

Molly stepped out along with several of Duck's old friends. "You bet you can," she said. "God love you, Duck. We missed you." They all walked out and gave hugs to Duck. Since they were friends of Duck's, they gave Mya, Fritz, and Tony hugs as well. Duck announced, "I hope you don't mind, but we brought some of Carl and Mary's bagels, povitica, coffee, and juice." Molly said, "Bring it in."

Duck made introductions all around between his new friends and his old buddies. As the introductions were being made, Mya, Fritz, and Tony started handing out the goodies. As Duck and Cilus talked about old times, he glanced around to see where Fritz, Mya, and Tony had run off to. He saw Mya and Molly chatting in a corner as if they were old friends.

In fact, the more the two talked, the more they found they actually had in common, with Mya having been raised a Catholic and Molly being a former nun, though she chose to live with the homeless on the streets as her calling, leaving a richer life in hopes of enriching someone else's soul.

Across from Mya and Molly sat Tony and another of Duck's old friends, perched on what you might call the front porch of a cardboard house, laughing and chatting away, both men being very knowledgeable about sports. Tony found out his new friend had quite a golf handicap when he was out in the real world. The visions of this sent Tony's sports-agent mind into high gear, wondering if lightning could strike twice.

Fritz was discussing art with Van Gogh, who had just stopped by to show some new work to Sister.

Cilus, playing the self-proclaimed leader, said, "So Duck, let's get to the point. What's up?"

Duck thought for a minute. "Well, I don't know if you've heard about the new blessing I've received in my life. The first, of course, was my dad, and the second, believe it or not, was living here with you. I still consider you all some of my oldest and best friends, and for that, I am forever thankful."

He reached into his pocket and pulled out the golf ball that he found in the dumpster years ago and continued. "Do any of you recognize this?"

He tossed it to Cilus, who looked at it quietly and said, "Ketchup. Man, I remember the day you found this. You were staring at it so hard; B.F.D. and I thought for sure that you were going to eat it."

Molly chimed in, "Yeah, and you used to drive me crazy with it, constantly fidgeting with it and tossing it in the air and listening to it hit the ground. We used to call it your gazing ball."

Duck continued. When I found this ball that day, it brought back memories. And somehow, it was what I needed to step back outside. And that is exactly what brought us here today. We want to build a place that will give each and every one of you the opportunity to find your gazing ball. Not that you need any opportunities outside of here. But if any of you want a chance to fit back into the fold, a chance like I used to look for—and I'm not saying that living here is bad, 'cause it's not—"

Mya interrupted. "What Duck was trying to say is that he loves you guys. And I can see why. It doesn't take long to get to your hearts. We need people like you to help us help some of the lost individuals who are aimlessly roaming the streets. We want to start a Duck's Run Foundation. With our initial donation of $2 million, we would like to build a rehabilitation campus for the homeless, and we would like for you all to help us reach that goal. What do you say?"

They were awestruck, not expecting this and not knowing quite what to think. Chattering broke out. Molly's voice rose out of the chaos as she asked, "Can you give us a minute? We need to discuss this matter privately." Mya got up, motioned for Duck, Fritz, and Tony to follow her out of the alley, and said, "Sure. Take your time. We'll be out front."

After a while, Cilus and Molly came out.

Cilus started out, "Duck, Angel, Fritz, Tony, this is a lot for us to consider, and because of the magnitude, the—"

Molly interrupted. "For crying out loud, Cilus, just say yes."

"Yes! My God, yes! This is a godsend. Now, come back in. Let's hammer out the details. We have a few ideas of our own that may require your help."

Mya perked up at that. "Oh, yeah? What's that?" she asked.

Everyone sat around, discussing their plans. The old friends told Duck, Tony, Mya, and Fritz about how they would like to teach some old weathermen a lesson, and Duck chimed right in, having had the same idea they did. They talked about how they thought they could raise even more money through the organization of celebrity golf tournaments and a special pictorial book project Duck's friend's son had been working on for years.

Duck said, "Take a look at these." He handed out several photos of homeless people taken in black and white. Cilus said, "That looks like me."

Molly looked at another photo, and remarked, "If I didn't know better, I'd say that one is me."

Then Speedo looked at a photo of what he swore was himself wearing a red swimmer's skullcap and said, "Look at that handsome devil. If that picture gets out, the whole world will be wearing caps like mine."

Duck said, "Those are photos of you guys. Do you guys remember Tommy? You know, the kid who used to come around here with his camera. These are his pictures. He hopes, with your approval, to put them in a book to chronicle your lives. He'll want to get a few stories from you. Heck, who knows? Maybe someday you'll be signing autographs. And this would give Tommy a jumpstart on what he hopes will be a career as a writer/photographer. What do you think?"

Molly said, "These are great photos. Your Tommy seems to have a real talent here. Count me in."

Cilus was skeptical. He stated, "I don't know. I really don't like having my picture taken."

Molly answered for him, saying, "He's in."

Speedo said, "I've got some great stories to tell, like the time I—"

Duck interrupted, "All right, then. It's decided. We'll have Tommy come by and see you and get to work on this."

Molly, wanting to seize this opportunity without delay, said, "This all sounds great. When do we start?"

Mya answered that one by saying, "Is tomorrow morning too late? We'll start by getting some equipment we're going to need."

In the car on the way back from the meeting, Tony said, "Man, that couldn't have gone any better. It was like, well, like it was supposed to happen."

Duck, smiling at this observation, said, "Yeah, I know. It's like what Sister Molly used to say. Don't worry. Put everything in the hands of the man upstairs, and he will show you the way. Thanks, guys."

Tony cleared his throat and said, "Duck, there is something I have to tell you."

Duck just looked at him expectantly. He knew this tone, and he knew he needed to shut up and listen.

"Duck, I'm moving back to Duluth."

"You're what? Not now."

Tony continued. "I got another letter from my dad today. He said mom wasn't doing real well, and she missed me. Hell, Duck, it used to be I'd react to something like this and say, okay, someday I'll start spending more time with them. They're both getting up there, man, and I only get this one chance to spend time with them. I've got to go. No, I want to go back home to them."

Duck sat quietly, staring out the windshield as the passing streetlights shone on his face. He was in deep thought. Then he said, "Tony, I'd give everything I own for that opportunity. Everything. I think the man upstairs is telling you something. Selfishly, I want you to stay. I love you, man. But both of our hearts know this is right. When are you leaving?"

"I'm heading out as soon as I can. This meeting today with your old friends from the street was like a lightning bolt to my soul. I can't let another day float by. After you spend a moment with Sister Molly, you realize it's just too short, and it's not just about your own wants and needs. I just can't put it off any longer."

"You give your mom and dad big hugs for me," said Duck. "And if you need me for anything, well, you have my number.

But don't take the bus. It takes too long, and the vending machine food can be a little stale." Duck affectionately mussed Tony's hair and said, "Thanks, pal."

CHAPTER 17

Troy Mastersomn, in a way, ended up getting a weather-related job. You see, the construction company he was working for bought the local franchise for Bull's-Eye porta-potties. He never was really very good with a hammer, so his boss called him in one day and gave him a "promotion." His boss sent him off to Bull's-Eye corporate to go through what they called Potty Training for a couple of days. When he came back, Troy's boss called him into the office and handed him a set of cards. Opening the box of cards, he took one out and read it. It said, "Troy R. Mastersomn, Vice president, Bull's-Eye Portable Toilet." At the bottom of the card was the company's slogan, "We aim to Pees." He didn't get a pay raise, but he got a title. He knew his mom would be so proud of the title.

Troy was everything—the site coordinator, the delivery guy, the clean-up and the pick-up guy. At some point, Troy's boss grew disinterested with the aspect of running a porta-potty business. You might say he didn't give a crap about it anymore, so he offered it to Troy. Troy jumped at the opportunity and went to his mother for the money. And here he was, 2 ½ years later, still in business for himself and doing quite well. Sometimes when he thought no one was looking, he would stretch the clean-out hose from the portable potty to the city sanitary storm system and let it drain. By doing this, he saved time and money. The fee for getting rid of this stuff was getting more expensive by the month.

Unbeknownst to him, this day he was being photographed from the bushes by a band of characters that he had long since forgotten about. In the bushes, Molly, Cilus, Speedo, B.F.D., and some of the other gang from the alley were watching him. They were armed with some supplies that Mya and Molly had picked up the morning after their initial meeting. Today they had with them two cameras—one a top-quality movie camera manned by Sister Molly, and the other was a very nice 35mm camera with lots of lenses. Cilus had control of this one. And they had all the film they wanted. Duck even gave them a charge card in case there was something else they needed.

They had been following Troy around for some time now and had a pretty good feel for where his route took him and the routine he went through when he delivered and picked up his "Aim-to-Pees" Bull's-Eye portable bathrooms. First, he would remove the discharge hose from the back of his truck, drag it over, and hook it up to the outlet on the unit. Then he would walk back to his truck; put the other end of the hose into the large holding tank, which was also on the back of his flatbed truck. Next, he would turn on the switch that activated the pump that pulled the night's deposits into the holding tank. Once done, he would unhook the hose, place it back onto the back of his truck, grab his refrigerator dolly, roll it down the ramp, walk over to the unit, stand the dolly up straight. Then it was time for a break. He would reach into his pocket and pull out a pack of cigarettes; he would remove one, place it into his mouth, drag his metal-hinged lighter out of his pocket, flip open the lid and light up his smoke. With cigarette in mouth, he would move on to the next step of his routine, which was picking up the Bull's-Eye "Aim-to-Pees" unit.

They noticed that Troy always picked up the portable potties from the back side by sliding his refrigerator dolly under the rear edge, and then he would wrap the canvas belt around the unit so that it would hold the door shut. Then he would tilt it back toward himself and head toward the ramp that lead up the back of his flatbed truck. Loaded with this research, they hatched a plan; actually, Sister Molly had the idea. She had quite an ornery streak running through her veins. During the night, they fastened a shallow bucket to the top of the unit so that it wouldn't be visible from the ground. Then they filled it with a yellowish type of drinking liquid, several melted candy bars, all mixed with a cup of apple blossom for aroma. It was a harmless mixture, but it sure looked and smelled like the real thing. Cilus and the others argued they should make the cocktail surprise from natural ingredients, but Sister Molly just wouldn't allow it. That wouldn't be right, and they all reluctantly gave in.

Today was the day that they were going to be attempting to play their first "weather-related" payback prank on Mr. Mastersomn. The cocktail was in place, and they wanted to catch the whole thing on film. You see, part of the reason they used the cameras was because it would be fun to look at the images while having coffee back at the alley; and second, they hoped they could capture on film Troy in the act of "accidentally" discharging the collected waste into the sanitary sewer opening. And that is exactly what he did this time. Imagine the look of the law enforcement agencies when a group of street folks delivered such incriminating evidence.

The first images they captured were of Troy looking around to see if anyone was around. They witnessed him hooking up the drain tube and then stretching the discharge hose—not to the holding tank, but into the drain. They all wondered if their surprise would work. With the metallic sound of the lighter closing, Troy put the cigarette in his mouth, grabbed the handle of the dolly and pulled the unit toward himself. As he did, the cocktail in the bucket on top of the unit shifted toward him and oozed down onto his head.

He stood there in shock, with foul-smelling yellow liquid dripping from his hair and soaking into his clothes. It worked perfectly. He was drenched. He screamed out a loud "shit" and let go of the unit. The "Aim-To-Pees" unit went crashing to the ground, still hooked to the refrigerator dolly. As the unit rested on its side, he noticed the shallow bucket attached to the top of the unit. As he looked closer, he saw a note, sealed in clear laminated plastic in the bottom of the bucket. Slowly oozing down the front of the note was the yellow liquid and streams of melted brown candy. The note read, "Well, hello, Troy. Bet you forgot all about those Tuesday Evening Weather Reports. Well, guess what—we haven't!"

Troy was no longer mad—he was a little taken aback. He looked around to see if he could see who had done this. He thought he saw something move in the bushes, but shrugged it off. Must be a bunch of disrespectful kids. 'What's with the kids these days?' he thought to himself. Troy decided not to report it to the cops. Besides, if he did, they might catch him with his illegal dumping. Better play it straight for a while.

For the next few weeks, he did his routine strictly by the book. However, he now carried a ladder on his truck and expanded his ritual to include climbing up and checking the top of the unit before pulling the dolly back toward himself.

Enough time slid by, and Troy let his guard down. In his mind, he had to. Since he hadn't been pumping the waste down the sanitary sewers, his profits were way down. Those thieves down where he emptied the tanks were charging even more these days.

Over the next few days, Molly and the crew got more of his illegal dumping on film, and then they decided the time was right to strike again. Her idea this time was to approach from the bottom of the unit. They rigged up a flat, pan-type sealed container about as wide as the unit and about three inches deep and made sure when they attached it, it was recessed from all outer sides of the porta-potty far enough so Troy could still get his refrigerator dolly under it. They watched from the trees as Troy climbed down from the ladder after checking to see if any surprises were left for him up there. By now, this was as much a part of his routine as lighting his cigarette.

After putting his ladder away and fetching his dolly, Troy strapped the canvas belt around the unit and tilted it back. As he leaned it back, the pan underneath, which had holes drilled into it on all four sides, started leaking. At first, he didn't notice the leakage. Heck, these things leaked all the time. Feeling full of energy and rather manly, he decided he would push the unit up the ramp instead of pulling it up backwards like he normally did. He realized if he was going to make it, he'd need a little bit of a run at it. As he gained momentum, reliving some high school football game that he never even played in. As he crossed the parking area heading at a slight trot toward the ramp, he announced the game. "He breaks one tackle; he cuts toward the middle of the field. It looks like he's going to go all the way." You could see the trail he was leaving as he reached the ramp about halfway up. With the unit in front of him on the dolly, most of the cocktail underneath spilled on the ramp ahead of him. He lost his balance, slipped and fell. His face splashed down on the ramp, right into the mess. The unit, still attached to the dolly, fell back on top of him, pushing his face and his body down even further into the nasty gunk. Then, with the "Aim-to-Pees" unit and the dolly still attached on top of him, he slowly slid back down the ramp. After reaching the bottom of the ramp, and lying there a second, spitting God knows what out of his mouth, Troy pushed up with all his might, and off came the dolly and the unit.

He slid a little as he attempted to get up. As he reached his feet, he had yellow filth dripping from his hair and brown chunks of something smelly, containing, among other things, several pieces of corn pushed into his hair and running down the side of his face. Again, he spit out a chunk of slime and wiped something else from his face. Thinking candy bar like last time, he took a taste and promptly gagged. Still dripping, he walked around the Bull's-Eye unit. As it laid there on its side, he noticed a note attached to its bottom. The note read:

"A man's got to be prepared. You never know when the weather's going to turn and dump nasties on you. Especially on Tuesdays."

He ripped the sign off the bottom and noticed the pan on the bottom. It started to sink in that this was revenge. He yelled out, "I'm sorry! We were just kids!" Back in the trees, they had it all on tape.

Sister Molly said, "Boy, that was fun, and you're getting good with the props. That stuff looked more real this time."

Cilus sheepishly responded, "Uh, yeah, it did, didn't it?" He looked away and wouldn't make eye contact with her.

"Cilus, you didn't."

"Sorry, Sister. 100% natural."

She grinned and put her hand on his shoulder and said, "What am I going to do with you?" She continued, "I've been thinking. We have all of this film and movie footage. We could walk right over to the sheriff's department, the health department, the City—any number of government agencies, just like we talked about. Any of them would love to have this info, but what if we used it to raise money for Duck's Run? You know, send a partial copy with a note to Mr. Mastersomn."

"But wouldn't that be blackmail?" asked Cilus.

Sister Molly looked down at her cat, Princess, that she was holding in her arms, then she looked back up at Cilus and said, "No, not if it helped me do the Lord's work."

Cilus liked it and said, "Sounds like a plan to me. We'll tell the others."

CHAPTER 18

Joey Parma was doing really well for himself and becoming quite imbedded in the local political scene. For Joey, this was what he hoped was only the beginning. His self-serving aspirations and dreams had him eyeing the national arena. As the residents of the alley sat around pouring over yesterday's newspaper, they read in the Metropolitan section that next Tuesday, Joey Parma would hold a Town Hall meeting. He was going to be giving a speech down at St. John's from 6:30 P.M. till 8:15 P.M. He was presently immersed in a very close, heated battle for election as mayor. Molly and Cilus informed Mya of this meeting, and she used some of Duck's connections that he'd made through golf these last few years and arranged for admission and seating for everyone. Tuesday evening came around, and Mya, Duck, Molly, Cilus and a few of the other inhabitants of the alley who wanted to see this firsthand were there at the rally, which Joey had filled with a partisan crowd of supporters.

Joey concluded his speech by saying, "And that, my friends, is why I wish to serve you, the good residents of this city, for four more years." The crowd chanted, "Four more years! Four more years!" Joey raised his hands to quiet the crowd. Joey, feeling all pumped up by the chanting of the partisan crowd, did something he didn't normally do. Joey's manager tried to discourage him, but Joey, feeling all full of himself, shrugged off his manager's pleas. He announced, "And now I would like to take a few questions." Cilus and every one of the gang immediately raised their hands. Joey acknowledged Cilus. "You back there—what's on your mind?" Cilus pointed at himself, as if to say 'me?' "Yes, you, what's your question, sir?"

Cilus stood up, looked down at Molly and got the encouraging nod he needed, and said, "Thank you, your honor, for this opportunity. My friends and I were wondering just what it is you do for fun on Tuesday nights these days. We want to thank you for finding something else to do with your time besides coming down to the Cardboard Hotel on Tuesday night and delivering us the Weather Reports."

His manager's pleas started to sink in. He couldn't have this brought up. Joey was nervously adjusting his tie, pulling at his collar and doing that twitching thing he did when he was stressed. He motioned for his assistant to come over to him. When he arrived, he whispered, "Uh, you'd better call security." Cilus, still standing, continued. "Mr. Mayor, one thing we could never figure out is why you and your friends were so mean to us. And what ever made you think you could take those pliers and pull Sister Molly's teeth? Do you know she nearly died from the infection from that?"

Joey was getting more and more nervous, and then he said, "Look at what my opponent, Mr. Carl Mecation, is up to these days, sending in this group of people full of lies and untruths. Folks, these dirty political tactics have got to stop. This candidate won't stoop to such lows—never have, and never will."

Still seated and blocked from view by those standing, Bob Duckins had heard enough. He stood up and spoke. Instantly, almost everyone there recognized him from his golf success, much of which was on TV in front of millions. The Duck spoke. "Mr. Mayor, ladies and gentlemen, my name is Bob Duckins. Some of you know me as the Duck. I want you folks to know that what my friend here has been talking about is what's called the truth. I know. I was there. Your mayor and his friends helped put me to sleep on at least one occasion, by kicking and beating me until I was unconscious. And then, just like he has been doing and will continue to do to you—only in your case figuratively—he and his cronies urinated on us until their bladders were empty. Now, most of you know I live in this town. And frankly, I've made it a habit not to get involved in politics, but this time I'm making an exception. I can tell you this," he pointed at Joey, "This man will not get my vote. And I hope to God he doesn't get yours." Duck turned to his friends and said, "Let's go, guys," and turned and left the now-quiet room, leaving Joey standing there stunned and speechless at the podium.

CHAPTER 19

Frankie Armattan was now The Reverend Frankie Armattan and pastor of his own non-denominational church, which had quite a following right here in town. There was even talk of a syndicated radio talk show brought on by his popularity when he appeared as a fill-in for the regular weekend preacher on the radio. You see, Frankie was big on incorporating slide shows into his regular sermons, believing totally in the saying, "A picture is worth a thousand words." Through her research, Mia found the name of the guy who was in charge of loading the slides into the projector. Frankie used these slides at predetermined points of his sermon by using his remote control device. Mia also discovered that Frankie's projectionist was a man named Jimmy, who showed up on Saturday evening like clockwork and loaded the projector slides into the sequence dictated by Frankie in a note left taped to the projector. Mia informed Duck of this, and he decided he was going to go talk with Jimmy on Saturday.

Duck arrived at the church and walked over to the projectionist and said, "Excuse me, Jimmy, could I have a word with you?" Jimmy was looking down, working on inserting the slides. As he looked up, he instantly recognized The Duck.

Jimmy was immediately star struck to have The Duck—the famous Bob Duckins—walk up to him. And he actually knew that his name was Jimmy! Bob extended his hand, and Jimmy stood up and shook Duck's hand.

"Jimmy, could I have a few minutes of your time? I need your help with a bit of old, unsettled business."

"Of course, Mr. Duckins. Sit down—please sit down."

Duck sat and said, "Thank you. And call me Duck." Then he told Jimmy of the Tuesday Evening Weather Reports. After finishing the story, he showed Jimmy the slides he brought with him as proof. Jimmy was shocked, but somehow not totally surprised. He had seen the other side of the reverend. Duck continued, "Jimmy, here's the deal. I'll give you $1,000 if you will place these slides of mine into the projector you are preparing for tomorrow's Sunday Morning slide show."

Jimmy thought about it for a second and said, "So, is what you just told me and showed me the truth?"

"You have my word on it."

Jimmy took the slides from Bob and said, "I'll do it with pleasure. You know, there aren't many people around here who really know him and work with him that wouldn't pay for the opportunity to do this. Do you believe in the golden rule, Duck? Do you know he fabricated a story that accused our original beloved pastor of a hideous scandal? It was a lie—we all knew it—but once Frankie took it to the press, there was only one choice in Pastor Mike Spanky's mind. Even though the allegations were totally false, for the good of the church, he resigned. And guess who was there ready to go with a pre-packaged show?"

"Let me guess," Duck interjected, "The Reverend Frankie Armattan."

"Bingo," was Jimmy's one-word reply. "Duck, I'm comfortably retired. You see, my invention, the Wedgy Master, was very, very good to me."

Duck asked, "You invented that? Wow, I have one myself. Those things are awesome."

"Yeah, thank you. So, I don't need your money, and I wouldn't take it myself even if I did. But would you put the money in the collection plate on Sunday? You will be here tomorrow, won't you?"

Duck thought this might be his answer, and he stated, "Oh, yeah, I'll be here, and yes, I'll put the money in the collection plate. I'll see you tomorrow, Jimmy. And thank you!"

Duck got up, shook Jimmy's hand, turned and turned to leave when Jimmy said, "Hold on for a second, please. Do you suppose I could get an autograph?"

Duck stopped and said, "Sure." Jimmy produced his golf hat from behind him and handed it to the Duck. The Duck signed it, "To my friend, Jimmy."

Sunday morning at 10:58, just like clockwork, Jimmy activated the fog machine and filled the stage with Frankie's mystic smoke. Jimmy threw another switch, and the strobe lighting flashed. The band was cued, and the bass drum started the beat, which you could feel in your chest. The music joined the drum beat and got louder and louder. Then, with the strobe lights bouncing off the smoke, like lightning would on a cloudy, stormy day, the Reverend Frankie appeared in the middle of the mist. The music paused, and Frankie began singing a song that he wrote. He was a very bad singer who thought that he was the greatest. Duck, Mya and their friends were sitting there with 'I can't believe he's really doing this' expressions on their faces. It was hard to contain the laughter. Finally and mercifully, the song ended. Polite applause was heard coming from the crowd. Then Frankie said, "Thank you, my brothers and sisters. Welcome to all our members and our visitors as well. Does anyone have a visitor they would like to introduce to us today?" Frankie was always looking for more members. As he looked around the audience, he was pleased to notice Bob Duckins, and he said, "Well, look here. I see we have a famous visitor in our midst today. Ladies and gentlemen, please join me in welcoming Mr. Bob-the-Duck Duckins. He continued, "Duck, welcome to our call to worship."

The Duck stood and politely nodded to the crowd, then quickly sat back down. "Hey, stick around after the service; I think I can help with that glitch in your backswing. Jimmy, hand me my remote." Jimmy brought him his remote.

Frankie began his sermon. "Today, my children, I have chosen to guide you through my experience of buying a new car and show you how it can affect the horsepower of your spiritual engine." He clicked the remote. "This is the very first car that I ever bought—back in 1967. I loved that car. It made me feel proud. It made me feel complete. That was a long time ago, and I have changed. Today, my faith is the vehicle that makes me feel whole, at peace, proud, and complete. Material things are not my—nor should they be your—guiding light, and certainly not our source of pride."

"This next slide is me talking to the new car salesman about trading my old car in for a brand spanking new one. Do you see the symbolism here? I thought I loved my first car. It was all I thought I ever needed, but the light which that new car brought in was that much brighter. Are you beginning to see what I'm talking about?"

Most of the audience was confused and clueless about what he had just said, but hey—what else is new? But they loved his smoke and mirrors, and somehow he made them think. Frankie had all those bright lights shining on him, and therefore he couldn't see the congregation turn toward each other with those puzzled 'I don't get it' looks on their faces. Duck and the guys were having fun with this.

Frankie continued, "I knew you would. Now walk with this humble mechanic of the soul, and I will show you how to keep oil in your spiritual engine. Now, this next slide..." As he pushed the button on the remote, he heard the congregation gasp. Frankie looked up over the top of his bifocal glasses at Jimmy, then paused and said, "What are you waiting for? Dim these spot lights, you idiot." As Jimmy dimmed the spot lights, Frankie saw the shocked looks on the faces of the congregation. They were looking at the big screen above his head.

Frankie stepped out away from his position and looked up at the picture on the screen. Suddenly, there was a voice from the back as Duck said, "Let me tell you what this slide symbolizes."

Frankie gave Jimmy a look of hate, but Jimmy just looked at him as if to say, 'It's about time you got what's been coming to you.' Bob Duckins started walking toward the stage, and Frankie was frantically trying to change to the next slide, but the photo wouldn't go off the screen. Jimmy held in his hand an over-riding controller. As Duck walked toward the front, Frankie—always quick on his feet—said, "That's right, Duck, if you're feeling the need for healing, come on down to the front, kneel before me, and I will place my very own hands on you."

Duck replied, "It's Mr. Duckins to you. And I'll pass on your whole laying-on-of- the-hands process, but I know several people who would love to get their hands on you. Does anyone in here know the definition of a hypocrite?" Duck was interrupted by a little child who had the answer. "That is absolutely correct. And this is a photo of one." Duck pointed to the projected slide. As he walked by Jimmy, he said to him, "May I borrow that from you for a minute?"

Jimmy gladly handed the over-riding control to him. Duck clicked to the next slide. "As you can see by this enlargement of the previous photo, your very own Reverend Frankie is shown here delivering his sermon and something he called a Weather Report to his fellow man. From the looks of this picture, I'd say that Frankie and his friends really didn't care too much for their fellow man after all."

Duck clicked the remote again and showed a photo of Sister Molly shortly after Frankie and his friends pulled her teeth. Duck continued, "This is Sister Molly. It seems Frankie and his pals thought of themselves as God's messengers even back then, as they decided to pull her teeth with a pair of pliers! Can you feel the love coming from this man? The only love coming from this man is for himself." Duck clicked the button again and said, "And this photo is your congregation's accountant. My attorney and I have been to visit him, and he tells me he has some significant concerns regarding some of your unaccounted-for funds. I think we'll turn this meeting over to him now."

The accountant walked up and stood next to the Duck, and the Duck said, "Oh, and Ms. Angel, would you stand up, please?" She stood. "Thank you. Ladies and gentlemen, this is my attorney. She will be available to you and your church free of charge should you need her assistance." Duck pushed to the next slide and said, "These are her phone numbers. Would someone write them down, please?" As Duck looked around, he saw the congregation and everyone in there feverishly writing down the numbers. Duck and his friends were pleased to see this. "It sure looks like big trouble for little Frankie," Duck commented to Mia. Duck turned and looked at Frankie, who was white as a ghost.

"At this time, my friends and I will leave you. Have a great day." Duck and his friends walked out the doors.

CHAPTER 20

Deano Alonzo received separate phone calls from Joey, Troy, and Frankie—all telling of the unpleasant events that had taken place in their lives over the last few days. They agreed to meet. At the meeting, Frankie said, "Deano, talk to your Uncle Tommy. We've got to stop this. If they haven't ruined us already, they surely will if they keep this up. I've got a national radio show at risk here. They've been to see all three of us, and you can bet you're next. We've got to put a stop to this right here and now."

Deano said, "Okay, I'll talk to Uncle Tommy. Yeah, I can't have them coming around here causing trouble." Deano was now chairman of the board of directors for a large national charitable organization. Mya had already done a lot of research, delving into the past of Mr. Alonzo, and she had found plenty of irregularities. Like seven very expensive trips to Las Vegas, each of which had him flying first class, both in the air and on the ground. He was not attending conventions, but he produced receipts for reimbursement for the trips. And she found plenty more. You see, the Duck believes in the Golden Rule, and before all this went down, he went to talk with his old pal, Tommy. Duck had asked Mya to keep all the information she had on Deano on ice somewhere, where it could be easily accessed if needed. Uncle Tommy's friendship with Duck dated back to childhood, and through the years they had remained trusted best friends. Duck was Godfather to Tommy's son, Tommy Jr., and he took it seriously. For years, he had co-ventured on only one project with Tommy, and it was an investment into Tommy Jr. Duck and Tommy had been supplying the money and helping any way they could to help get Tommy Jr.'s photography career started.

Tommy Jr. had been working on a book chronicling the homeless for some time, and it just needed a few more good photos and some additional stories before it was ready to go to press. Both Uncle Tommy and Duck wanted this book to get published for the same—yet different—reasons. They both wanted to see Tommy Jr., who had real talent, get into a legitimate business. Uncle Tommy didn't want him in the family business. Duck wanted to see the book on the homeless published. He thought some of the photos were absolutely right on. Some, in his opinion, were amazing. He thought the book could really help with the plight of the homeless, and he hoped to have the book ready so that copies could be offered for sale at the press conference/groundbreaking ceremony for Duck's Run.

Duck and Uncle Tommy had this whole thing figured out. They knew that once the retribution started taking place, the others would approach Deano and ask him to come to see Uncle Tommy. And Deano, fearing for his own hide, would no doubt do so. Deano was Tommy's nephew, the son of Tommy's sister.

Deano called Tommy and said, "Uncle Tommy?"

"Deano" was Tommy's one-word reply.

"Uncle Tommy, would you allow me the opportunity to visit with you about a matter of concern?"

"Sure, Deano. Be here at 1:30 today."

"Thank you, Uncle Tommy."

"Deano, give your mother a hug for me."

"Sure thing, Uncle Tommy."

Deano arrived at 1:15. He knew Uncle Tommy would not tolerate tardiness. Uncle Tommy told Deano to come in and sit down. Deano sat on the opposite side of Uncle Tommy's desk.

"So tell me, Nephew, how can I help?" Of course, Uncle Tommy knew from his conversations with the Duck exactly what was going on. Deano told his uncle about his and his friends' predicament.

"Uncle Tommy, my mother and I both want to thank you for giving me the opportunity to see you. You see, there are these people going around bringing up things that my friends and I might have done when we were 18, 19, 20, 21 years old." Deano paused. When he had come in, he noticed a guy sitting over by the window in a high-backed chair, smoking a cigar. Deano took notice of him again. All he could see was the back of his head, which was sporting a golf cap. He felt uneasy. The chair the figure was sitting in was facing the windows. Occasionally, he would see a hand move off the armrest of the chair and the bright orange glow as whoever was sitting in the chair took a puff of the cigar. The smoke rolled up and then over the top of the back of the chair as the wind from the slightly open window blew it toward Deano. Uncle Tommy had his own cigar lit and sitting in an ashtray. Deano looked at the chair as if to say, "Who's that, and is it all right to talk?"

Uncle Tommy answered his silent question. "He's just an old friend. It's okay. Talk to me, nephew."

"Like I said, Uncle Tommy, we were just kids, 18, maybe 20, 21 years old—still wet behind the ears. These people are going around telling stories about things we may have done. We never hurt anybody but a bunch of bums. These people have already been around and visited Frankie, Troy, and Joey— and Uncle Tommy, I'm next."

"So, are you hiding something, nephew?"

Deano answered, "Well, there are the trips—you know, a little gambling here and there." Suddenly, he once again remembered the guy in the chair. Deano paused. He looked at the chair in an 'oh, shit, I just said something I shouldn't have said within the range of the stranger's ears' manner.

Uncle Tommy inquired, "So Deano, just what are you asking me to do?"

"Uncle Tommy, could you have someone go talk to this Bob Duckins jerk? Maybe get him to see the light, if you know what I mean?"

"You want me to have him and the others whacked?" Uncle Tommy asked.

"That's a little drastic, but you're the boss—whatever you think."

Silence filled the room. Uncle Tommy spoke up and said to the person in the chair, "So Duck, you've been hearing this. What do you think?"

A stunned look came across Deano's face. A voice coming from the chair said, "These truly are fantastic cigars. As a matter of fact, I think this one is one of the best I've ever had, if I do say so myself. Thank you, Tommy, for sharing one with me."

"No, thank you, Duck, my friend. You always gift me with the best Cubans. But these," he took a drag off of his cigar, which had been sitting in the ashtray for quite a while, "look at this—still lit. These, my friend, are primo."

Duck stood up and walked over behind Deano and put his hands on the back of his chair. Deano had recognized the name from what he was told by Troy, Bobby, and Joey; and when he saw his face, he knew who he was. Deano was sitting there, scared to death, and even wondered if he might be the one who was about to get whacked. Duck said, "Tommy, may I?"

"Go ahead, my old friend."

"Thank you. Personally, I think whacking me might be a tad bit harsh, but your Uncle Tommy and I have a plan. You might have guessed by now that Tommy and I have been friends for many, many years, and we knew once word got out that we'd been visiting your old weathermen cronies, you would call your Uncle Tommy and come hightailing it over here to save your own sorry butt. So we've been waiting for you."

Uncle Tommy interrupted. "Duck, let me take it from here. You see, Deano, you are my blood—my sister's boy, for crying out loud. But you're not Tommy Jr." Uncle Tommy got on his intercom and said, "Tommy, come in here." Tommy Jr. came in with his nearly finished photography book under his arm. Deano said, "Tommy, how you doing, Cuz?"

"Doing great, Deano. Thanks."

Pleasantries completed, Uncle Tommy continued, "You see, Deano, Tommy here—sit down, Tommy—Tommy here has a talent, a real knack with a camera and a pen and paper. For years he's been doing his shooting with a camera. That's the kind of shooting he likes to do. As a matter of fact, he's nearly finished his first book—a book which chronicles the lives of the homeless. Duck and I have been working with him on this, and we're going to press sometime soon, depending on how long it takes Tommy Jr. to get some stories from Duck's street pals. But you see, Deano, there still are a few decisions to make."

Tommy Jr. handed his dad several photos. Uncle Tommy continued, "For example, we have a dozen or so photos here, and we have to decide—do we leave them in?"

He threw down a photo. The picture clearly showed Deano, Troy, Frankie and Joey peeing on one of the homeless. Uncle Tommy continued, "Or do we leave it out?"

Uncle Tommy pulled that picture back and continued, "Do we leave them in?" Uncle Tommy tossed down another photo. This one clearly showed Deano, pliers in hand, pulling out one of Sister Molly's teeth. "Deano, aren't those the pliers I lent to you? Oh, and the next time you say 'Screw Uncle Tommy'—blood or no blood, you will pay."

"Or do we leave them out?" Uncle Tommy pulled back the photo.

Looking at another photo, Uncle Tommy said, "Here's one of you, and I must say, nephew, it's a very disgusting photo. It's a top-quality photograph, but it's a terrible subject." He didn't bother to show that one to him.

Deano interrupted, "Uncle Tommy, I messed up. I was young."

You could see Uncle Tommy's face getting red, and he blurted out, "And disrespectful—then and now. If you interrupt me again, so help me…"

"Now, Deano, Tommy Jr., as I just told you, has been taking these pictures for years, and when he saw who he had captured in some of them, he was surprised, and he did the right thing. He came to me. He never said a word to anyone else. But now—now, nephew, we are at a crossroads." He paused and then continued. "Here's the deal. There will be no answer but 'yes' or 'no'—understand? You save your 'yeah-buts' for your board members at work. First of all," Uncle Tommy leaned up into his chair closer to Deano so that he could see that he was not kidding, "If you have scammed one cent, or if you cheated your charitable organization out of $10 million, you pay back every cent. And I will know. I have my ways. You bring me proof. Am I making myself clear?"

"Yes, Uncle Tommy. Very clear."

"Second, you will come out to the news conference that my friend Duck here will have, and I want you to announce that you and your high-powered organization are backing his Duck's Run project 100 percent. Again, am I making myself clear?"

Deano reluctantly started nodding his head 'yes,' and then he responded to his uncle. "Yes, Uncle Tommy."

"In return, these photos of you stay out of the book and hopefully out of the papers. One more time—have I made myself perfectly clear? Do we have an answer?"

"Yes, Uncle Tommy."

"Deano, give me your hand. With this handshake, our words are bound. Duck will tell you when and where to be available, and you will be available. So Deano, did you give your mother a hug for me?"

"Yes, I did, Uncle Tommy. She sends her love."

"Good sister, your mother." Uncle Tommy flicked ashes from his cigar into the ask tray and said, "Okay, this meeting is finished."

"Thank you, Uncle Tommy." Deano got up and headed for the door. As the door shut behind him, Tommy Jr. got up and walked over to his dad, who stood up, and the two of them hugged. Tommy Jr. said, "See you later, dad. Love you."

"See you, son. I love you, too." Tommy Jr. walked over to Duck and said, "Good to see you, Uncle Duck."

"Good to see you, Tommy. Now, I know nothing was said, but believe me, the folks down in the alley will expect you tomorrow morning at 3:30 a.m. They assume you know that."

"Thanks for the heads up, Uncle Duck. I'll be there. And I'll be there as long as it takes to get their stories. I can't wait."

Tommy's dad interjected, "I'll send Crazy Larry to drive you. I don't much care for that neighborhood."

Duck started to say something. Tommy interrupted, "I know, I know, Crazy Larry is not to go into the alley. But he'll be watching from the car."

Duck said, "That'll work." Not that Tommy Jr. was afraid of Cilus, Molly, and the gang. It's the sleazes that hang out in that neighborhood—guys like his cousin Deano used to be. Tommy Jr. left the room.

"So, how have you been doing, Duck?"

"Really? To be honest, I've never felt better in my life."

"So, is there anything else I can do to help?"

"You've done plenty. And thanks for not having me whacked." They both chuckled. Uncle Tommy said, "How's Mya? You ought to marry that little angel."

"No, can't be mixing business with pleasure. She's too good as an attorney. Besides, what would someone like her want with an ex-bum like me? Say, how about a round of golf next week?"

"Sure, a round sounds great. Besides, you could use some help with your putting. On second thought, I'd better take a rain check. I think we should wait until after your press conference. But I would like to borrow your caddy, Fritz, for a few rounds. That guy can really improve a game."

"Well, okay. But why?"

"I don't want you getting any bad publicity. Being seen hanging around a shady character like me might hurt Tommy Jr.'s book sales." Duck pondered and then decided not to argue with Tommy's decision. Duck announced, "I'm closing on the farm ground out west today, meeting Mya at 3:00 at the title company to sign the papers."

"You're actually doing it. You've always been a man of your word. That's your strength, Ducky, my boy. Just like your dad."

Duck continued, "Tommy, it's perfect. We've got enough ground to set up our 18-hole golf course, which will serve as a built-in revenue-maker for the center. We will have a practice range. There's a lake on the property already, and it's just perfect for pondering. We already have the color renderings of the plans for the learning/activity/dining building and the sleeping/rehab quarters. It's a way to give hope to those on the street. You know, Tommy, some of them may choose to stay lost for the rest of their lives, but there are some who are either just temporarily lost and need a little nudge, or who want help but don't know where to turn. If we can bring a few of them back to Ground Zero—well, maybe they'll get re-started, like I did. God brought me back, and maybe, just maybe, we can be successful in bringing hope into a few other lives. This is something I have to do, and you know what, Tommy? I owe it all to the man upstairs, my dad, good friends like you—Tony, Mya, Fritz, golf, and, of course, Sister Molly. Am I a blessed man or what?"

Duck reached into his briefcase and pulled out a small color rendering, which he handed to Tommy. It was a miniature layout of the entire project. The drawing showed the housing and all the buildings on top of a bluff which looked out over the golf course. There were observation areas all around the facility where the residents could look down to see what's going on.

Tommy looked at the plan, and when he was finished, he handed it back to Duck. He put them back into his briefcase and pulled out a rather legal looking envelope and said, "Tommy, if something happens to me, will you keep an eye on Mya for me?"

Without hesitation, Tommy replied, "You got it." Duck reached over and handed the envelope to Tommy and said, "I have some money set aside for her. It's all spelled out in my will, and now you have a copy. There's another copy in the safety deposit box at my bank. My other attorney, who drew this up, can be reached at the numbers contained in the paperwork in that envelope. Thanks in advance, Tony. Oh, and if you don't keep getting a fresh box of Cuban cigars every month, make a house call to that banker." Duck looked at his watch and said, "Gotta go. I'm running late. I'll talk to you later."

Duck reached over to shake Tommy's hand, and Tommy said, "Take care, my friend."

CHAPTER 21

Duck arrived at the title company, and Mya was waiting for him. Duck said, "Sorry I'm late. Did you look over the papers?"

"Yes, I did."

"So, do you think they look okay?"

"They look good to me."

"Well, give me a pen. Let's get this done. We've got some work to do." Duck started signing every paper they threw in front of him.

"You sure put a lot of trust in me, Duck."

"You're my attorney. And it was you who first put a lot of trust in me years ago, at the library."

"So, how much do you trust me?" She asked.

"I trust you totally and unequivocally."

"That's good, because today I hired a general manager for the facility."

"You did what?"

"Yep, and he's waiting down at Pickles around the corner for us. I told him we'd be there about 6 p.m., right after we were done here."

"Is he a local guy? Someone I know?"

"Yes, and no. You'll see." Duck just shook his head and kept on signing. She handed him the last paper.

"Last one?"

"Last one." Mya grabbed the stack of signed papers and evened them out by tapping them on the tabletop. She handed them back across the table to the closing person and said, "And here is the check. If you don't mind, I'll be back in the morning for my copies. We're running late for a meeting. Let's go, Duck. It's 6:15, and our new administrator is waiting."

As they exited through the doors and stepped out onto the walk, Duck said, "Let's walk. It's not far away, is it?"

"Only about a long par 5 away, I'd say."

"Let's do it." They turned and started their walk to Pickles. Duck said, "Thanks for being you, and thanks for jump-starting me back to life—twice. None of this would be possible if it weren't for you and Sister Molly."

As they walked by a park, Duck had an overwhelming feeling that he'd had many times in the past but had always simply suppressed. This time, he couldn't.

Duck stopped her under a shade tree and said, "Wow, I don't know where what I'm about to say is coming from. Wait. Yes, I do. It's from my heart. I love you. I've loved you ever since I first set eyes on you. I thought to myself, 'Look at me— I'm a bum living on the street, and she's a successful lawyer. Talk about a mismatch.' All these years I kept telling myself it would pass. But it hasn't. It's grown. I don't know if I have the words to describe how I feel about you. When you saw that bald doctor from Connecticut, let's just say I was not happy. Well, I don't know if 'not happy' was even in the ballpark. I mean, I was happy for you because you deserved—"

Mya reached up and placed her fingers on his lips to stop him from talking. She took her fingers down, stepped closer, and kissed him. Then she said, "You had me at the kiss on the cheek at the library," as they embraced.

Duck said, "Do you think it's too late for—" he paused.

"Too late for what?" she asked.

Duck dropped to one knee and said, "If I wasn't this tired old ex-bum, would you marry me?"

"What kind of 'almost question' is that?"

"Will you marry me?"

"Yes! Yes! Yes!"

Then, only half kidding, Duck said, "You'll still be my—I mean, our—attorney, won't you?"

"Of course I will. Even if someday I have to take our little Ducklings to work with me—I mean, us."

She looked at her watch. "Oh, my gosh. We'd better get to Pickles."

"To hell with Pickles. I've wasted enough time. I..."

Mya interrupted him again. "As your attorney," she said, with tears of joy in her eyes, "I must recommend that we get to this meeting."

"But I can't stop hugging you."

"I feel the same way. But if you think about it, well, it might be kind of hard to walk like this."

"Look at me, a full-grown man, and I can't stop crying. But they're tears of joy!"

Holding hands, they walked to Pickles. With excitement in his voice, Duck talked of future plans. "We'll both have offices at the ranch, and we'll have a day care. That could be Sister Molly's job. She'd be great with kids." As they entered Pickles, Duck immediately recognized a green leisure suit at the bar. And right next to it was a smaller, same-colored leisure suit with Fritz in it. Duck walked up, put one hand on Fritz's shoulder and the other on Tony's, and said, "What on earth are you doing here, Tony? Of all the luck! We pop in here to meet someone, and you are here."

Mya interrupted and said, "Duck, meet your new administrator."

"What? Are you serious? My God, this is perfect, Mya! Fritz, you knew about this, didn't you? But hey, what about your mom and dad?"

"That's all taken care of." Mya pulled out a set of plans showing a quaint little cottage. "I took the liberty of having these drawn up. You see, this is the gardener's quarters. And let me introduce you to your two new gardeners." Mya and Tony led Duck over to a table in the corner, and there sat Tony's mom and dad. Fritz took the last taste of his drink, slid off the chair, and followed them. Tony said, "Duck, you remember mom and dad?"

"Of course I do. It's nice to see both of you again."

"You see, they really love to garden, and those winters in Duluth make it a little hard to keep those green thumbs active. They're moving here, too. They're your new gardeners. Plus, I plan on putting them to good use at a few of my clubs—when and if they have the time," Fritz injected.

Duck was elated and said, "What a marvelous day! Now it's my turn for a surprise for you guys. Close your eyes. Do you have them closed?"

"Yes. What is it? I love surprises," Tony's dad said.

"Me too," replied Fritz, "but I'm not very patient, so surprise me already."

"Okay. Now, on the count of three, we want you to open your eyes. One, two, three…okay, you can open them now. I want you to be the first to meet my fiancée, Miss Mya."

Tony asked, "For real? Oh, my goodness, this calls for a toast. I didn't think you'd ever make the connection, you big idiot. Bartender—six Mai Tais, please." After the bartender delivered the drinks, Tony, with tears of joy in his eyes, said, "A toast to the future bride and groom."

After taking their drinks, Mya offered a toast and said, "And here's to our two new gardeners and our new general manager."

Fritz offered a toast to all of his friends, both new and old. Duck asked, "So how soon will you be moving back?"

"We're here today, reporting for work. Just so you know, as part of my condition for accepting this position, it has been agreed that occasionally I may have to go out of town for a few days and renegotiate a contract for some of my other clients. And Duck, thanks for not saying anything about my and Fritz's green leisure suits."

"I bit my tongue this time, Tony, old pal."

"And thanks for not leaving dirt smudges on our shoulders earlier," said Fritz.

"I've got to tell you, that was really the hard one," replied Duck.

"We've had the water, lights, and gas all turned on at the cabin on the farm. With a little paint, it will be a perfect temporary home for our G.M. and the gardeners; that is, until their new quarters are completed," Mya explained.

"So you'll be at the news conference, then?"

"It's in my contract, Duck. You've got a shrewd lawyer there. And besides, I wouldn't miss it for the world."

CHAPTER 22

As he was instructed by Uncle Duck the next morning—and right on time, I might add—Tommy Jr., known as Tommy J., and Crazy Larry, his driver, arrived at the alleyway leading to the Cardboard Hotel. Tommy J. grabbed his briefcase, which contained his laptop computer, a few pens, an old-fashioned spiral flip-up notepad, and some photos. As Tommy J. opened the back door to get out, he said, "Thanks, Larry. I don't know how long this will take."

"It's okay. It doesn't matter. Your dad said to wait and keep a close eye on you. I'll be right here, so just start yelling if you need me. I'll be there faster than a speeding bullet. You know, I always thought that sounded strange. How can a man be there faster than a speeding bullet? It's impossible; that is, unless you get there before you send the speeding bullet. Then that wouldn't be too smart, either, because then you might get in the way of the bullet. The next thing you know, you're reading in the papers about how you shot yourself from 150 yards away. Tommy J., I just don't know how I would explain that one to Uncle Tommy. And mom—oh, she'd kill me. But hey, I guess depending on where the bullet hit me, I might already…"

Tommy interrupted and said, "I get the picture." Crazy Larry was deep in thought, still trying to come to terms with that whole 'faster than a speeding bullet' thing. As Tommy J. looked out the window, he saw two cups of coffee and then the whole silhouette of a person stepping out from the dark and gradually into the light that was being cast off from the signage mounted on the old downtown brick buildings. Tommy J. remembered what Duck had said and reminded himself, 'It's a test and a judgment barometer. If you pass, then you will be warmly received. If you refuse to drink coffee from one of their cups, then you won't be welcomed into their home.' Crazy Larry watched as Tommy J. approached the figure he assumed was Cilus. Crazy Larry mumbled as he sat in the driver's seat with his hands resting on the wheel, looking out the windshield at Tommy J. "At least I'll be there as fast as a speeding Crazy Larry if you need me, Tommy boy. I really don't see how I can be there much faster than a speeding Larry, since I am Larry. It can't happen. It's just not possible. It would be real hard to get there ahead of myself."

As Tommy J. approached Cilus, he said, "Good morning. You must be Cilus." Tommy J. extended his hand to Cilus for a 'glad to meet you' shake. Cilus extended the cup of coffee in his right hand and said, "Would you care for a cup?"

"Absolutely. Uncle Duck said you make some of the best coffee." Tommy J. took the cup from Cilus and took a sip. Tommy J. said, "Mmmmmm, Uncle Duck was right. This is sooo good."

Cilus, now smiling proudly from ear to ear, extended his hand and said, "Cilus McQuitty."

"I'm Tommy J. Nice to meet you." They shook hands. "Won't you come in, Tommy J.? I understand we've got a book to finish. Did you bring any photos with you?" Tommy J. patted his bag and said, "They're all in here."

"Good. We also have a few photos and movies, and we would like to get your opinion."

"Sounds good—I mean, it looks good. What I'm saying is that it sounds good to look at. I'm…" Tommy was silent. He was stuck in mid-sentence and couldn't think of what he was going to say.

Cilus chimed in, "I'll have to admit that this is a first for me. I've experienced brain farts before, but never before have I been given such an accurate audio and visual live example of one. From now on, if that happens to me, I'm going to say I'm having a 'Tommy J.' moment. Just relax, kid. No one in here bites. You'll be just fine. So let's get you started." With that said, Cilus had taken the edge off. Tommy J. smiled and took Cilus's advice and relaxed.

The evening before, the group at the alley had a lottery drawing to establish the order in which they would be interviewed. The person with the shortest straw was Speedo, so he would be the first one interviewed. Cilus walked Tommy J. over to Speedo's home, and Cilus said, "Speedo, are you in there, son? You make sure you get fully dressed before you come out. Don't want to scar the boy for life."

Speedo stepped out of the box. Heck, you could hardly tell anyone was even in that box. He had been way back in what he called the back bedroom. As Speedo stood up, Cilus said, "Speedo, this is Tommy J."

Tommy J. said, "Nice to meet you, Speedo." They shook hands, and Speedo said, "So you're the kid that's been taking all those pictures. Let me see what you've got."

Tommy J. flipped through the pictures and found a couple of them that had Speedo in them. You could tell it was Speedo because of the bright red swimming skullcap that looked just like the one he was currently wearing. He grabbed those photos and handed them to Speedo, who took the pictures from Tommy J. and studied them.

Tommy J. said, "So, Speedo, just how did you come about getting the name Speedo?"

"It's mostly this swim cap. I wear it all the time."

"So, how did you get the cap? Do you swim a lot?"

"Swim? Me? Not anymore. I'm allergic to water these days. Nope, didn't get it from me swimming. It was this girl."

"So, there's a girl in your life?"

"No, no, not anything like that. I didn't know this one. She came walking by the alley one night and said to this guy with her, whom I guess was her boyfriend, she said, 'I never, ever want to see you in something like this again.' Then she heaved this plastic sack into the alley. She nearly hit me right in my left eye with that sack. It made a little mark on my face. You can still see it if you look hard." He pointed to the spot on his face and said, "It's right here. Can you see it? Do you see it?"

"Yeah, I think I do," Tommy replied.

"Anyhow, as soon as that sack hit the ground, I dove on it and claimed it. I heard the Romanian judges gave me a 9.9 on my dive. When I opened that sack, I found - amongst other things - this red skullcap. I remember the first time I put it on. It was raining, and I admit I was complaining about my head getting wet, and someone said, 'Why don't you put that stupid red hat on?' And I thought, 'why not?' I did, and I liked it. At first I wore it only when it rained. It felt so good and right that I started wearing it all the time. That was nine or ten years ago."

Speedo took the hat off of his head and held it out so that Tommy J. could see it and said, "It's held up pretty good, hasn't it? But you'll have to admit that until it gets put on my head, it just looks like a plain old hat. Someone came up with the name 'Speedo'; it stuck, and here I am."

Tommy responded, "To be honest with you, Speedo, I'm glad the hat is the reason for the name. Originally, I was afraid that maybe the name referred to a skimpy swimming suit that you would parade around in. All I can say - considering the nightmarish images I had dancing around in my head - is, 'Thank God for the skullcap.'"

"Oh, I have the suit. It was in the sack, too. I wear it mostly in the warm weather and on special occasions. I've got it in storage for the winter." Speedo pointed above his home, and there, hanging on a nail, was a tiny red bikini swimsuit. Speedo said, "Would you like for me to model it for you?"

"Uh, no, that's okay. So tell me a little about how you came to live here."

"Actually, when I was younger, I was a pretty darn good swimmer. In fact, in high school, my coach told me I had a real good shot at State. But I got distracted by an altered state of mind, got a little too involved with one of those girls in those cute little cheerleading outfits, got someone pregnant, dropped out of school, dropped out of a short marriage, dropped out of society, and ended up here. I read about folks today, and a lot of them say swimming is one of the best forms of exercise. Someday, when I win the lottery and get rich and famous, I'm going to have my own pool—someday." He paused.

Speedo stood up and said, "Enough about me. Let me take you over and introduce you to Fast Eddie." They headed for Fast Eddie's space. Speedo, who was wearing a long trench coat, and Tommy J. arrived at Fast Eddie's. They found him lying on his back, staring up into space. As he caught sight of Speedo coming closer, he shut his eyes and turned over onto his side, facing away from Tommy J. and Speedo. Tommy was afraid that Fast Eddie was shutting him out, but then Fast Eddie said, "Speedo, so help me, if you are wearing that suit under your trench coat again, and if you flash me for the umpteenth time and make me upchuck again, I'm going to stand up and kick your sorry butt right out of this alley and all the way down Main Street to the bus depot and then back again."

"Nope. Sorry, Eddie. No treats for you this time."

"Eddie, this is Tommy J., the author."

"Oh, yeah. Just about forgot you were coming." As he raised himself to his feet, Fast Eddie said, "How you doing, kid? Sorry about my morning breath. Now that I think of it, it's my afternoon and evening breath, too. I've got to get a new toothbrush someday."

Now standing, Fast Eddie turned his head to the right, positioned his right hand over his right nostril, and did one of those disgusting 'blow snot out of your nostrils' things. Then he did the same thing to his other nostril. With nose cleared of debris, he was ready to talk. As he extended his hand to Tommy J. for a handshake, Tommy J. could see the shining snot remnants on Eddie's fingers from the escaping snot wad as it made its way to the ground. Fast Eddie said, "Oh, how rude of me. My name is Eddie, Fast Eddie."

Tommy J., remembering Duck's words, didn't want to seem rude, so he reluctantly extended his hand out to meet Fast Eddie's still-lubricated hand. Suddenly, from out of nowhere, a third set of hands intercepted the handshake with a moist wet wipe, and then a voice was heard saying, "For crying out loud, Eddie, what on earth is wrong with you? You use these and wash your hands before you shake this young man's hand." Tommy J. could actually hear the Halleluiah Chorus in his head as he turned to see a little lady standing next to him. She was holding a box of easy dispensable wet wipes that had been given to them by the local mission. She was just finishing wiping her hands with one of the wet wipes as she said, "I'm Sister Molly. I'm next on your interview list. I'll be right over there when you're done with Fast Eddie. Here, you might need these again." She handed him the rest of the box of wet wipes. Tommy J. expressed his sincere thanks to Sister Molly.

Tommy turned, shook Fast Eddie's hand, and said, "Here are a couple of the photos I hope to use. I think you will recognize one of the subjects." Fast Eddie was pleased that Tommy J. had caught his good side, and as the interview began to wind down, Fast Eddie said, "Someday you'll read about me in the papers." He painted a headline with a broad stroke of his hand and said, "'Fast Eddie takes first place again in the fifties-and-over World Racing Federation International Championship. Oh, yeah, I can see it in my head as clear as day, and someday you will see it, too."

Finished with his conversation, Eddie turned and blew his nose - again without a handkerchief - and extended his snotty paw to Tommy J. for a handshake. This time, thanks to Sister Molly, he was ready and extended the box of handy-wipes to Fast Eddie and said, "You better take two. I don't think any of that even reached the ground." With Fast Eddie's hands now clean, he told Tommy J., "Remember, it's 'Fast Eddie,' not Eddy or Edward. It's Eddie. And don't forget to use my good side. Now, follow me. Oh, and watch your step. Sometimes this alley gets slick as snot."

This just about hit the gag-and-puke button for Tommy, but the sick feeling in his stomach quickly faded as he stood face to face with his next interview, Sister Molly.

"Sister Molly, this is my friend Tommy J. But I think you two have met before; snot too long ago, either, I'm thinking."

"Thanks, Eddie," Sister said. "Tommy, have a seat, won't you?" Sister Molly was sitting in an old high-backed leather chair, and at her feet was an ottoman. It didn't even come close to matching the chair, but it was a comfortable place to rest your feet. She motioned for Tommy J. to sit on the ottoman, and he did. Tommy sat there mesmerized by Sister Molly's remarkable story that was unfolding before him. Later, when his book was finished, the story read like this...

Sister Molly was the sixth of twelve children from a poor family who had immigrated to this country from Belgium. They seized the new opportunities given them in this land of promise and turned hard work and determination into a vast fortune. Money never was important to Molly. Her passion was her faith, and she knew at an early age that her life's calling was to become a worker for the Lord. When Molly reached the age of eighteen, she asked her parents for permission to join a Catholic order of nuns. Being staunch Catholics, her parents were overjoyed and, of course, said yes, so at eighteen, she entered the convent. With studies completed, it really didn't take long for Sister Molly to find her life's passion.

After getting to know many of the homeless people who stopped by the Convent for food, advice, and occasional shelter—but mostly for food—she quickly realized that these were simply people like you or me who chose to or were forced, through some circumstance or another, to step out of the mainstream. Many of us at one time or another have been one small step away from living in a box. She had observed a common vein that seemed to run through the majority of the homeless that she talked to. It was what she calls the 'Someday Newspaper.' She'd hear the same thing in different ways from different folks—things like "Oh, someday I'll do it. Some morning I'll wake up and step right back in." Someday this, someday that. She decided she had to do more to help these folks find their 'Someday Newspaper.'

She went to the Bishop and asked his permission to go live on the streets with the homeless. She explained her "Someday Newspaper" plan to him, hoping that he would see that her living with them on the streets would allow her more opportunities to deliver messages of encouragement to them daily. And maybe—just maybe—she could help some of them step back in. The Bishop denied her request, citing that such a life for a nun would be too dangerous and inappropriate. After appealing to his decision several times, Sister Molly accepted his decision. He was, after all, her boss—at least in this world. She settled for the fact that she would have to do all that she could to help them from the kitchen and den of the convent.

That all changed one morning. She answered the doorbell, as she had so many times before, to greet the day's group of homeless friends. Earlier in the morning, her prized pupil, Clarice, was a no-show for their early morning coffee, but she thought for sure she'd be there for breakfast. As the last visitor filed in the door, there still was no sign of Clarice. Sister stepped out the door and looked up and down the street. She was nowhere in sight. Chalk Line asked, "Are you looking for Clarice?"

"Yes, I am. We have a lesson today. Has anyone seen her?" Responding in a matter-of-fact way, Chalk Line said, "Oh, I guess you haven't heard. She won't be making the lesson. She died Monday. Yeah, we think she froze to death. Some think it was from an overdose. Hey, did you know you're out of sugar?"

"She did what? My God, why? That's it? That's how you tell me she died? Don't you have any feelings?"

"Sorry, Sister. It's a way of life. It happens all the time." Sister was stunned. She and Clarice had been making headway as they were preparing her for her G.E.D. As a matter of fact, the very next Wednesday was to be Clarice's test date. Overcome by emotions, Sister Molly remembered sobbing uncontrollably. She recalled how she grabbed the notes she had prepared to give to Clarice, wadded them up, and threw them to the floor. She looked at this author and said, "Tommy, if I had been there, maybe I could have helped. No—I know that I could have helped." That's when it all changed. She knew what she had to do. A look of resolve came over her entire being. She grabbed a banana cream pie and some plates out of the cupboard, laid them on the table and said, "Have some dessert, but don't you leave until I come back down. I'll be right back."

With as much determination as she had ever mustered up in her life, she marched upstairs to her room. As she reached the entrance to her nice, clean, cozy room, she opened the door, stopped and glanced around. She could see the neatly made bed. "To this day," she said, "each and every night when I lie down to sleep, I can still see that lovely bed that was covered with a beautiful quilt handmade for me by my grandmother." She knew she would miss all the creature comforts. She stepped in and headed right for the closet and grabbed a small suitcase. As she was pulling a few things from her nightstand drawer, she came across the rejection letters from the Bishop. She picked them up, glanced at them, then put them back into the drawer and shut it. She walked over to her study desk, pulled out the chair, and sat down. With a deep sigh, she reached for a pen and a pad of paper and wrote a note.

"Dear Mother Superior,

Please find it in your heart to forgive me for not following your orders and Bishop McCoy's. I have to follow what my heart is telling my soul to do. I know I can better serve my friends if I join them and can be there if they need me. I can't let another single one of them die alone without me being there. I will always be indebted to you for all you have done for me.

Sincerely,

Molly"

She purposely signed the note "Molly," and not "Sister Molly," for she knew that as she left against their decrees, they would have no choice but to disassociate her from the Order. She stood up from the desk, now dressed in civilian clothes, walked over and laid the note on her bed's pillow. After patting the quilt with the palm of her hand one last time, she grabbed her suitcase and walked back downstairs—right past a group of fellow sisters who silently watched her descend the stairs.

Arriving at the kitchen with suitcase in hand, she addresses the group seated obediently at the kitchen table and said, "Let's go home." They all walked out together, back to the streets. Sister Molly turned back to see her fellow nuns filling the second-story windows as they watch her walk away. She was leaving a life she dearly loved, but she was okay with being an ex-nun. It didn't change her heart. She knew this was the work that God wanted her to do, and nothing was going to stop her.

As she finished telling her story, she said, "And so, Tommy, here I am. You know, that is the first time I have ever told that story to anyone. To this day, when I smell muffins, I can hear Clarice's voice saying, 'This must be what Heaven smells like.'" A tear ran down her cheek.

Unbeknownst to Tommy J. and Sister, Speedo was standing there listening. Speedo spoke up and said, "I know this to be the truth. I was there at the table. I was even wearing my skimpy trunks."

"Speedo, you're sick. Always have been, always will be. But I love you. Have to love you. You're one of God's children.

Now, get out of my face." Speedo gave the okay sign with both sets of fingers and walked away.

Tommy J. said to Sister Molly, "Wow, that is a truly remarkable story. Thank you for sharing it with me. This is a story people need to hear about. Would you mind if I change the title of this book to the 'Someday Newspaper'?"

"Sure, Tommy, that sounds nice to me. I think the man upstairs might like that, too." Sister Molly got up and takes Tommy J. over to meet the next person on the interview list—a man known as B. F. D. Arriving at his space, Sister Molly introduced them. "Tommy, this is Bottom Feeder Del. He likes to be called B.F.D. B.F.D., this is Tommy J."

They shook hands, and B.F.D. said, "So Tommy J., what's the B.F.D. about writing a story about us? Man, who's going to care?" Tommy J. was still shaking his head about the initials that Bottom Feeder Del liked to be referred to. Then he said, "Oh, you'd be surprised to know that what happens to you is a B.F.D. to a lot of folks. Folks like Sister Molly, Duck, the people down at the Mission, and me, just to mention a few. To us, you and your friends are a B.F.D."

Bottom Feeder Del tried to make a stab at humor and said, "So what you're saying is that we're all a bunch of bottom feeder Del's."

"Bottom Feeder Del, now sit down and tell me about yourself." Tommy J. sounded more like his dad, Uncle Tommy, with that command than he did himself.

"My story actually is no big deal, really. I was fresh out of law school and hired by a large legal firm in Lincoln, Nebraska. Being the new guy, I was given all the B.S. things to do— things that no one else wanted to do. At the firm, they called the lowest guy on the totem pole the Bottom Feeder, and that's the kind of tasks I was given. I found out very early that the whole 'legal truths' thing wasn't for me. You know, the truth wasn't always the truth. I could do the dog and pony part all right. In fact, I was quite good at acting, but apparently I stank as a lawyer."

"Finally, one day, I was given what I thought was my first really good criminal case. I found out later that it was a case nobody else would touch. I mean, this kid was framed, and I do mean framed. The clearly fabricated case had an innocent young man hopelessly boxed in. It was more than an uphill battle. It was the impossible dream. Someone had to defend him since his father was a big client of the firm. They made me take it on. The further I researched the case, the more I should have seen the web of lies and deceit were so well-woven that it was all but over before it started, but I refused to see it. At first, I wanted to prove to the firm that I was more than just a bottom feeder, so with both feet, I stepped deeper and deeper into it. The more evidence I uncovered, the more I knew he couldn't have committed that murder. Over time, he became more than my 'coming out as a lawyer' case. He became my friend, and his destiny became my passion. It was clear someone more important was being protected. No matter what we did, and no matter how the case was decided by the court, he would remain the guilty one."

"I always thought it was funny that in those two and a half years, his dad—this highfalutin client of our firm—never once came to the courtroom to show support. Oh, he funneled plenty of money into the firm to pay for the case, but that was it. I couldn't quite figure it out until one day a mysterious tipster called me. I checked out his story, and it jibed with my suspicions. Imagine a dad letting his own son take a fall for a crime he himself committed. My client wouldn't listen to my theory and refused to have me pursue it. We lost the case, and he was found guilty of murder in the first degree and sentenced to life in prison without parole."

"I realized that I and the system had failed him. The only good thing is that we nearly bankrupted his old man with the ridiculous fees charged during the trial. My company liked the bottom line—they made money—but it cost me my soul. I thought, 'all these years of study for this.' I just couldn't, In good faith, continue what had now become a lucrative career. I just couldn't continue the status quo, knowing that my client was spending the rest of his life in jail—behind bars for a crime that he did not commit. I tried to convey my theory to my superiors about my client's dad, but they wouldn't listen. In fact, they told me to drop it or else. I chose the 'or else' and walked out that day."

"So here I am. I've been here seven years now. Maybe someday I'll prepare another appeal for Sammy P., and someday I'm going after that rotten sack of shit S.O.B. dad of his. You watch and see, Tommy boy. Someday. Well, I told you that my story was no B.F.D., but that's my story, and I'm sticking with it. That's enough about me. Let me take you over to our mystery man."

B.F.D. took Tommy J. to Cilus. It was his turn. On the way, B.F.D. turned to Tommy J. and said, "Cilus has been here since dirt. I can't remember—and neither can anyone else, for that matter—a time when he wasn't around. We're not exactly sure what his deal is, or even if he has a deal. Maybe he'll tell you. Rumors have been flying around for years. F.B.I., D.E.A., and lately even homeland security. He has these guys who come by to see him every once in a while. They go off and talk, and he disappears for a night or so quite often." B.F.D. leaned over and whispered in Tommy J.'s ear, "If you find out anything, make sure you put it in that book of yours so that we know for sure. Don't tell him, but it drives us all nuts not knowing."

As they approached, Cilus extended his hand and said, "Tommy J.—good to see you." "Good to see you, too, Cilus."

"Oh, that's right," B.F.D. said. "You two have already met. See you later, Tommy. If you ever need any legal advice, I'll be right over here."

"Thanks for your time, counselor." Then Tommy J. turned to Cilus, "So tell me the truth about Mr. Cilus McQuitty."

"The truth. Well, the truth is I used to be a damn good cop, but that was years ago. Looking at me now, this might be hard to believe, but I was a detective with the San Clemente P. D. That is, until I got caught with my hands in the cookie jar with some drug money we took in from a big bust. I was convicted, thrown in jail, served my time, and here I am."

"Short and sweet. So that's it. That's the truth. This is who Cilus McQuitty is?"

In silence, Cilus thought, "Wouldn't it be nice if I could tell Tommy J. the truth? I could tell him I'm Trace Marcello, an undercover F.B.I. agent living on the streets investigating organized crime and conducting surveillance for homeland security. Maybe I should let him know that I have been investigating his dad's and his business associates for years, collecting information that is leading us to an upcoming bust. I wonder if he'd talk to me if he knew all of that. I wish I could divulge to him the latest information that I've not yet shared with my partners. This stuff could be helpful in keeping Tommy J.'s dad alive. I wish I could tell him I have no vendetta against his dad, and that we're closing in on many crime families in town and keeping an ear to the ground for terrorist activities. What the hell! I owe it to Duck. Tommy J. and his dad are good friends of Duck's. Maybe I'll give him a strong hint."

Cilus said, "You know, Tommy, all the attention and publicity you and Duck will generate is going to make it hard for me to maintain my peace and quiet. I'm going to have to escalate my timetable."

Tommy J. just stood there and watched as Cilus headed out of the alley. Cilus stopped and turned to Tommy and said, "Come on. Walk with me. I've got something to say to you in private."

Tommy was seeing the mystery man in action himself. He thought maybe he'd get a glimpse into the mystery.

"So are you coming?"

"Sure. Should I bring my briefcase?"

"No, it'll be fine right where it is."

Crazy Larry was sitting in the car, staring at the opening to the alley, and saw Tommy J. and Cilus coming out into the light. Crazy Larry started to get out of the car, but Tommy J., knowing Crazy Larry would be anxious when he saw them emerge from the alley, signaled for Larry to stay in the car. But Crazy Larry got out of the car, anyway. He knew he was under strict orders from Uncle Tommy not to take his eyes off of Tommy Jr. He was determined not to let him out of his sight. Larry walked over to Tommy J. and said, "So what's up, kid? Are you two planning to go somewhere? If so, you're going to need a ride."

Tommy J. turned to introduce Cilus to Crazy Larry, but before he could speak, Cilus said, "Crazy Larry. So we finally meet face-to-face."

"How do you know my name?" a shocked Crazy Larry replied.

"Oh, I know people." Tommy J. was surprised and impressed that Cilus knew who Crazy Larry was, and Tommy J. said, "It's okay, Larry. Why don't you get the car and follow us?" Crazy Larry took another long, hard look at Cilus, as if he must surely know him from somewhere. He turned and headed back to the car, but about halfway to the car, he turned to make sure they were still in eyesight. Reaching the car, he took one last look, and then he climbed in. With his watchful eyes trained on them, he started the car, put it in gear, and drove over to where they were. Crazy Larry kept the car in gear and rolled slowly behind them, keeping enough distance between him and them so that they could talk privately. Crazy Larry had been the driver for Uncle Tommy several times as he conducted meetings with some of his clients in a manner similar to this. To himself he said, "I don't know how safe Tommy J. should feel, because at my age I'm not sure that I'm as fast as a turtle."

Cilus said to Tommy J., "I want you to give this to your dad. It seems there are some people who want to harm him." Cilus handed Tommy J. a large yellow envelope and said, "Go ahead. Open it and look inside."

Tommy J. opened the envelope and pulled out some photographs and one of four V.C.R. tapes. Cilus said, "Your father will want to know what some of his so-called friends are thinking about these days. And Tommy, tell him to stay out of the club on 31st for a while. I've heard on the street that something might be about to happen. You'll have to trust me on this. Oh, and tell Tommy that Trace Marcello said hello. I'll be going away fairly soon. Tell your dad that we will take care of his friends. Tell him—no, beg him to please stay out of the club for a while. Convince him it's time for a vacation."

"So Tommy, we'll see you here tomorrow morning, correct?"

"I'll be here bright and early. You have the coffee ready."

Tommy J. walked back toward the car. Crazy Larry put the car in park and jumped out to open the door for Tommy J.

"Thanks, Larry."

"Anytime, Tommy J., anytime." As he stepped into the car, they heard a voice coming from the alley. "Hold up. Hold up a minute. You forgot something." As Tommy J. and Larry looked back toward the alley, they saw Tommy J.'s briefcase in the hands of Speedo as he emerged into the light. Speedo walked over and handed it to Tommy.

"Thanks, Speedo. We'll see you tomorrow."

Larry closed Tommy's door, slid into the diver's seat, and said, "Man, Tommy J., watching you walking along conducting a private meeting with one of your clients was like old times. You remind me so much of your dad. So, are you going to whack him?"

"Am I going to what??"

"Sorry, Tommy J... old habit." Tommy J. was looking into the sack, and he pulled out some very interesting photographs. As he looked through them, he was trying to decide whether he should tell his dad what Cilus had just told him. The more he looked at the pictures, he decided it was worth the risk of looking stupid if it meant he might have a part in saving his dad's future.

Arriving back, he walked right into his dad's office and handed the photos and the tapes to his dad. He explained to him how he got the tapes and said, "He also said, 'tell your dad Trace Marcello said hello.'"

Tommy's ears perked up as he heard this old name from the past, and then he said, "Thanks, son. I'll look at all this stuff tonight. How'd the interviews go?"

"Great, but I've got several more to do before I can finish."

"Just take your time. Now, go on, I've got some videos to watch. I hate those late fees, you know."

CHAPTER 23

The next morning, with Crazy Larry at the wheel, Tommy J. arrived at the alley, and this time he was eager to get more stories. A smaller silhouette stepped out of the darkness of the alley to greet him. He noticed it was not Cilus. This time, it was Sister Molly. "Good Morning, Tommy my boy."

"Good morning, Sister. Where's Cilus?"

"He came back to see me after your walk, and then he disappeared. Nothing to worry about; he has a habit of vanishing now and then. He asked me to tell you not to print everything you talked about last night. He said to tell Tommy J. to be discreet. So Tommy, be discreet. Sounds like Cilus; always the mystery man. Come on in. Time's a wastin'. It's Buck Eyes' turn, and he's waiting for you."

Buck Eyes was another in a series of interesting characters that Tommy J. would interview over the next couple of weeks. It seems Stan Smarts, A.K.A. Buck Eyes, an old auto mechanic, always walked around with that 'deer in the headlights' on his face, so they named him Buck Eyes.

Then there was Half Deck. After five minutes of conversation with him, there was no question where he got his name.

Then Sister Molly introduced him to one of her friends from the next alley over. They called her Van Gogh. She showed him some of the drawings she carried around with her in a large artist's carrying case. On another visit, Tommy J. and Van Gogh took a walk, with Crazy Larry following close by, of course. She wanted to show Tommy J. some of the building graffiti she had created. Tommy J. was impressed. She was one of the best artists he had ever had the privilege of meeting. She just couldn't make any money at it.

The list went on and on. A girl named Speed Bump, and then there was Chalk Line. It seemed he'd lie down in one position so long and often that they drew a line around his body with chalk. That didn't bother him. He'd just come back night or day and lie inside the chalk figure sketched on the paver bricks. It became his bed.

A man called Juggler. It seems he ran away from home to join the circus, but the closest he came was watching the end of the circus train drive off into the sunset at a Chicago rail yard. He was quite good at juggling. He even demonstrated how he could juggle three plastic gallon milk jugs and a small rock, all at the same time.

A girl named Indy. She loved to play with a remote-control kid's car she found one day in the trash bin. She raced that thing up and down the alley, making precision high-speed turns with the grace of a race car driver, while dodging obstacles in her path, as if she were actually sitting behind the wheel of that thing. The folks at the mission kept her supplied with batteries.

Finally, the interviews were done, and Tommy spent his evenings making corrections on the stories he had accumulated on his laptop. One evening, while finishing and polishing one of his stories, he glanced up at the TV. He had kept it on in the background with the sound muted, and recognized the front of the building and noticed it was the Club on 31st. He reached for the TV remote, and he caught the reporter's voice saying, "Several arrests were made today at the Club on 31st—the result of what we are being told was years of undercover investigations." Tommy J. was sitting there with his mouth open, thinking, "How on earth did Cilus know that?" Suddenly, he thought, "Shit—Dad!"

He picked up the phone and called his dad's cell phone. His dad answered. "Dad, are you watching the news? Where are you? Are you okay? Do you want me to call an attorney?"

His dad interrupted, "Whoa, whoa—am I watching what? Tommy, you really need to pay attention to your father a little more closely. Don't you remember I told you I would be in Hawaii on a much-needed vacation for a couple of weeks? And you know I don't watch TV while I'm on vacation. Got to go now. The flames are lit, dinner's here, and the Luau is about to start. See you soon."

Tommy J. breathed a deep sigh of relief. His dad had listened and was nowhere around when all of this happened. The reporter doing a live shot was now on the screen. Tommy turned the volume back up. As he listened, the reporter said, "Sources who wish to remain anonymous have told this reporter that they believe most of the information was gathered by an F.B.I. agent who has been posing for years as a transient, living on the streets and alleyways."

In the crowd gathering around the commotion, Tommy J. thought he saw Cilus, and then the image disappeared. Cilus was never seen again by the folks down at the Cardboard Hotel.

For the next few weeks, Tommy J. worked night and day proof reading all his notes. He had already selected the photographs he was going to use. The next morning, he dropped all of his information off at the publisher's office.

CHAPTER 24

Duck and Tommy were sitting in high-backed chairs looking out the window, puffing on some of those fine Cuban cigars. Duck said, "So how was Hawaii, Tommy?"

"Gorgeous. Just gorgeous. You really need to go back there some day."

"Yeah, someday maybe I will. It's a long flight, though."

Duck reached down into his bag and said, "Oh, almost forgot." Duck pulled out a square package wrapped in cellophane. It was a fresh box of Cubans, and he said, "Here you go, Tommy, my boy." Duck handed the box to Tommy, who took it from Duck, removed the plastic, opened the carton, brought the box up to his nose and took a close whiff and said, "Thanks, Duck. Now, how about these weathermen? I've been thinking about this. They need to learn a little more about the word 'respect', and I definitely think they are all going to want to contribute to your Duck's Run Charity. So me and Crazy Larry here, well, we're going to"—he paused—"oh, let's just say we'll see what kind of donation we can solicit from them."

"Tommy, thanks, but don't waste—" then Tommy interrupted.

"You leave this matter to us. It's what we do. Enough said— end of story for now. Like I told you, we'll handle it. So, are we all set for the news conference/groundbreaking event? I've been told by the publisher that the book will be ready Thursday afternoon. Did you get a chance to read the final draft?"

"Did I," Duck answered. "I tell you what, Tommy. Your Tommy J. has a gift."

Tommy, the proud father, said, "He really does, doesn't he?"

Duck continued, "And yes, the news conference is set for two weeks from today, Tuesday morning, 10 a.m."

"Good. It looks like Larry and I better get to work on those voluntary donations."

Duck started to talk. "Tommy, I—"

Tommy interrupted him again, motioned for him to stop, and then said, "Duck, it's only right, although I have to admit it's been a while since I made my last house call." Larry's eyes lit up at the sound of this. He threw his fists into the air and yelled, "Eeeeeyesss!"

CHAPTER 25

Mayor Joey Parma returned to his office about 6 p.m., after having dinner with a group of school teachers down in Barns Town. The election race for mayor was running close and very heated. It was exhausting keeping up with the schedule, but Joey loved the job and the fringe benefits, and he wanted desperately to keep things status quo. As he stepped into his office, he took off his coat and scarf and threw them over the back of a chair. Suddenly, he heard a voice coming from the shadows of the chair in front of his desk.

"Cashmere, isn't it? You really should take better care and hang it on a nice, curved wooden hanger. It will last longer. Larry, would you mind grabbing his coat and hanging it up for him?"

Startled by the presence of someone in his office, the mayor said, "Who are you, and how did you get past my security?" Smelling smoke, he said, "And put that thing out. You can't smoke in here."

He was interrupted. "Shhhhhh. I'll let you know when I want you to speak." Uncle Tommy took a puff of his cigar, and as he did, the orange glow of the end of the cigar lit up Uncle Tommy's face, revealing to Joey who the shadowy figure was.

Joey instantly recognized Uncle Tommy and was now scared to death.

Joey said, "Uncle Tommy," he paused, "can I get you an ashtray?"

"An ashtray would be nice," replied Uncle Tommy. Joey bent down and reached into one of his desk drawers, and with a shaky hand, grabbed an ashtray out of his left top drawer. It felt like every muscle in his body was shaking as he walked around his desk and over to Uncle Tommy, carrying the ashtray. The glass ashtray made a tittering sound as it hit the table several times as Joey tried to set it down with trembling hands next to Tommy.

Joey headed back to his desk and said, "Do you mind if I sit down and have a cigarette?"

"Be my guest—but I thought this was a no-smoking area." Crazy Larry walked over and stood over Joey, making sure that he had full sight of the mayor's hands and the contents of his drawers. It's been some time since he had made a house call with Uncle Tommy, and the first time Joey got into the drawer for the ashtray, he watched him from a distance, not up close like he used to when he and Uncle Tommy made all their house calls together. This mistake wouldn't happen again.

Mayor Joey opened the drawer, and nervously he pulled out a pack of cigarettes, a book of matches, and an old lighter that he always fidgeted with when he was nervous. As he tried to tap out one cigarette from the pack, a cold chill caused a nervous twitch that sent about five from the pack sailing to the floor. Automatically, Joey bent over to pick them up. As he did, Crazy Larry reached out, put his hand on Joey's shoulder, and pushed him back down into his chair. He motioned for Joey to stay seated; then Crazy Larry bent down, picked up one of the fallen cigarettes from the floor, placed it between Mayor Joey's lips, and nodded to him it was now okay to light it.

The cigarette was jumping around, and his hands were trembling with fear. Joey struck a match and chase the nervously moving cigarette with an equally unstable match. Finally he got it lit and took a drag, completely forgetting about the lit match still in his fingers. He said, "So Uncle Tommy, to what do I owe this—" suddenly, the searing pain of the lit match burning his fingertips made Joey shake his hand violently, and then he stood straight up and yelled, "What the …oh man, that burns."

Crazy Larry, seeing him stand up, immediately swung into action and had Mayor Joey's arm pinned against his back and the 'Pearl' at his head in the blink of an eye. Instantly, a spot of water which kept getting bigger and bigger appeared on the front of Mayor Joey's pants as he uncontrollably peed his pants. Uncle Tommy said to Crazy Larry, "Hold on there, Larry. He just got burned, that's all. My guess is that he, just like old Vic, forgot that if you play with fire, you just might get burned. Relax, Larry, but don't let go just yet. Now, Mr. Mayor, before my good friend Larry lets go of you, I want to talk to you man to man. Jeez, I see you peed your pants. It's a good thing for you that you peed your pants rather than trying to deliver to me that Tuesday Evening Weather Report you used to do."

At first, Joey was puzzled by what Tommy had said. Then he realized what he was talking about. "You see, Mr. Mayor, you did some bad things to some of my friends. I should just let Larry here do what he does best and let him have his way with you. Maybe that would teach you a lesson. How does that sound to you, Larry?"

Crazy Larry, always eager to please Uncle Tommy, said, "Anything you say, Boss. It'll be fun—just like old times. Remember the time you let me break that guy's kneecaps on my birthday?" Crazy Larry's eyes got watery, and then he said, "Boss, sometimes you are just too good to me."

The spot on the front of Joey's pants now grew even larger. Seeing this, Uncle Tommy said, "Oh, for crying out loud, Joey, get a grip. This is why I don't make house calls anymore. So help me, Joey, if you crap in your pants… well, where was I? Oh, yeah. And Crazy Larry, let go now."

Joey's face was looking a little blue. "Sorry, Boss. I guess working out with the Pilates tapes has helped my overall strength, including my grip."

Uncle Tommy continued, "Next Tuesday, Bob Duckins is going to be having a press conference/groundbreaking ceremony for Duck's Run. You will be there, and you will support him. I've prepared a little speech for you that I want you to read." Uncle Tommy pulled the speech out of his jacket pocket, leaned over, and set it on Mayor Joey's desk and said, "The conference is at 10 a.m. next Tuesday. Also, here is a list of the local TV stations I want you to personally call. I'm counting on you to make sure they cover this event. And one more thing; Duck's Run is to have no zoning, no planning problems. In short, no problems under your control will confront them. Have I made myself perfectly clear, Mr. Mayor?"

"Yes, sir, Uncle Tommy. Anything you want, you got it."

"Good. I also expect a sizeable contribution from you personally to the Duck's Run Organization. Oh, and don't be surprised if you get a dental bill. Sister Molly is going to have her teeth fixed. When you get it, don't argue—just pay it. However, I suggest you split the expense with Deano, Frankie, and Troy."

It was easy to read the look on Joey's face as he thought, 'How did Uncle Tommy know about all of that?' Joey said, "Anything. Sure, sure."

"Larry, my old pal, let's leave the mayor to clean himself up. That's a nice lighter." He leaned over and picked it up. "It's got a girl on it and everything. And would you look at that—you turn it like this, and now she's clothed only in a bikini. I've seen these before. They used to have these down at Carl's. You know, Joey, Mary, and Carl and I never could figure out why you guys kept stealing from them." Uncle Tommy leaned over and put his face within breathing distance of Jocy's and said,

"Looking back, I should have let Larry here pull your Tuesday Night Weather Reports off the air years ago. So be a good little mayor and do as you have been instructed. And Joey, do not whisper a word to Deano, Frankie, Troy, or anyone else about us being here tonight. You see, unlike me, Crazy Larry here loves to make house calls. And next time, I won't be with him."

At this, a foul smell wafted through the air. Smelling it, Uncle Tommy said, "What on earth is that?"

"I think he soiled himself, Boss."

Uncle Tommy pointed at Joey and said, "Not a word."

As a sign of respect, Joey scrambled to his feet and stood as Uncle Tommy left the room. Uncle Tommy pulled a handkerchief out of his pocket and covered his nose.

Once Uncle Tommy and Crazy Larry left, Joey, still standing, reached down and picked his nearly burnt out cigarette butt out of the ashtray, put it in his mouth, and sank down into his chair. As he sat down, he got a rather unpleasant look on his face—a look that I guess anyone would have as the deposit in his shorts spread all over his butt.

Just at that precise, uncomfortable moment, the buzzer went off on his desk. It was his secretary, who had just gotten back from her dinner break. She always ate early when she knew they were going to be working late. She said, "Mr. Mayor, the women for the gay rights movement are here for your 7 p.m. meeting." Realizing he wasn't in any kind of condition to be accepting the public, he said, "Wait. Tell them…" They barged right in. "Good evening, Mr. Mayor. What on earth is that smell….?"

CHAPTER 26

Being a close-knit, self-governing church with huge hearts, Frankie's congregation was satisfied to have Frankie resign. They agreed that what they knew about Frankie would stay amongst themselves. Frankie, after being hired by a national radio talk show programming station, simply told his new employer that he decided that his calling was for, apparently, a much larger audience. And he stated, "Who am I to argue?" The national radio audience seemed to eat up his self-promoting ways. Although they never quite understood his sermons either, they knew they could count on being entertained by him.

Things actually turned out well for the church. Frankie, behind closed doors, told the whole truth about the previous pastor, and with a lot of coaxing, Reverend Mike Spanky agreed to once again lead their congregation. Jimmy, the projectionist, was made a deacon and often filled in for the new pastor when he was away on church business. This turned out to be a win-win situation for Frankie and the church. After they had sold the smoke machines, the drum sets, and Frankie's other extravagant toys at their annual garage sale, the congregation netted enough money to send twelve missionaries to Sri Lanka for two and a half years. Up to this point, Frankie—well, let's just say he was getting off lucky.

One Sunday morning, while fielding calls on his nationally syndicated talk show, the call screener in Frankie's headphones said, "Frankie, we have this guy on the line who said to tell you it's Uncle Tommy. Some kind of kook is my guess. I tried to disconnect him three times, but I couldn't. He is insisting on talking to you—something about the Tuesday Evening News and Weather Report."

Frankie's face turned a noticeable shade of white as he realized Uncle Tommy wasn't calling him about the current news and weather. Frankie thought to himself, 'This can't be a social call.' His face apparently turned from ghost white to gray as his screener said, "Frankie, you don't look so good. Are you okay? Anyhow, this Tommy character said that if I tried to disconnect him one more time, he and someone he called Crazy Larry would pay me a house call. What do you want me to do? Are you sure you're okay?"

Frankie muted his microphone and said to the screener, "Take over for me. Tell the listeners that I'm on the other line tending to some needy soul. Play some old records, and just fill the air with something until I'm done. What line is he on?"

"Line one."

"I'm not on the air, am I? Make sure I'm not on the air."

"Trust me, Frankie, you're off the air."

Frankie picked up the call. "Good morning. This is Reverend Frankie."

"Frankie, how's it going? We are off the air, aren't we?"

Frankie knew that voice anywhere. "Uncle Tommy, is that really you? I'm fine. How are you doing? And yes, we are off the air."

"I'm cutting out all the pleasant B.S. right now. Here's my reason for calling. You now have a national radio show with a good following, right?"

"Well, yes. And frankly, Uncle Tommy, I'm flattered that you know this much about my career."

"Don't be. I have a favor that you need to do for yourself. I want you to announce today that you are going to be doing a live remote next Tuesday morning from Bob Duckins' scheduled press conference and groundbreaking ceremony. I want you to interview Tommy J. and help him promote his new book. I expect you to come out in full support of Duck's Run. You are to encourage your followers to financially support this cause. In return, I let your little Tuesday Night Weather Reports and your history at your last pastoral assignment blow over for now. But don't miss this last-chance opportunity. I really can't believe the way you treated those homeless friends of mine. And covering the cost of what you, Deano, Troy, and Joey stole and broke at Carl and Mary's place still sickens me to this day. But Deano's mother, my sister—God rest her soul—asked me to watch out for her precious Deano. I did, and you guys reaped the rewards of Deano's mother's request. Big mistake on my part—big mistake. Mary and Carl were right. You guys never did learn. Tell me something. I have to know. Are you really a Christian, Frankie? Notice there is an envelope by your microphone with all the instructions you need."

Frankie looked down and saw the envelope. He looked around the room, thinking to himself, 'I know this wasn't here a minute ago. How did he…'

Uncle Tommy said, "I guess Larry is faster than a speeding bullet, after all." Frankie sat up in his chair at full alert and said, "What was that about a bullet?"

"Frankie, just shut up and listen. Now, Frankie, I'm about to ask you if you intend to do this favor for yourself. Now, before I ask and before you answer, take a look at your phone bank. Do you see blinking hold button lights for lines 2, 3, 4, 5, and 6? Now, look at the caller identification names on the screen of your computer."

Frankie looked at the screen. "Are you looking at the screen, Frankie?"

"Yes, I am, Uncle Tommy, sir."

"Do you see any familiar names? You see, you should recognize all of those names. Line 2, for example, is Sister Molly.

You should remember her from the days when you apparently thought you were going to be a dentist. Why else would you have helped pull her teeth with a pair of my pliers? The rest of those names are my friends from the alley, and I'm sure they all have interesting stories to tell. And Frankie, your cough/mute/ cut-off buttons, or whatever it is that you call them, they just won't work, thanks to my resident electronics genius, Crazy Larry. Yep, with a flip of a switch, we could be live with one of the most interesting conference calls that have ever been heard on live radio. Hmmm, I wonder what would happen to your sweet job then. Would it go the way of your most recent pulpit? So, have you been wondering how that envelope got placed by your microphone?"

Frankie, now sweating bullets, looked around again, frantic this time. Then he heard Uncle Tommy's voice. "Now, I ask you, Frankie, are you willing to do yourself a favor?"

"Yeah, sure. Anything for you, Uncle Tommy. You know that."

"Good. Now, I want you to get back on the air and immediately announce your plans to do a live remote from the Duck's Run news conference and groundbreaking ceremony. I want you to continue promoting this event every half hour."

"I'm going to need my producer's approval before I can do that, Tommy."

"Larry and I have already taken care of that. Now, get on the air and make your first announcement. We'll all wait right here in the land of hold."

Frankie opened the letter left by Uncle Tommy and read it. He turned his microphone back on and said, "Hello, everyone. Sorry about that. I had to help an old friend in an hour of need." Of course, he failed to mention that the old friend in time of need was none other than himself. "Hey, did I mention that next Tuesday morning we will be live at the Duck's Run press conference and groundbreaking ceremony? You will want to come down and join us. This will be an event you won't want to miss; one of the—if not THE—biggest events of the year. I am asking you personally to come out and back this worthwhile event, both personally and financially. Let's all show up and get this thing started right."

Having said that, Frankie saw the blinking hold button lights go dark one by one, as Sister Molly and her friends hung up. Frankie breathed a sigh of relief.

At first, Frankie did as he was told. By the third day, he skipped one of the half-hour announcements, thinking enough was enough. Frankie's call screener said, "Frankie, we have this guy on the line. He gave me his name as Crazy Larry. Then he said to tell you he's good with electronics, and that he hoped he didn't have to tie up all your lines again. He wants to talk to you live now. Should I call the police?"

"No, put him on. Hello, C.L. You are live with Reverend Frankie. What's on your mind today?"

"My name is Crazy Larry. Nobody calls me C.L. but my boss."

"Sorry. Just what can I help you with today, Crazy Larry? What seems to be troubling your soul?"

"Right now, I'm not the one who needs to be worrying about his soul. I have a question about the Duck's Run press conference and groundbreaking ceremony. You haven't mentioned it in the last hour. Is it still taking place? Are you still doing a live remote from there? If so, what time does it start? I have this uncle who wants to know."

Frankie, realizing what this was about, said, "Why, sure, we'll be there. Like I said, it is going to be one of the biggest events of the year."

Crazy Larry said, "You know, I guess I do have something I would like to discuss with you. You see, I have this boss who is like an uncle to me. Right now, he's a little concerned about an issue. It seems he had a deal worked out with a person. That person is not living up to his end of the bargain. What do you think my uncle should do? Should he turn the other cheek, or should he consider him a lost soul and write him off?"

"Well, sir, I think your uncle should give him the chance to say it won't happen again and allow him the privilege to re-earn his trust."

"Do you really think so? Wow, thanks, Frankie. Thanks for the words of advice. I'll tell my uncle what you said. I'll get back to you after I see his reaction." Crazy Larry abruptly hung up.

Frankie's screener said, "Man, Frankie, you look like a ghost. Is everything okay?" Frankie, in an attempt to get himself out of hot water with Uncle Tommy, announced information about Duck's Run every fifteen minutes everyday right up to and including the day of the news conference.

CHAPTER 27

Troy Mastersomn was easy—just like Uncle Tommy said. Sister had hatched a plan. It was a little something that she and Indy could do together. Indy loved the idea, so they went to work on gathering supplies and perfecting the technique. Then one day when Troy stepped into one of his portable toilets, someone pushed the door shut behind him. The next thing he heard was the sound of duct tape as it came off the roll. It was Crazy Larry wrapping a single line of duct tape around the entire portable facility, sealing Troy inside.

Troy, who, as we know, was naturally paranoid anyway, was scared and wondering what in the world was going on. The sound of the tape being dispensed stopped, and then there was silence. Troy could hear someone walking up to the unit, and then he heard a voice. "Troy, this is Sister Molly. You might remember pulling my teeth out down in the alley." Sister was trying to act tough, but she was just about to break out in laughter. She had forgiven them long ago. Trying to keep a straight face, she said, "Uncle Tommy sent me. He said you didn't believe that I was really a nun. Let me tell you, son, I am a nun with every fiber of my body and soul. My faith is the reason I forgave you and your friends years ago."

Troy was silent as he digested what was just said, and then he said,

"Oh, my God, Sister, I am so sorry! I thought—I didn't—I, I am so sorry. Is there anything I can do to make it up to you? Anything at all?" A broad smile came across her face as she realized everything was going smoothly, just like Uncle Tommy said it would.

Then she said, "Well, there is something." The whole thing reminded Sister Molly of a scene right out of the confessional. She walked up to the ventilation grills on the side of the portapotty, turned her head so that her ear was to the grills—just like a priest would do in a confessional. While on the inside, Troy spoke to the side of the nun's habit through the grills. Sister explained how he could help. Once she was finished, she undid the tape and let him out.

As Troy exited, he looked and saw the back of a person dressed in full nun garb disappearing into the night. Reaching the base of the street lamp, the figure turned back to him. He couldn't see her face; all he could see was the dark shadow of what appeared to be a nun and the white of her long collar. Stunned, silent, and full of remorse, Troy stood staring into the faceless shadow.

The silence was broken by the sudden loud hiss of a cat. Startled, instinctively Troy turned to run. He made it about a foot before he ran his nose smack into the hard corner of the plastic "Aim-to-Pees" Porta-Potty. The sudden blow knocked him to the ground. As he raised his head, blood was trickling down from his nose. He found himself looking directly into the face of the biggest, most unfriendly looking tooth-filled hissing cat he had ever seen. Waiting in the shadows was Indy. Sister Molly and Indy's plan was to add a twist of mysticism to this situation. Indy, having received the supplies from Mya, had rigged up a sturdy platform that was attached to two remote control vehicles that were set to operate in unison, on the same frequency that she had dialed into the wireless control she was holding in her hand.

Sister, as they had been practicing at the alley, stood on the platform just out of the light. Comfortably standing on the platform, with a nod from Indy confirming that she was ready, Sister called for Princess. "Princess, come here, girl." The cat, recognizing her voice, turned to look at Sister Molly. Seizing the opportunity, Troy jumped to his feet and wiped the blood from his nose on the sleeve of his shirt. Princess turned back, looked up at Troy, and gave out a cry that sounded like 'whyyyyy'? At that moment, Sister, standing on the wheeled platform, still dressed in her full-length nun's outfit, floated effortlessly toward Tony. She looked as if she were gliding through the air. Her arms and feet weren't moving, even though she was heading toward him. Tony's eyes grew wide, and his jaw nearly touched the ground as he saw Sister's floating approach. Out of the corner of his eye, Tony saw movement on the ground as well. He glanced down and saw Princess turn and limp slowly over toward Molly. Troy noticed the black cat's limp. Molly stopped about 20 feet from Tony. When Princess reached Molly, without saying a word, Molly extended her arms, and right on cue, Princess jumped up into them.

Once again, Princess hissed directly at Troy. Then Molly looked up from her cat to Troy and said, "I guess Princess hasn't quite forgiven you boys for throwing those rocks."

Sister Molly, with Princess in her arms and the help of Indy and her remote control device, moved effortlessly backward, disappearing from the light into the darkness. Tony was frozen, staring at the darkness, and then he said to himself, "She really was a nun, and that was her cat." Then he yelled, "I'm sorry. I'll make it up to you, I swear. Well, I don't really swear, because it wouldn't be right to swear to a nun."

Over the hill, Sister and Molly headed back toward the alley, Indy carrying the board and remote, and Sister carrying Princess. Sister admitted something to Indy—"I really enjoyed that, and I always wanted to do that whole 'nun-glides-across-the-room' thing. Good job, Indy."

CHAPTER 28

On the Monday before the big event, Duck and company were at the site preparing for a last-minute addition to their news conference. It seemed three of Duck's golf buddies from the tour who were coming in for the wedding and the news conference called and suggested that they, along with Duck, should put on a golf clinic while they were there. So Duck was having a tee box built. Of course, the golf course wasn't completed, but they had the drawings, and they knew right where the first tee box was going to be put. They built their seating and centered all the other activities around the tee box. Finally, all the preparations were completed. The folding tables and chairs were out, the banners were up, and the schedules were copied and distributed to different locations for easier distribution.

It took a lot of work to put on this type of event. Mya made most of the arrangements, with the help of Tony, Sister Molly, the gang from down at the Cardboard Hotel, and an eager-to-help new volunteer named Troy Mastersomn. Troy made sure there were Bull's-Eye "Aim-to-Pees" portable bathrooms everywhere. He even set one up at the Cardboard Hotel free of charge. This was part of the deal he and Sister Molly had struck. That unit would stay there permanently, and he would service it on his regular route.

To top it all off, there were two other ceremonies planned to take place that day. One was Mya and Duck's wedding, which everyone knew about and helped plan. And there was another that was to be a special surprise for Sister Molly. Mya, Duck, and a few of their friends had secretly been talking with the Bishop, and he agreed that Sister Molly should receive full reinstatement as a sister of the order. They would do this at a surprise ceremony for her on Tuesday.

Up on top of the hill, in an area where the residential/assistance area for the homeless would be constructed, a large white tent had been erected. This was the site for Mya and Duck's wedding ceremony, which would be conducted by the Bishop. Assisting and co-monitoring the wedding would be Sister Molly, only Sister didn't know it yet.

With preparations made by Monday evening, Duck, Mya, and the gang all said their goodbyes. Duck had limo drivers take them all home—all, that is, except himself and Mya. This was a special night for Duck and Mya. It was the night before the beginning of a dream. An iced bottle of champagne sat in a silver container on its stand right next to a table covered with a white cloth and two chairs. Hand in hand, they walked over to the table and sat down.

Mya said, "Well, Duck, this is it. In a matter of hours, this will become a reality. I propose a toast to you." She poured champagne into the long-stemmed glasses.

Duck grabbed his glass, raised it up, and said, "Without you, I wouldn't be here. You stuck your neck out—no, you did the whole hokey-pokey thing and stuck your whole body out for a bum. This," he said as he fanned his hand and arm across the landscape, pointing out the farm ground, "is all because of you. Who knows where I'd be today if you hadn't come along?"

"Okay. Then let's toast to us," she said, "and our dream team."

Duck replied, "I'll drink to that. You know, I'm nervous all over again. What if we have the news conference, the clinic, the book sales, and nobody shows up? Then what?"

"Duck, you're worrying over nothing. What if the crowd overflows? And you know what? Duck, even if no one but us shows up, we will be here, and we will do this. This, my little Duckling, is the right thing to do, and it's being done for all the right reasons. We all know that. Now, I suggest you have the driver take me home. And you need to go, too. We've got a big day ahead of us tomorrow."

The driver took Mya home and then took Duck to his place. Duck sat alone in his office, going over last-minute items. He re-read his speech, all the while rolling on his fingertips and tossing into the air his golf ball with a smile on it. Finally, he laid down his ink pen, reached over and turned off the lamp, and headed for his bedroom. Climbing into bed, Duck turned off the lamp next to his bed. The room now was lit only by the glow of the moon as it shone through his window. Lying there with his head on his pillow, still staring at his golf ball, he heard, 'They call that a smile.' As Duck sat up and rested his weight on his elbows, he saw his father sitting in a chair across the room. He noticed he was wearing his favorite golf outfit right down to the pair of golf shoes he was wearing the day he died. As he looked closer, he noticed his hat had a different logo on it. As he stared even closer, he noticed that the logo on the hat read, "Duck's Run." Duck said, "Dad?"

"Duck, I'm so proud of you, son. I thought you would never find that ball in the dumpster. Welcome back, son."

"You put it there?"

"There and about a hundred and thirty-three other places—all of which you never found. I had to do something. You were wasting your God-given talent." Runner, always a kidder, took the hat off and turned it around so that he could read the name on the logo and said, "Now, about this name, I was thinking something more like Runner's Duck's Run. What do you think?"

"I like it. I'll have Mya, my attorney, instruct Van Gogh to change it first thing in the morning."

"No, no, I was just kidding. I think the name Duck's Run is perfect. Speaking of Mya, I definitely approve. You're perfect for each other." Runner got up out of his chair and walked toward Duck. He placed his hands on each side of Duck's face and kissed him on the forehead and said, "Know this. I am right beside you every step of the way. I've got to go now. Please tell Sister Molly thank you for arranging this opportunity."

Having said that, Runner disappeared. Duck settled his head back down on the pillow, and the biggest smile, coming from his heart, lit up across his face.

Suddenly, he was awakened by his alarm clock. Duck rolled over and looked at the clock, and it was 5:45 a.m. As he got up to head for the shower, his phone rang. It was Mya. "Good morning, Mr. Duck-meister."

"Good morning, Mrs.—I mean, soon-to-be Mrs. Duck-meister."

"I've been lying here thinking—this being our wedding day and all—that maybe I shouldn't ride with you. Maybe I'll just meet you later at the tent. You know, the old 'groom isn't supposed to see the bride' thing."

"But I can't—are you serious? You…" The Duck stammered.

"Duck, I'm kidding. I just thought I'd get that old wives' tale out of the way. I have to be by your side this morning, and I want to always be there. Looks like my ride is here; we'll see you in a bit."

"You scared ten years off me."

"Sorry. See you soon."

"Hold on, hold on. I've got to tell you something. I had a visitor last night. I know this will sound strange to you, but my dad came to see me last night in my room."

Mya interrupted. "Did he tell you to thank Sister Molly?"

"Yes, he did. How did you know?"

"He stopped by to see me, too. I told him we would set a place for him at the wedding and the press conference. He really liked the idea of naming our firstborn Runner."

CHAPTER 29

As Duck and Mya were driving to the press conference/ groundbreaking/wedding/ surprise celebration, Duck said to Mya, "In a short bit here, you will officially be My Angel Duck."

"Yeah, and someday we'll add My Angel Duck and her little ducklings."

As they turned in, they saw news trucks with all the national and local logos on them all over the place, setting up their remote vehicles. A truck from Cool Carl's delivered free donuts and coffee. An outdoor workout area displaying Fritz's latest fitness machines was set up. The gang from the street and Troy were there, setting up even more tables and chairs. Tommy J. and Crazy Larry were busy arranging Tommy J.'s books on the table in and around the area where Tommy J. would be sitting.

Looking around the area, there was Speedo being interviewed by Scoop, who, coincidentally, was now an up-and-coming reporter with a major network. Sister Molly was over being interviewed by Frankie, and somehow the topic centered on the virtues of forgiveness. Juggler was entertaining kids and adults alike with her juggling prowess, and Indy was giving lessons on the fineries of remote-control devices.

About a hundred feet behind the staging area, Duck and Mya noticed a helicopter sitting there. As they walked closer, they noticed a huge red ribbon around the helicopter. There was also a card, and on the envelope a note read, "Mya & Duck, open later after the wedding. But don't get too excited. You don't get to keep the helicopter."

As Duck and Mya looked around, they saw more and more cars coming in. Lines formed at various information tables, people asking to whom they should make their checks payable. Many of them wanted to know if their contributions were tax deductible. And thanks to the hard work by Mya and her legal assistant B.F.D., the answer was an easy one. 'Yes, they are deductible.'

Lines were already forming at Troy's Bull's-Eye "We-Aim-to-Pees" toilets. Just then, Troy walked by Duck and Mya, pointed at the Bull's-Eye Porta-Potties and said, "Free of charge. And I'm heading back to the shop for more. Looks like we're going to need them."

Duck turned to Mya and said, "Can you believe this?"

Mya's reply was, "It's amazing what the Lord and a little help from our friends can do."

It was 8:15 as Duck walked over to Tommy J. and said, "Where's your dad?"

"He said he'd be watching from home. You know how he hates big crowds. He told me to tell you he'd see you at the wedding. Gotta go, Uncle Duck. My sixth interview of the morning starts at 8:20. Me on TV. Can you believe this, Uncle Duck? Thank you."

"No, thank you, Tommy. Your book is everything your dad and I had hoped it would be, and more."

"Hey, don't forget about your old Uncle Duck when you get rich and famous."

"Never. And that is a promise." Tommy J. gave Duck a big hug and then turned to head off to the interviews.

Tommy left his booth in the capable hands of Crazy Larry and B.F.D. Speedo came walking by and whispered something in Duck's ear. Duck said, "Speedo, so help me, if you're wearing it, do not, and I mean do not even think about that right now."

"Relax. I was just kidding about the whole unveiling thing. But I am wearing it." Duck just smiled and shook his head.

Duck looked at his itinerary: 8:45, meet the two Nicoles, Jay, Jamie, Aaron, John, Chris, and Alia at the tee box. It seemed a lot more of his pro golfing buddies showed up for the clinic than he thought would. The clinic went well and lasted about 45 minutes. According to his itinerary, he was to meet Tony and Mya at 9:30 to go over any last-minute details, and he was running tight on time.

As he was just about finished talking with them about the details, a well-dressed, clean-shaven man came up to Duck and said, "Can I visit with you in private when you have a minute to spare, Mr. Duckins?"

"Well, this is my fiancée and attorney. I don't do anything without her present."

"Very well, then. Will you two come with me, please?"

They all walked together over behind an evergreen tree. Mya asked, "Just what is this all about? We're sorry, but we don't have much time since our press conference starts in a few minutes. You look familiar to me."

"Relax. This won't take long." He handed an envelope to Duck that said, 'To Mr. and Mrs. Duckins.'

"What's this?" Duck asked.

"What's it look like? Open it, for crying out loud."

Duck opened the envelope, and there was a card and a gift certificate from Cool Carl's for $250. The card said, 'Best wishes to both of you.' Handwritten on the card was a note that said, 'Thought you might want to try Cool Carl's food from the inside while it was still fresh.' At the bottom it was signed, your friend, Cilus. Duck looked up from the card and said, "You—by God, it's you!"

Trace smiled. "I clean up pretty good, don't I?"

Duck turned to his fiancée and said, "Mya, you remember Cilus."

Trace put his finger to his lips. He stepped up and gave Duck a big hug; then he stepped back and looked at Duck. He was waiting for Duck's permission to give Mya a hug. Duck nodded 'yes,' and Trace gave Mya a hug, stepped back and said, "Not a word, please."

"You have our word. Thanks, Cilus." Mya gave Cilus another hug. Noticing how tall and handsome he was, she said, "Thank you. And it's a good thing for Duck that I didn't meet you first. Hey, just kidding, Duck. You know that."

Cilus—Trace—turned and disappeared into the crowd, keeping his identity concealed.

CHAPTER 30

Mya looked at her watch. It was 9:45. She said, "We need to make sure everyone and everything is in place." As they came around from behind the evergreens, they saw that Tony, sporting his lime green leisure suit, already had everything under control. Tommy J. was seated at the far left of the long table, along with a copy of his book. Next to Tommy, Speedo in his red cap and overcoat was seated. Next to Speedo was Sister Molly. She was sitting just to the right of where Duck would be. On Duck's left, just next to him, would be Mya. Next to her, Tony, Fritz, and the gardeners.

Duck and Mya walked up and took their seats. Duck reached over, grabbed a pitcher of water, and filled a glass for Mya and himself. At 9:50, just as Uncle Tommy had instructed him to do, Mayor Joey's limo pulled up, and out stepped the newly re-elected mayor. He worked his way through the large crowd toward the front tables. Arriving at the front table, he took time to shake the hands of everybody at the table.

As he reached out to shake Sister Molly's hand, she flashed a huge bright new smile at him, showing the new implants that had reinstated her beautiful smile. As she was shaking his hand with her right hand, she handed him an envelope with her left hand. Joey opened it while he was still standing in front of her. He was shocked when he saw it was a bill from the dentist. Sister Molly said, "Uncle Tommy told me to give this to you and said you and your friends would be more than happy to pay for it. Thank you, Mr. Mayor."

Joey looked at the total of the bill. It was $11,111.11. He gulped. Sister added, "Oh, and Uncle Tommy said it's a little reminder that he's watching—whatever that means." Joey was stunned but resigned.

Just then, Tony came up to him and said, "It's 10 o'clock, Mr. Mayor." Joey turned and headed up to the podium and began his speech. "Good morning, everybody. Wow, what a beautiful day for the groundbreaking for this great complex. Mr. Bob Duckins, 'The Duck,' if you will, had a dream, and I am here to tell you that this town shares fully that dream. You can be assured, Mr. Duckins, that you will have all the support you need from this mayor for as long as I am in office and after. I am urging every one of you here today, and those of you at home watching on television, to take this project to heart. It is, in this mayor's eyes, a win-win situation. So please open up not only your head and hearts to this project but also your wallets. Let's all get behind this program one hundred and fifty percent. And now it is my pleasure to introduce to you the general manager at Duck's Run, Mr. Tony Bezmouskee."

Tony stepped up to the podium. "For those of you who don't know me, let me introduce myself. As the mayor said, I am Tony Bezmouskee. Let me tell you a little something about the man I am about to introduce to you, Mr. Bob Duckins, more affectionately known as The Duck. You see, Duck and I go back a long, long way. We were both young aspiring golf players and the best of pals. Even when we competed against each other in tournaments, we stayed true to our friendship. The more I tried and the harder I practiced, I'd look at Duck and realize there was a big difference. Duck has always had that something extra. I learned to call his gift the 'It.' We've all heard about the 'it,' but believe me, he defines the word. He was more than just a notch above the rest of us mentally, physically, and talent-wise. He was miles ahead. His good foundation for life and golf was formed through the parenting and teachings of Runner Duckins. He was a man we all looked to, and we took pride in saying we were his friend. If you look over there at that table, you see the place we set for Runner, and you can bet just as sure as we are all here, so is he. He's looking through eyes of pride at this fantastic person he molded. You all should take pride in the fact that Duck chose your community in which to build Duck's Run. So do yourself a favor and put your support behind him, because what he is doing here is good; and good done for the right reasons isn't bad at all."

"I guess I'm sounding like I'm throwing fire and brimstone at you. I ask you to please allow us the privilege of securing your trust. And now, it's my pleasure to introduce to you Mr. Bob 'The Duck' Duckins!"

Duck stood up and headed toward the podium. The crowd was cheering, and everyone was standing and applauding. "Thank you—please." Duck waited for the crowd to quiet down. "Thank you." He held up his well-worn golf ball with a smile on it—the one he had carried with him all these years, and said, "I don't know if you can see this or not, but this is a golf ball with a smile on it. A long time ago, my dad told me that a smile is caused when a club strikes the ball incorrectly. Isn't it funny how some of the smallest things can have such a huge impact on your life? You can't even imagine what kind of smile is radiating from my heart today. You see, I'm a lot like this golf ball. I've been struck with some pretty tough blows in my life, some beyond my control and some self-inflicted. I venture to say there is not a soul in this crowd that hasn't been through their own bad hits. Days like today show why you never should quit. Rest a little, maybe, but never quit."

"Yeah, I have a lot of reasons to smile today; for one, the fond memories of my father." Duck pointed and looked over to the place they set for his dad and then continued. "The realization that a dream is about to come true, the future Mrs. Duck. And support from all my friends. I pledge to you that what we are starting here today will be among the finest facilities of its kind in the country."

"I would now like to direct your attention once again to Tony Bezmouskee, our general manager. He's got a little something to show you. Tony."

"Thanks, Duck. What you are about to see," Tony paused and tapped on the wireless microphone and said, "Is this thing on?" Manning the control box for the P.A. system was Jimmy from the church. He turned up the volume on the monitors, and as Tony heard himself through the monitor, he said, "That's better. Thanks, Jimmy. As I was saying, what you are about to see is a rendering drawn by this young lady." Tony pointed to Van Gogh. "Nice job, sweetheart. It depicts what you will come to know as Duck's Run." Tony pulled the cover off and revealed the full 4 foot by 8 foot color rendering of the entire facility, including a Tony Bezmouskee/Duckins designed golf course. "Our goal is to be fully operational by spring of 2007. If you have any questions, just come on up after the news conference and pick up one of our full color brochures, which has a tear-off pledge card attached to it."

"Duck, if you don't mind, we have someone who says he has a surprise special announcement you will want to hear."

Deano walked up to the podium and said, "Hello, everyone. My name is Deano Alonzo. You may know of my affiliation with our charitable organization, and it is with that capacity that I have come to speak to you today. Me and my co-workers have come to a unanimous decision that we are one hundred percent in support of Duck's Run, and we pledge that at least seven percent of our received annual charitable contributions will be pledged directly to Duck's Run. And if any of our national donors wish to pledge a larger portion of their annual contributions direct to Duck's Run, we encourage them to attach a note to their contributions checks. Flyers to this effect will be mailed out with all annual contribution packages. This, my friends—this whole concept is long overdue. Thank you for the opportunity to bend your ear. And thanks, Duck, Tony, and Mya, for the opportunity to partner up with you."

Tony stepped back up to the podium. "How about that, Duck?"

"Wow, I'm speechless. Thank you, Deano, and please express our gratitude to your board members."

Duck stepped back up to the podium and said," Wow. How about that? As some of you know, I met quite a woman six years ago, and this afternoon, shortly after the events of today are over, there will be another event held here. This one will be up there in that tent you see on top of the hill. Today I get to marry her. How does one man get so lucky? Before we let you all go today, Mya and I have a little surprise of our own planned for one of our special guests. I would like to direct your attention at this time to the line of trees just to your left."

Right on cue, a helicopter came over the treetops and hovered directly overhead. Then it landed near the temporary tee box. As the engines were shut down and the blades slowed to a stop, Duck said to Mya, "Hon, come on up here, please."

Mya walked up and stood next to Duck. Duck handed her a second microphone. Mya turned it on and said, "Sister Molly, will you come up here and join us, please?"

In the background, a figure stepped out of the helicopter and into a golf cart that had been sent out to greet the helicopter. Duck and Mya instructed Sister to stand between them, and they turned her so she was facing the figure now in the golf cart. As the cart got closer, she recognized the Bishop who had disassociated her from the Nunnery. As the golf cart pulled up in front of the crowd, the Bishop stepped out. It was at this moment that Sister noticed a second golf cart behind the Bishop's, and in it were two of the nuns from her vent. One she recognized as her Mother Superior. The other was her close friend, Sister Lorana. Now she was really beginning to wonder what the heck was going on. As Bishop McCoy approached, Sister Molly could feel her heart beating in her throat. In her mind, she was saying, 'Why are they here?'

Mya broke the silence and said, "Believe it or not, Duck and I were expecting this helicopter. It's part of the special surprise for Sister Molly, but we had no idea the other helicopter would be here. Ladies and gentlemen, let me introduce you to Bishop McCoy."

Duck handed his microphone to the Bishop. "Molly, would you step up here and stand between Sister Lorana and Mother Moranda?"

Molly moved up and obediently stood between the two other nuns. Bishop McCoy continued. "Molly, in a special meeting held on your behalf on November 20, 2004, after taking into consideration your consistent dedication to your calling to serve the homeless in our community, the high esteem you have focused on our order, and the immeasurable good you have accomplished, by a proclamation signed by me, Bishop McCoy, and Cardinal Beloy, we hereby offer you full reinstatement to the order of the Sisterhood. We would be honored if you would accept our invitation to re-enter the order. If you decide to accept our offer, please know that from this day forward we will fully back you in your excellent work with the homeless. In short, this old man you are looking at was so wrong, and you were, oh, so right. So it is with the strong desire to hear an acceptance that I ask—Molly, do you accept our offer of reinstatement, and the apology of an old, foolish man?"

Molly said, "Let me ask my attorney. I'm kidding! Of course my answer's yes."

"Thank you. By the power vested in me, I proclaim you, Sister Molly. Sister Molly, I am so sorry for the past and yet so happy for your future."

Sister said, "What I have been through has made my faith even stronger. I have never lost my love for my work, and today you have made my life complete. Who would have thought this day would come? I'm even more elated about today than I was the first time I was married to the Lord's work."

Sister Molly gave the Bishop a hug, and then she turned to Duck and Mya and gave them the biggest thank you, teary hug ever received by anyone. Then Sister Molly turned to the Bishop and said, "I still get to live on the streets where I belong, right?" The Bishop nodded. The crowd, which up to this point had been so quiet, reacted to what they had just been privileged to witness. Slowly, a few started to clap, and then the whole place stood and showed their appreciation. As they all joined in applauding Sister Molly, she gave a salute to God that a baseball player might do after getting a key hit or making a spectacular play. Then spontaneously, she grabbed an autographed football from the silent auction table and slammed it to the grass and did her own crazy legged end-zone dance. Then she ran over and grabbed the Bishop by the hands and swung him around in a circle. His large religious hat at first bounced around on his head as they twisted in circles, then it fell to the ground. "Oh, sorry, Your Holiness. Old habits are tough to break." She picked his hat up from the ground and put it on his head. It was a little lopsided. A huge smile came across his now beet-red face, half out of embarrassment and half because he hadn't had this much exercise in a long time. Fritz rushed over and handed him a card to his gym.

Duck stepped up to the microphone and said, "Wow, what a day so far. On behalf of Duck's Run, we'd like to thank you all for being here today. We hope to see all your names on checks."

Tony turned his microphone back on. "And don't forget about the silent auction items. We will close the auction down in about 15 minutes."

Tony turned to Duck and said, "Duck, have you seen the bids for that old library card of yours? Man, do you have any more of those?"

Then turning again to the crowd, "If you have questions, call us at the number printed on your donation card, or you

can reach us on our website that you will also find printed
there. May you always have a safe and wonderful trip to the
destinations of your choice, a safe and wonderful time while
you're there, and a safe and wonderful trip home."

Duck and Mya stepped back over to Sister Molly, and Duck
said, "Sister Molly, would you honor us by assisting Bishop
McCoy in our wedding ceremony? We've got a little something
we would like you to say."

"I would be honored if it's okay with the Bishop."

"That's been arranged. Duck had Mya negotiate that up
front."

Jimmy turned Tony's microphone back up, and Tony said,
"Thank you—every one of you—for being here today, and
thank you for your support in the future." Tony dropped his
microphone down to his side and said to the wedding party,
"What are we waiting for? Let's get up the hill."

The groups of invited guests took off walking up the hill,
followed by the two golf carts which were bringing the Bishop
and the two nuns from the vent. As they crested the hill and
reached the tent, they found that all was in place. Duck noticed
a camouflaged catering truck with the name 'Cool Carl's
Catering,' and dotting the "i" in catering was a big golf ball
with a smile on it. Next to the truck were Carl and Mary, both
of them posing for Scoops's camera. Mary had on her black
stocking cap and khaki military shirt. Carl sat with his hand in
Mary's as they both took a short break from the catering.

Mya said, "The guys thought it would be perfect to have
Cool Carl's cater this, and I have to agree. What do you think?"

"Absolutely perfect. Wouldn't have it any other way!"
replied Duck. The Bishop and Sister Molly were escorted to
the front by Speedo. Speedo was wearing his long overcoat, and
he set it off nicely by wearing a bow tie—red, of course—tied
around his neck, and his red swimming cap. Speedo took his
place to the left of the Bishop. Next, up walked B.F.D. He took
his place right next to Speedo. Then up came Uncle Tommy

and Tommy J., and Tony and Fritz in their matching Lime Green leisure suits. Tony took his place, which was right next to where Duck would stand, and Uncle Tommy would stand on the other side of Duck. And Fritz next to Tony. There they will stand, Duck's three best friends standing as bookends, plus one on each side of him. Several of Mya's friends came walking down the center aisle and took their appropriate places on the opposite side of Speedo and the boys. All were in place. They looked to the back of the tent and saw Duck and Mya as they began walking side by side, heading toward them. Both of them were dressed casually, in something old. Duck had his old worn-out golf shoes on, the ones that he was wearing the day they met, and Mya was carrying the briefcase she was carrying the day they met, plus she was wearing a necklace with a locket on it. The necklace and locket were her mom's. Inside the locket, she had replaced the old photo with one of her mother and father. Today, the briefcase carried the couple's rings. For something new, they were both wearing matching T-shirts which said 'Duck's Run' on the front, for something borrowed, Duck had one of Tony's frilly orange shirts on under his T-shirt, and Mya was holding one of Sister Molly's rosaries and for something blue, both of them were also wearing blue golf hats which had the new "Duck's Run" logo on them. The logo, by the way, was designed by Van Gogh. She did a super job on the logo, and soon she would be in charge of the art department at the Duck's Run. On the bill of Mya's golf hat was sewn a veil—a cute touch thought up by Van Gogh.

As they reached the group at the front, Mya stepped forward and walked up to Sister Molly, grabbed her by the hand, and lead her to where she would stand by Mya's side. Mya whispered to Molly, "This bride needs her angel to stand by her side. You can step up to the front when it's time for your blessing." Mya placed her hand in Sister Molly's hand. Sister Molly gently squeezed Mya's hand, letting her know she was there for her. Duck nodded to the Bishop, and the ceremony began.

Near the conclusion, the Bishop said, "I, Bishop McCoy—"

"And I, Sister Molly—"

"Pronounce you, man and wife," they finished together.

Mya whispered to Sister, "It's your turn." And she nudged her to the front.

Sister Molly walked to the front, turned to the couple, and said, "May the good Lord continue to shower you with his blessings and always keep you safe and warm, and may He forever bless you two."

Sister Molly opened an envelope handed to her earlier by Mya and read it. It said, "Remember to always follow your hearts, and never, ever forget to do the little things that you didn't forget to do in the beginning."

The Bishop signaled for Sister Molly to do the honors. Sister Molly said, "Mr. Bob Duckins, you may kiss the bride." Duck parted the veil hanging from the bill of Mya's hat and kissed her.

As they turned to face the crowd, Sister Molly said, "Ladies and gentlemen, I give you Mr. and Mrs. Duck Duckins."

Duck and Mya both looked at each other, then looked down the row at Speedo. Speedo had his head leaned forward and was anxiously looking at them. Both Duck and Mya nodded their heads. Then, faster than you can say "yuck," Speedo took off his trench coat and let it hit the ground, leaving him standing with only his red bow tie secured around his neck, his red skullcap, and his red skimpy trunks. The Bishop's face was beet red again; however, after a few cocktails at the reception later, he admitted he took a second look.

After a second nod from Mya, Speedo finally moved. Speedo stepped out of line and walked over in front of the newlyweds and said, "Follow me." He led the procession slowly, making sure he milked every second out of this opportunity down the aisle and out the other side of the tent. After a couple of hours at the reception, having given the newlyweds plenty of time to have mingled with their guests, Uncle Tommy came up to Duck and Mya and said, "I'm going to have to be going pretty soon."

"Yeah, we're just about ready to head out ourselves," Duck said. Then Uncle Tommy said, "You two didn't plan a honeymoon, did you?"

"Nope, you told us you had some work for us to do. So we figured since we'd waited all these years to get married, we can wait a little while longer for a honeymoon."

"Good. Now, say your goodbyes, and then come with me."

Duck and Mya make their rounds. Duck stepped up on the bandstand and took the microphone away from Speedo and said, "Just because we are leaving, it doesn't mean the party's over. The bar will remain open." Duck continued, "Good night, and thank you all for everything."

Tony grabbed the microphone. As always promoting something, he said, "For those of you who are ready for coffee, you'll find several pots of Cilus's coffee blend right over there." Tony turned to Speedo and said, "I don't know if the crowd's ready for another of your songs. You may have worn out your welcome." Tony turned to the crowd and said, "How about it, everybody? Are you ready for another of Speedo's songs, or should we give someone else a chance?"

Without delay, someone shouted, "Give us Barabas!"

Uncle Tommy was waiting for the newlyweds in the passenger seat of a four-seated golf cart. At the wheel was Crazy Larry. Mya and Duck climbed into the back two seats as they were directed to. Crazy Larry headed down the hill and drove them right to the helicopter, which had been parked there all day. As they got closer, they could see a couple of figures sitting in the pilot and the co-pilot seats. Uncle Tommy said to Larry, "Stop here, and keep the engine running. You two come with me." Stopping at the spot where they could reach the card that was still taped to the helicopter, Uncle Tommy said, "Now you can open it." Duck reached up and pulled the card off the lower windshield of the helicopter. The pilot, that he could now see clearly, saluted him. Duck handed the card to Mya to read and said, "You read it, Mrs. Duckins."

"Okay." She opened the card, and they read it together. The card said, "To my very special friends. To my old friend, Duck, and my new friend, Mrs. Duck. The two gentlemen you see inside the helicopter are here at my request. They have been instructed to fly you to Brown County Municipal Airport where you will find waiting for you a private jet that will fly you directly to Kauai, Hawaii, where you will enjoy an all-expenses-paid month-long honeymoon, courtesy of Tommy J., Crazy Larry, Tony, Fritz and me."

Duck, in a habit of stammering lately, said, "Tommy, we—" Uncle Tommy stopped him and said, "Not another word. You guys are wasting time. We've made all the arrangements. Besides, you've got Tony and that damn green leisure suit to handle everything while you're gone. Have a great time, my friend, and we'll see you when you get back."

Mya and Duck looked up the hill and saw Tony and Fritz there waving at them. They waved back, then turned and looked at each other and at the same time said, "Let's go, then."

Duck said, "After you."

As they walked up the ramp to the helicopter, Uncle Tommy said, "Hey, Duck." Duck turned to see what Uncle Tommy had to say. "Aren't you forgetting something?" Uncle Tommy tossed Duck his golf ball with the smile on it. Tommy was holding it for Duck during the wedding ceremony. Duck caught the ball, looked at it as he held it in his fingertips, then held it up in the air and waved goodbye to Tommy. He turned and stepped into the helicopter.

As they took off, the pilot flew over the reception, and as they did, he signaled for Mya and Duck to look down. They could see their friends on the ground standing in precise positions, forming a human golf ball sitting on a human tee, and on that golf ball was a smile, and every one of them was looking up and waving goodbye. Right in the middle of that smile were Tony Besmouskee and Fritz in their lime green leisure suits.

Duck reached over and grabbed Mya's hand and said, "It was the best thing that I didn't ever do."

"What?" a puzzled Mya said.

"I said it was the best thing that I didn't ever do."

"What on earth are you talking about?"

"When I was down and depressed, I saw no way out, felt no hope. At one point, I walked down to the bridge overlooking the rail yard and waited for a train. I was through with all the darkness. I climbed up onto the side railing of a bridge and was holding onto a support cable as I waited to jump in front of the next train. I stood there waiting for the right moment as I watched a locomotive charging down the tracks toward me."

"Then I heard a voice say, 'Duck, is that you?' The voice startled me, and it was a good thing that I was holding onto that cable, or I would have fallen for sure. I looked toward the voice and saw Sister Molly. She was looking over the rail, trying to see what I was so intently staring at. All I could see was the back of her head as she looked down over that rail. I said, 'Molly, is that you?'"

"She looked up at me, smiled, and said, 'Yep, it's me.' Well, I asked her how she found me, and she reminded me how we always talked about following Cilus as he headed off to one of his secret rendezvous. Turns out, she followed him that day, only it turned out that she was following me. I had been wearing his coat and hat that morning."

"Then she told me how if I jumped, my wife and kids wouldn't appreciate me bowing out before they had a chance to meet me. 'My wife and kids?' I said. Mya, I hadn't even thought that far ahead. And then Sister pulled an envelope out of her pocket and handed it to me. Do you know what was written on it? It was a future front-page story for her 'Someday

Newspaper.' She said she didn't have the whole story yet, but she wanted me to hold on to it and open it at a point in the future when I felt that I had been blessed. Then she said she wanted me to write the story that came after the headline. She said, 'Duck, I know it's hard to believe right now, but you have a rainbow awaiting you at the end of all of this darkness.'"

"I just felt like everything was such an effort, but she said, 'Duck, don't do this to your wife and kids; don't do this to yourself; and don't do this to me.' She had lost Clarice, and she said she didn't want to lose me, too. She said, 'The end of this ride that we're on will come all too quickly on its own.' Then she told me to come back with her where she would get a good fire started in the barrel."

"I stepped back off of the bridge's railing holding that sealed envelope in my hand, and we watched a train speed by some one hundred feet or so below us. As each car from the train passed, the sound of its heavy wheels rolling against the steel tracks clanging out a rhythmic beat, I thought to myself how that could have been the sound of my death march."

"She put Cilus's hat on my head and said, 'It's a good thing I didn't pop a paper sack behind you like I did that day behind Fast Eddie. If I had done that, you probably would have jumped right off of this perfectly good bridge.' That brought a smile to my face, and we talked all night long around that fire. I'm so glad she was living with us on the streets."

Mya said, "Duck, what was in that envelope?"

"Well, one day as I sat around counting my blessings, I opened it, and the letter simply read, 'The best thing I didn't ever do,' by Bob Duckins."

"Look at what has happened to me. I found you and all of this. Man, just think what I would have missed out on. Like Sister Molly said, it was the best thing that I didn't ever do."

"I'm glad Sister Molly was there, too," Mya said. Then she laid her head on Duck's shoulder, and the pilot turned the helicopter and headed over the tree line toward the airport.

The End...

Wait! Wait! Don't go away yet. Don't you want to know what happened to the four former hoodlums?

Troy, the only one who expressed true remorse and later backed it up with action, fared the best. In fact, today he is a very active member of Reverend Spanky's congregation. The reverend is quite pleased with his transformation and is constantly bragging about Troy's soprano voice emanating from the choir.

Frankie's charade as a preacher at the national level didn't last long. He was caught behind a log cabin at a youth summer camp with an underage member of his flock who had been traveling across the country with him. He was fired from the pulpit once again, only this time there were no closed-door hearings. It was there for all to see. Frankie's fifth wife left him, the F.B.I. became interested in his transportation of a minor across state lines, and the local police arrested him. Today he works for Troy, servicing the porta-potties while out on bail awaiting his trial.

Deano never learned his lesson, either, and he got caught after one too many dips into the cookie jar. He was forced to resign from his cushy job, and you can now find his photo at the post office. Rumors have it he's now living on the streets in Quebec, Canada, under an assumed name.

Joey Parma, contrary to what was first thought, actually lost his bid for re-election. The challenger, acting on what he considered a reliable tip, demanded a recount and got one. The election board quickly found discrepancies in the balloting process. It seems someone had stuffed more than a few ballots into the box, and it was alleged and later proven that Mayor Joey had gone out and filled several vans with as many homeless people as he could gather, then delivered them to the voting polls, bribing them with cash and goodies in exchange for their vote. It was the sworn statements voluntarily given under oath by these same individuals that led to the recount and change of the election. To this day, Joey still wears his fancy coat and hat as he travels back and forth from his job at the sewage treatment plant.

Okay. You can go now. Thanks for sticking around.